JUNGLE RESCUE

JUNGLE RESCUE

TO: MY LOVING BROTHER
EUGENE MARSH
FROM: ARLENE WITH LOTS OF
LOVE

Geoffrey Gilbert

JAN. 04/2014

authorHOUSE®

AuthorHouse™ LLC
1663 Liberty Drive
Bloomington, IN 47403
www.authorhouse.com
Phone: 1-800-839-8640

Published by AuthorHouse   11/12/2013

ISBN: 978-1-4918-1689-9 (sc)
ISBN: 978-1-4918-1687-5 (hc)
ISBN: 978-1-4918-1688-2 (e)

Library of Congress Control Number: 2013916932

This book is dedicated to all the special people who in some way impacted my life.

My dear Mother, Cecilia Gilbert and an adorable Grand Mother, Emelda Bartholomew (deceased) for instilling the values of honesty, discipline and hard work at an early age. My Father, the late Leslie Gilbert. Sister Yolande, the dedication and unwavering commitment shown during my early childhood would always be remembered.

Mr. Michael Philbert, former Principal of my Alma mater—St. Theresa's (Vincennes) RC School. A sincere and special "thank you" to my wife Joan for all the encouragement during those long nights of writing and research. And Justice Lyle St. Paul and Mrs Margaret St. Paul, for their words of wisdom and moral support throughout my entire career.

Chapter 1

As the Liberian registered freighter plowed through the dark murky ocean water, the man lying beneath the deck turned slightly to relieve the pressure on his back muscles. He has been in this position for well over three hours, and the extremely cramped conditions were having a debilitating effect on his body. He looked at his watch and then gazed at the creaky narrow stairway. He reached for the heavy tote bag and carefully removed a 9 mm Semi Automatic Pistol from an inner compartment. Gradually, he eased himself from the confined space and adjusted his eyes to the dull dark conditions.

The passenger is travelling under an alias to conceal his true identity. A forged travel document gave his last name as Smith—Arthur W. Smith, American professor and research scientist heading to Colombia to begin a geological research project. The captain and some crew members knew of his presence, so for this reason the man had to be extremely cautious. The traveler stretched again as he made his way up from the claustrophobic bunk and climbed the rusty stairway to the top of the deck.

He got to the deck just in time to hear a clanking metallic sound in the bow area of the ship and another bang, this time around the mid section. The mystery traveler leaned over the side just as another object clattered against the metal guard railing. When the last thump was heard, the traveler almost instantly knew that something unusual is happening. Nothing must get in his way now—getting to the City of Santa Marta early on the following day is extremely important. The man is prepared to use any means—including lethal and deadly force to ensure that his mission is accomplished.

In the pale and fading moonlight, as the freighter rode the ocean waves, the American professor of geological studies saw two dark and shadowy figures moving towards the middle of the ship. From his concealed position behind the stack of sheet metal he could hear them. Pirates had boarded the freighter! He had to move quickly and decisively; they cannot be allowed to take this ship—no way! This could have a terrible impact on his mission to the South American mainland.

The man drew his Semi Automatic pistol and moved forward in the direction of the advancing pirates. He attached the silencer to the weapon, crouched and waited. The dark figures got closer; the taller of the two paused and pointed to the upper deck and spoke to his counterpart. The words were barely audible, but the traveler knew exactly what they were up to.

To gain control of the ship, the pirates had to commandeer the main control room—the captain and crew must be taken hostage quickly; that's the method these roving high sea bandits use in all their operations. Some naval analysts believe that this follows the blueprint written by Al Shabaab—a notorious Somali based terrorist group.

Still crouching, the American made one final check of the area around him. In the darkness, he relied heavily on his keen sense of hearing to determine how far the pirates were from the steps which led to the ship's control room. This is his kind of game—stalk wait and pounce; he expected them to be armed and extremely dangerous. Pirates operate under their own rules and are known for gruesome and barbaric acts. Just recently, off the coast of Somalia they boarded another Liberian registered oil tanker and took the entire crew hostage. The captain and four of his crew were murdered in cold blood, but in the end the bandits did not escape unscathed. During the attack, a coded message was sent out by the ship's mate. Fortunately, at the time of the attack a joint United States and East African naval exercise was being staged in the area; they responded quickly by sending three commando units, backed up by two Apache helicopter gunships and a frigate. The commandos stormed aboard the tanker, and in the ensuing firefight, four of the five pirates were killed.

While the thought of outside military intervention crossed the professor's mind, this situation called for immediate and urgent action. He had to stop the pirates from taking control of the ship—no matter the cost. He slipped out from his concealed position and got closer to the stairway; above him, the reflection from the glass panels slightly improved the visibility. He saw them a bit better now, the taller guy leading the way paused again, this time to secure the mask which partially covered his face. The American traveler leveled the Glock 17 Semi Automatic pistol, pointed it then squeezed the trigger. There was a muffled pop as the pirate jerked sideways then fell flat on his face. His counterpart, on hearing the impact of the body hitting the hard deck, quickly spun around. He had little time to recover from the shock.

The mystery traveler, well positioned after he shot the first pirate pounced on him in a flash. Grabbing the tall pirate by the left arm he side stepped as he brought the pirate's hand crashing down onto the firm upward thrust of his knee. The bone-jarring impact jolted the gun from his hand, causing it to catapult into the air and crash land onto the metal railing. Even though the pirate sustained a broken arm, in desperation he attempted to fight back. His attacker never gave him a chance; the wounded pirate brandished a long machete and began to swing it wildly with his right hand.

His adversary picked up a meter long piece of rusted metal pipe and swayed out of the path of the swinging blade. Turning quickly he swung the pipe in the opposite direction hitting the man a smashing blow on the forearm. This time, the injured man had no chance to launch any form of counter attack. The American quickly followed up with three hard blows to the victim's the knee cap, rendering him totally immobile.

In the meantime, three other pirates using grappling hooks, made their way onto the upper deck and were closing in on the control room of the ship. The Russian Captain and his First Officer heard the commotion and hit the alarm button. Sirens were blaring and the ship's emergency lights came on. The American raced up the stairway. Three other crew members appeared on the deck below, the short stocky guy started to bludgeon one of the wounded pirates, previously beaten up by the American. By now, the captain had barricaded the entrance to the control room, and for the moment he remained in command of his ship.

The three pirates realized this and started firing their weapons at the solid metal door. The man made it up to the upper deck as the gunfire erupted and bullets ricocheted against the door of the captain's quarters. Moving in from the rear, he fired into the chest of the closest bandit. The American dropped to the deck and rolled to the other side, quickly taking cover behind a stack of containers. The gunfire continued as he climbed to the top of a container. From this vantage point, Professor Smith quickly reloaded the Semi Automatic pistol and pumped the entire clip into the attackers below. He quickly reloaded the weapon and made his way down to the command center. Other crew members joined the American and they pried open the barricaded door. The Russian captain looked quite startled as the American and three of his crewmen busted into the control room.

"Captain, your ship came under attack by pirates. Fortunately, I saw the fucking bastards and repelled them; you and the crew are safe and secure now, there's no need to worry."

The relieved captain, still slightly dazed from the ordeal, extended his hand to the American. "Thank you very much, you've saved us from certain disaster."

The American spent another twenty minutes chatting with the Captain Balhosikovic. The captain offered to use his contacts at the Port of Santa Marta to get him ashore safely; but the traveler preferred the more subtle and covert entry into the city. Captain Balhosikovic then agreed to have two of his crewmen carry the American ashore in one of the ship's lifeboats. This would take place around 4:30 AM. They shook hands again, and the man went back to his bunk beneath the deck; he estimated that he'll get at least another three hours rest before leaving the MV Perestroika.

Chapter 2

The small wooden craft heaved and rolled against the incessant barrage of the swirling waves, and a rather strong tide made maneuvering quite difficult. The tall square shouldered and muscular man kept clutching the handle of the military grade duffle bag. He had travelled well over two hundred and fifty kilometers to get to this point—Santa Marta, the capital city of the Department of Magdelena, on the Colombian mainland. The journey was filled with several challenges; in the swamplands of Maracaibo he ran into many predators, and a close call with a huge Green Anaconda nearly ended his life.

And the situation could have been much worse, when he boarded the MV Perestroika at Boca de Camarones en route to Santa Marta under the pseudonym, Professor Arthur Smith; Bradley didn't have the slightest clue that several hours after leaving port he'll be caught up in a bloody fire fight to prevent the ship from falling into the hands of a vicious gang of pirates.

So much work went into the planning of this mission, and since the timing is of extreme importance; the American just could not deal with anymore setbacks. Of course it had to coincide with the extremely dark periods prevalent around this time of year.

The Former Navy Seal visited Colombia previously, but this time around, the trip had an added sense of urgency. The life of an American citizen hung in the balance and this warrants quick and decisive action.

John Bradley saw the perplexed look in the captain's eyes when he inquired about a trip up the Santa Marta Coast. Actually, it wasn't really the request, but rather the timing. What kind of tourist or visitor makes a trip up the coast at midnight? In all the years plying his trade, Captain Alvarez had done some night drop offs; but at midnight—never!

The last one he remembers so vividly—the young German couple. They were doing a documentary on the reefs and coral. The site chosen was about six miles from the Inca Inca Cove near the pristine Rodadero Beach. The couple were in Santa Marta to capture some of the exhilarating underwater footage. That's usually an hour long dive which started from around 7:30 pm.

Again, Captain Alvarez felt rather uncomfortable with the request of this American visitor. However, the prospect of getting a big payoff significantly diminished his underlying fear and concern. What really brought this mysterious visitor to Santa Marta? Captain Alvarez continued to ponder about the job he had accepted. A clandestine trip in the dead of night ferrying a strong and powerfully built man with a military style tote bag? The Colombian seaman made a very conscious effort to rid his mind of these troubling thoughts as he guided the craft through the water.

The captain tried to keep the wooden boat steady despite the turbulent waves, and at the same time blot out the suspicious questions constantly bombarding his mind. It's none of his business anyway. The man had agreed to pay him well for the trip, so his main focus should be to take him to the agreed destination safely; nothing else really matters.

The waves continued to swirl; stinging shafts of water zapped Bradley across the face as the captain navigated his vessel through the choppy waters. At least this is the price the retired American military man had to pay. A little discomfort from the rolling waves doesn't matter—it's the tradeoff that really mattered. Around this time of the year, longer periods of darkness prevailed and this is a critical factor in any covert operation. Darkness enhances the surprise factor and it's usually the ideal time to instill fear, shock and uncertainty in the mind of an adversary.

John Bradley looked at the old captain as he expertly cajoled the craft; the turbulence appeared to be subsiding though. The former Navy Seal pulled out a small flashlight and pointed the shining rays of light on the laminated map held against his bag of luggage.

"Hey skipper, how long again before we reach the cove?" John is referring to the designated point near Bahia Concha. This location would get him close enough to the Tayrona National Park, named after Colombia's indigenous Indians. Bradley read extensively about the natives and had a great fascination with their culture and formidable resilience.

"Should be getting there in about 35 minutes," answered Captain Alvarez.

"OK, not bad, would want a good look around at first light."

"Visited Santa Marta before?"

"No, but seen a lot of some other areas. Cali, Bogota and Medellin, even Buena Ventura and Barranquilla."

"Hope you had a good time; we got so many lovely places to see, you'd need a long vacation to really enjoy all of what we've got to offer."

"Sure, there is quite a lot. I really enjoyed my last visit—you have a marvelous country. What impressed me most are the charming, warm and hospitable people. You guys are just wonderful!"

"Thanks, come again; that's just our way of life—despite all of the bad things you hear on the news. Yeah, that's our way of life—It's our culture you know."

Captain Alvarez continued to steer the boat along a path which appeared less turbulent. He has been plying these waters for over three decades so he knew almost every bay, cove or inlet along the entire Santa Marta Coastline. He kept a firm grip on the handle of the outboard motor and started to steer the craft towards the inlet.

The Captain estimated that he needs to travel another one and a half nautical miles before he lands his passenger. Previously, to reduce the effects of the surging tides and ensure a more comfortable ride for the visitor seated on the rough cut plank across the middle of the craft; a diversionary course was taken by Captain Alvarez. While this tactic did reduce the rolling and swaying to some degree, it did increase the duration of the journey by another 20 minutes.

John appeared pretty much unperturbed by this anyway—he seemed so focused, intense and rather distant. And when old Captain Alvarez tried to engage him in conversation, the visitor gave him a good hard look before responding. "I've got so much on my mind buddy; no need to burden you with all that stuff."

As they neared the stretch of water a bit closer to the inlet, John Bradley felt the boat rocking violently and he instinctively clutched the handle of his Duffle bag. He had good reason to hold on firmly to it; as a former Navy Seal he knows the importance of staying close to your supplies and equipment. No matter what happens, Bradley made a vow not to be separated from all his military paraphernalia. The success or failure of his mission on the South American Continent depended heavily on the gear he carried.

The American Special Forces man is a true professional, with a career in the military spanning well over twenty-five years. If you are going to war, this five foot eleven battle hardened soldier would certainly be your first choice. John, had quite an impressive resume: four tours of duty in Afghanistan, service in Iraq during Operation Desert Storm and the post 911 Iraq war. Bradley also saw action in several fire fights—including Mogadishu, Somalia and has two purple hearts and many citations for valor. He also served in in Bosnia Herzegovina, and as a tactical support advisor to the Chechen rebels during the war with the Russians.

After Bradley retired from the military, he became somewhat of a freelancer. His involvement with the Chechen rebels was initiated by Russian Oil Magnate Igor Romonov, a staunch anti-government activist. Romonov, arrested by KGB agents twice in 2007 escaped the usual long and harsh jail sentence due to the unrelenting pressure from human rights groups and international media publicity, particularly in the United States. He served only three and a half years. Ironically, after his release, Romonov vowed to use any means necessary to humiliate or embarrass the Russians for putting him in jail on fabricated corruption charges.

And what better way to do it than to help them get a bloody nose from neighboring Chechnya? This sparked the beginning of the relationship with the former American Soldier. Romonov had very strong ties with the Americans through the many business connections he had in the United States, so recruiting Bradley did not require any exceptional effort. He had connections with many US policy makers and other highly Influential people in Washington. Five years have gone by since John retired from active military service, and when the call came he certainly had no reservations.

The soldier in you never dies, he would say to himself while hiking in the trails near his home in Houston Texas. Bradley spent nearly seven months with the rebels, and his presence surely made a difference in what transpired during one of the most bloody urban conflicts in recent times. Grozny was reduced to rubble but the Russians paid a heavy price. With an increasing body count and adverse international publicity, they had no choice but to withdraw.

And today post war Grozny is a thriving city, dazzling with modernity and architectural brilliance. John was quite impressed during his last visit as a tourist just over a year ago. He would certainly be back when his assignment in Colombia is complete.

Chapter 3

Captain Manuel Alvarez was looking for a safe area to land his passenger. He knew the waters off the Santa Marta coast better than the average sailor or fisherman as he has been plying the seas for the last thirty-five years. This is his turf—his exclusive domain. Of course, there were some bad experiences; he still carries a large jagged scar on his left cheek, from the wound inflicted by Carlos Del Monte, a notorious guerrilla leader "AKA" El Capitan. Del Monte and a group of his henchmen were scheduled to make a midnight delivery to a freighter in a secluded bay some 15 nautical miles southwest of Santa Marta. The shadowy rendezvous point is a favorite drug drop off bay for the notorious drug baron. No glitches were expected on that night, just the normal routine. A passing ship would deploy two rubber dinghies at the designated time; the illegal drugs would then be picked up by the waiting crew for transfer to the freighter moored off the coast.

Del Monte and his group operated with impunity along the entire Caribbean coastline, from as far north as Puerto Bolivar to Buenaventura. Allegations have been making the rounds in both Washington and Bogota, that El Capitan pays significant sums of cash to high ranking members of the Armed Forces in exchange for immunity and tip offs. As fate would have it, Captain Alvarez had major engine trouble earlier in the day. After several failed attempts to start the motor, the fishing vessel was eventually hauled up onto the shore. Captain Alvarez made the decision to take refuge and stay overnight; the other crewmen were all in agreement with this. For the old sailor, the safety of his crew must never be compromised.

Sometime around 2:15 am, El Capitan and his men who had reconnoitered the secluded bay earlier, detected the presence of the marooned fishermen. Del Monte and his cohorts were taking no chances; nothing should stand in their way! They stormed ashore in a Yahama powered speed boat to confront the stranded seamen. Captain Alvarez, oblivious of the impending danger signaled with three quick flashes from the sturdy rubber coated flashlight, to confirm the location.

Del Monte and his henchmen, suddenly and without warning unleashed a murderous barrage of gunfire from their blazing AK-47 assault rifles on the Captain and his helpless men. "Este es territorio de Capitan de carril elevado, y no tomamos ningun prisionero maldito!" (This is El Capitan's turf—and we take no fucking prisoners.") It all happened so quickly; miraculously Captain Alverez was not hit by the gunfire. He managed to jump and take cover in the surrounding thorny shrubs, remaining calm and motionless—holding his breath and mimicking death. A short time later, Del Monte stumbled on the captain. The guerrilla leader jerked the old man's head backward, pulled a sharp knife with a seven inch blade from his ankle holster and sliced him diagonally across the left cheek. The captain felt the razor sharp blade cutting deep into the facial muscle—his entire face instinctively became rigid and taunt. But he did not flinch or make a sound as the henchman relaxed his grip and wiped the bloody knife on his jacket.

The three other crewmen were not so lucky though; they all succumbed to their injuries. To this very day, the veritable and expert seafaring stalwart has immortalized the memories of that cold and dark November Morning. He credits his miraculous escape to the rosary he has been carrying with him for the last 30 years. His wife Marabel never allows him to leave home without this important symbol of spirituality and good luck omen.

As John handed him the sealed envelope in a watertight plastic pouch containing Two Thousand Five Hundred U.S Dollars, Captain Alvarez smiled revealing a set of pearly white teeth. He extended his strong right arm for a handshake as he spoke.

"Adios amigos—via con Dios."

"Thanks buddy, leave your contact number—may want to use your boat again," replied the former navy seal as he helped the old sailor push the bow of the wooden sloop back into the water. It faded into the darkness, and the Captain Alvarez was soon on his way home to Taganga Bay.

The route back from El Rodadero was a bit shorter. The experienced seaman had earned his stripes; he really knew the coves, bays and inlets. Captain Alvarez instinctively touched the scar left by the blade of El Capitan's knife four years ago, as the boat sliced through the churning waves. What he did not know was that another encounter with the marauding henchman— Carlos Del Monte may not be too far away.

A short distance away, the lights of his home port, located just about seven kilometers from the main Harbor in Santa Marta, appeared to be drawing closer. He kept a steady right hand on the rudder while thinking about the tourist he took to the secluded cove earlier. The man had this look about him, but the most subtle indicator as to his background was the firm handshake. After releasing his hand, Captain Alvarez thought that some kind of metal vice had squeezed him. The grip was so strong and firm; several years at sea, pulling at the heavy nylon ropes and rigging had given Captain Alvarez a strong grip and handshake as well—but wow! This American guy had something extra in those brawny arms.

He continued to maneuver the boat into the narrow channel leading up to the bay of Taganga; Alvarez switched off his outboard engine and used the momentum of the waves and tide to glide the craft safely to shore. He gathered his gear and secured the engine—this is absolutely necessary. Many of his fellow sailors had the rather unpleasant experience of arriving at the bay, anxious and ready to head out to sea, only to realize that bandits had stolen their engines overnight. Captain Alverez couldn't risk that. He earned a living by fishing, and his wife and five children depended entirely on him for their survival.

Tomorrow, he would share the good news with Marabel his dear and loving wife. Two Thousand Five Hundred United States Dollars given to him by this stranger is much more than he had earned for the last six months. Fishing conditions were no longer the same; Captain Alvarez reminisced on the good days when the catch used to be plentiful. In recent times, the fish stocks and other Crustaceans, so vital to the delicate Ecosystem have been slowly disappearing. Fisheries and Environment Ministry officials cite several reasons for the decline.

Indiscriminate logging and the subsequent increase in landslides and soil erosion, together with the improper usage of pesticides and fertilizers in the agricultural sector. The Ministry official, in a Town hall meeting also stated another threat to the fishing industry.

"The drug trade is another factor, many complex operations exist deep in the rain forest and some of the chemicals help to pollute the rivers and streams. Sometimes all this toxic stuff is deliberately poured into the river or left carelessly on our hillsides. Eventually, they all end up in the food chain."

Captain Alvarez remembers very well the words of the Ministry official; for now he is just grateful for the visitor. This American—a total stranger, had given him the largest paycheck he'd seen in years. He strode briskly through the last 50 meters of the cobble strewn path towards home. The house stood majestically above Taganga Bay, and as Alvarez made his way he did not miss any of the meticulously positioned stones, embedded in the pathway. Captain Alvarez pressed on; tiring slightly, he knew that the journey home has a very special meaning. His strides were almost involuntary as he got closer; the old seaman had lost count of the number of trips he had made to and from the lovely Taganga Bay—his ancestral home. Alvarez knows that he is just continuing in the footsteps of his forefathers—fishing and plying the sometimes treacherous waters to put food on the family table. He is so proud to carry on the family tradition, and now at the age of 65 he still had the energy to carry on for quite a few more years.

The old Captain lengthened his strides as he got closer to the house; just a few more steps and he would be home. He had an extremely long but very productive day and could not wait for daybreak to share the great news with Marabel. He reached into his left jacket pocket and felt for the brass key, tied in a knot with the same old string. This time though, his pocket is bulging with a very unusual catch. The old sailor squeezed the envelope given to him earlier by the American and felt overwhelmed. He tossed the rope and other gear under the protruding eave; he is extremely tired but managed to insert the brass key into the quaint rusty lock. The mechanism, quite worn and battered from the harsh tropical elements yielded after a few sharp twists and turns. The door swung open as the hinges squeaked and strained. It's 1:15 am and Captain Alverez can kick back and have a good shot of tequila before retiring for the night.

Tomorrow would be a brand new day, and although he felt sleepy he just could not stop thinking about his encounter with the stranger from America. Was it just by chance or maybe destiny? His route for the day's fishing expedition based on his normal routine, should have taken him further up the coast—at least, a few kilometers to the north of Taganga Bay. He planned to purchase extra fuel so he decided instead to travel south to the resort Town of El Rodadero. This was a life-changing decision! The tall well—built man he stumbled upon, wanted to know how well the Captain knew the Santa Marta coast. He offered to pay a large sum of money if Alvarez would pick him up at a prearranged time later that night.

At first the old man was hesitant; memories of El Capitan four years ago flashed through his mind. Indeed the recollections were quite vivid—the scar on his left cheek, a chilling reminder. But for all that money—it was a chance worth taking. Alvarez tucked the cash filled envelope under the pillow; he felt his eyelids getting heavier. It's time for a good rest, but he could not wait for the light of day. He had made many promises to Marabel—a new stove, furniture for the house and replacing the old weather-beaten rotten window. To think that all these things were now within his reach—it must be the hand of God! What an amazing turn around. After months and months of returning home empty handed or sometimes with just a few fish to supplement the family diet—but now, he had money—not just any money—American money!

Chapter 4

11:00pm Thursday, the foothills of Sierra Nevada, Santa Marta, Colombia. The towering peaks looked so impregnable from DelMonte's hideout; he had such a great fascination with this landmark and it is his dream to scale its almost perpendicular cliffs one day. Against the backdrop of the gigantic full moon this magnificent mountain range is really a sight to behold. El Capitan had an extra bounce in his step tonight though. It's very evident—he seemed restless and paced about relentlessly. What's the matter? Something is bothering the chief tonight and all the insurgents felt it. The entire camp felt its debilitating tentacles. What was it? What could it be? El Capitan sucked hard on a Cuban Cigar to inhale the dry arid smoke; the guerrilla commander spent almost the entire day supervising the construction of three new guard towers and a spacious log cabin. Before becoming a rebel, Carlos Del Monte worked for a large construction company but he also managed the family farm.

The son of poor peasant farmers, Del Monte graduated from Universidad del Norte in the Northern Colombian city of Barranquilla with a degree in civil engineering. His parents scraped every penny they had to ensure that their son got the best education and he certainly made them very proud.

The Del Monte family was slowly moving away from the debilitating poverty which afflicted the entire community—thanks to their son Carlos. The new university graduate started showing his real worth. In less than a year, he totally revamped the family farm and with the help of a foreign funding agency, gained access to grant funding to purchase fifteen hectares of arable land. Soon, the family business became a template for other aspiring peasant farmers, all of this due to the genius of Carlos Del Monte.

Then on one fateful day, the Del Monte utopia and euphoria came to a screeching halt. An anonymous developer had purchased several Thousand Hectares of land from the Government—he had big plans for logging and mining. Shopping malls and other mega commercial complexes were to be constructed as part of the package deal with the Government. Sounds great! Except for one problem—The Del Monte farm falls smack in the path of a proposed four-lane highway. The young and energetic Carlos stood firm, militant defiant and uncompromising; he was at the forefront, leading the protest.

After several weeks braving a merciless barrage from water cannons, rubber bullets and choking tear gas fumes, the government sent in bulldozers and other demolition equipment to demolish the farm to make way for the development. In the end, Del Monte's parents moved south to Buenoventura, where they re-settled with relatives to live out their remaining days on the meager reparations paid by the developer. The younger Del Monte vowed to avenge their monumental loss and fled to the hills.

As the cool crisp night air swept across the lush verdant hillside, the men at base camp Diaz were also becoming restless and with good reason. Last summer, a similar scene played out at another camp and indeed, this situation bears some similarities to what unfolded at Camp Navajo. Exactly one year ago as the moon sprayed its brilliant rays over the jungle forest, El Capitan started walking back and forth, burning up cigars like an angry maniac. Then at the stroke of midnight, he ordered five of his elite body guards to prepare their weapons and report to the parade square where they executed three of their brothers in cold blood. El Capitan later told the stunned troops that the three were traitors and informants who supplied intelligence to the enemy. The wooden plaque hanging over the Colombian black devils Command and control center reads: "Lealtad, compromiso o muerte." Loyalty, commitment or death. These words serve as a poignant reminder for potential informants or anyone who dared to double cross El Capitan.

The hustle and bustle at Camp Diaz continued way into the early morning hours; Carlos Del Monte completed his inspection of the compound just around 1:45 am. He spent an inordinate amount of time focusing on a log cabin built on a freshly cleared lot. Earlier today, the construction crew labored in the sweltering tropical heat to put the finishing touches to the structure. The crew ensured that the plumbing worked well. Whoever is going to occupy those quarters must certainly be very important.

Although El Capitan's men were extremely curious about the newly built structure, even more so the many amenities which came with it, they dared not raise any objections or concerns. El Capitan presented himself the ultimate and supreme leader— he ruled the men with an iron fist and any hint of the slightest recalcitrance is swiftly and brutally snuffed out. Camp Navajo serves as a painful and vivid reminder for anyone brave or foolish enough to breach El Capitan's code of conduct.

By 2:00 am most of the men had already retired for the night, but few of them could sleep anyway as an uneasy air of expectancy and uncertainty enshrouded Camp Diaz. Whatever tidings tomorrow brings—good or bad, would be taken care of one way or the other. A ghostly silence fell over the hillside; even the wind subsided, and only the occasional flashing revolving lights mounted on the perimeter guard tower, broke the monotony. Camp Diaz fell silent; the tired insurgents finally went to sleep.

Chapter 5

Christina changed her position as she tried to sleep on the rough hard bed; she tossed and turned quite a lot. It's been well over a month since she was abducted in broad daylight in the Colombian capital of Bogota. What started off as a fun-filled trip for the daughter of Texas billionaire Mike Preston ended in tragedy on that fateful Saturday Morning, when an armed group stormed the bus filled with exchange students. Christina was researching the impact of logging on the environment and chose Colombia to complete her project, despite the passionate plea from her dad to look for a suitable alternative in another country.

Preston felt that her choice was overly weighted with risk as certain parts of the country had developed a kind of notoriety unrivaled in all of Latin America. Despite his overly protective stance as a loving and devoted father, he acceded to her request after much careful consideration. Mike Preston loved his daughter too much to stand in her way. He had to part with her someday—marriage perhaps, having a family of her own. That's just the way life is—always changing and never constant. He had another good reason for wanting to keep Chrisy close to home; she bore a striking resemblance to her mom Anna—his late wife, the source of his inspiration for almost thirty years.

Since her passing, nearly five years ago, the bond between Mike and his beloved Chrisy became much stronger.

Ironically, it was her late mother who first introduced Christina to environmental issues like land degradation, coastal erosion and the adverse effects of pesticides within the food chain. Mike had to deal with a dilemma here. Anna is no longer in his life, and now the only reminder of her wants to migrate to a foreign land. Yet, if he did not give his blessings and support, deep down inside he knew that apart from the disappointment and frustration Chrisy would feel, he would not be honoring the memory and legacy of his dear wife. And that would be a great sacrilege—Mike can't allow this to be on his conscience. No more indecision—his mind is made up. Christina would have his full and unequivocal support; and at the same time have an opportunity to experience another culture.

Colombia is truly a magnificent country with breathtaking and spectacular scenery; the people and culture are quite fascinating to say the least. Regrettably though, more of the negative stuff gets covered in the press. When was the last time you heard about the great strides the country has been making in the area of adult literacy? How many times? These and several other questions weighed heavily on Preston's mind as he prepared himself mentally for Christina's sojourn to the South American mainland. Mike had the confidence that Pontificia Universidad Javeriana would take all prudent measures to ensure the safety of his beloved Christina and the other exchange students. His angel would be just fine, no need to worry. Preston, by this time had fully made up his mind and all previous inhibitions or apprehension surrounding Christina's choice were gone.

Christina remembers clearly the late night call from her dad giving her the green light: "Hey Chrisy, I've given a lot of thought about your decision to travel to Colombia. It's very difficult for me, but as your dad, I know that I should not stand in your way. You've always made me proud, so you have my blessings— when do you plan on leaving?"

"Oh Daddy! Oh Daddy! You are so sweet." replied Christina, her smooth cheeks glowing with excitement.

"Well, once all the necessary travel documents have been finalized, I should be on my way. The US embassy in Bogota expects the paperwork to be completed by the end of November. When that's done, it's just a matter of making the flight arrangements. I think the middle of January is a realistic date."

"That's great! Hope we can go to the game then?

"What game dad—don't tell me, let me guess—ah, it's baseball I'm sure dad!" said Christina inquiringly.

"Yeah you're so right; It's the Texas Rangers versus the Seattle Mariners, the game is at Arlington on October 26."

"That's great! Yeah, actually the Rangers are quite a thrill— I'd love that," replied Christina, her eyelids flickering with anticipation.

"Daddy, I want to thank you so very much for always being there for me; surely, I won't disappoint you. I've got to go now, got another assignment to complete."

"Ok my dear, be good now, and see you soon."

Christina would always cherish those special moments; there was more sentimentality at that time, as she flew out the following year to begin her studies at Pontificia Universidad Javeriana. The memories of the conversation with her father continued to flood her mind as she tossed and turned on the hard bamboo bed. Trying desperately to fall asleep, the words of her father kept coming back to her. Christina even started to blame herself for being abducted. She summoned every bit of her will power in an effort to keep the depressing thoughts at bay, but they kept infiltrating her mind.

Her captors had not treated her badly anyway. She lost some weight though, and this is normal given her situation. Captivity and being away from home and family had taken a toll on her. Of course, coming from a highly affluent background, the adjustment to life in the bush necessitated radical lifestyle changes. The warm shower, marble bath and Jacuzzi and toilet with gold accessories were now only fading facets of her imagination, as she languished in this vast jungle enclave. A latrine, roughly constructed by lashing tree saplings tightly together with thick jungle vines, and two plastic buckets are the new amenities.

In her first week of captivity, Christina had to wear a blindfold only when her abductors were moving her around. They went to great lengths to ensure that she remained safe. This made perfect sense—as long as she remains alive, the group had a major bargaining chip. Additionally, this is a United States national and if any harm should come to her, the consequence could be quite grave. The rebel group knew of the pact between the Colombian Military and the United States Armed Forces so they are aware of the possible consequences if things went wrong. This is primarily a kidnapping for ransom and also a way of sending a very strong message to the Colombian Government: Cease all military collaboration with the United States or face continued destabilization and social anarchy. The rebel groups see this as blatant interference in the affairs of a sovereign country and an attempt by Washington to re-establish neocolonialism.

Chapter 6

Christina had been in the country just over a year and was really getting to know the local culture; her Spanish is now fluent. Another 13 months and she'll be back in her beloved United States. Christina impressed all her tutors with her impeccable work ethics and great discipline. University Faculty and staff spoke in glowing terms about her exceptional commitment, dedication and positive attitude.

Then, on one fateful October morning all her dreams were shattered; the tour of Quinta de San Pedro Aejandrino, organized by Pontificia Universidad Javeriana turned into a nightmare. Gunfire erupted all around the bus carrying 25 exchange students. The driver, Ernesto Abrillo was shot in the head; and as he bled profusely through the gaping wound in his left temple, six heavily armed masked gunmen stormed the bus. Christina remembers the chaotic scenes on that day. One student leapt through a shattered window when the bus veered violently off the road. A medium built, bearded gunman dragged Ernesto from behind the steering wheel to quickly regain control of the bus. It was a brazen and well executed attack; the whole episode lasted no more than four minutes. The attackers then bundled Christina into an unmarked pickup truck and whisked her away.

As Christina stared at the rough logs and coarse gravel and floor of her makeshift prison, her thoughts were back in Texas—the vast family estate, several swimming pools—the servants and all the luxuries that money can buy. Christina thought about her father and the fears and concerns they shared prior to her departure. Her mind went back and forth as she tried to get some sleep on the uncomfortable bamboo and rough sisal contraption. For some unexplained reason, her thoughts were still on the lavish lifestyle back home. Chrisy, as she was affectionately called by her dad was not prepared though to depend only on her dad's wealth. At age 15, she had already decided with the help of her mother, what her career goal is going to be—a research scientist specializing in tropical rain forests. Of course, Mike wanted the very best for Christina. He could barely control his exuberance when she first shared her dream with him. And of course Preston immediately committed to her tuition and other financial support.

Mike's only concern was her choice of university. He had some reservations about his daughter going off to university in Colombia. There were so many other alternatives available; but in the end all Mike Preston wanted to know was that Christina, his pride and joy—the very essence of his life found an opportunity to fulfill her dreams.

As the cool night breeze wafted through the forest, Christina made a concerted and determined effort to get some sleep. She knew very well that her survival was primarily dependent on her mental attitude and resilience. Christina again forced herself to limit the thoughts of home and focus on the reality; she is held captive deep in the Colombian bush. Wishing for the comforts and opulence of her father's sprawling mansion was certainly a waste of precious energy at this time. As she wrestled with a steady infusion of negative thoughts, Christina made a commitment to herself: She would not die in this jungle wilderness—she is going to make it out alive and well. I swear on the memory of my late mother to find a way out of here, thought Christina as she tried desperately to get some sleep.

Miraculously, the mere thought of her mother brought an immense feeling of calm over her; suddenly all the fear and panic disappeared. Christina not only felt stronger emotionally but physically as well. Her captors seemed less intimidating and Christina knew that nothing could stand in her way anymore! What a sudden transformation—she had a new burst of vigor and vitality. Christina looked at her watch, it showed 2:00 am; the breeze turned into a light wind and the smell of the guard's cigarette smoke drifted across her three meter square jungle jail house. This had minimal impact though, and soon Christina fell into a deep sleep.

Chapter 7

John lifted the heavy duffle bag and started advancing along the rocky stretch of beach. After his midnight rendezvous with Captain Alvarez, Bradley thought about getting some rest. Wary of venomous snakes and other predators he decided against it and continued on his coastal trek. Bradley is quite comfortable with these conditions having done several jungle training stints with the Marines and the US Navy Seals.

Bradley shifted the shoulder strap of his tote bag and advanced up the steep incline. He had entered an area of thick thorny vegetation. The spikes from the hard woody stems occasionally pierced the fabric of his camouflage trousers, but this had a minimal effect on the seasoned veteran. By now he had covered quite a considerable distance and really felt for a short break. Having taken the grueling cross country hike from the marshlands of Maracaibo, Venezuela all the way across to Boca de Camarones on Colombia's Caribbean coast; the American had to weigh the pros and cons before deciding.

The trek tested every bit of Bradley's skill and endurance. Danger lurked around every turn—from the stealthy alligators to the deadly Boa Constrictors it seemed to have no end. But eventually, he made it safely across and nothing must stand in his way. The search for Christina Preston had begun in earnest.

He stopped briefly under a secluded Coconut grove to double check his gear. The Bushmaster Semi-Automatic rifle with extra magazine pouches is never out of his sight. Bradley's arsenal also included an Israeli made Uzi sub machine gun, a crossbow and two large hunting knives. He also had several flares, camouflage paint, night vision goggles and duct tape. His supplies also included: a pair of pliers, a bundle of tying wire, extra items of clothing, rations and a camping stove.

As John examined each item, he could not help but think about the strange and ironical circumstances which brought him to South America - Colombia to be exact. This is not his first trip to this beautiful and ethnically diverse country. Of course, the last one in 2002 would always stand out.

Operation Lethal Fire—a joint United States and Armada Nacional de Colombia military exercise, aimed at rooting out the cocaine production plants deep in the highlands of Medellin. The operation was a resounding success—large swaths of territory controlled by the drug cartels were captured, and a huge amount of cash confiscated. But perhaps most important of all, the demolition of the drug processing facilities. John saw first hand the huge labyrinth of caves and tunnels housing these factories of death. In one particular case, the homemade armor at the entrance of a cocaine producing facility was so tough that the rockets fired from the Apache Helicopter gunships were just ricocheting off with minimal effect. It took Bradley and five Navy Seals almost an hour after fast-roping onto the compound, to finally blast the entrance open with C4 and other high explosive charges.

John had been travelling now for well over eight and a half hours; he knew that he had to get some rest very soon. The military gear coupled with the extremely rough terrain sapped his energy so Bradley really had to make a conscious effort to stay on course.

After leaving the military, Bradley continued his own training and remained fit, but the tough conditions and sleep deprivation started to affect him. He had to find a place to rest soon. At 2:15 am, local time the darkness created a rather creepy and eerie feeling. Occasionally, a cluster of bats would make low strafing passes to swallow up swarms of nocturnal insects and other prey. The ex-soldier's night vision equipment certainly helped. To be out in the South American rain forest at this time takes a special kind of strength and exceptional courage. Apart from the risk posed by hostile human contact, there is the prevailing threat from the vast array of jungle wildlife. The man-eating reptiles and other venomous snakes waiting in deadly ambush is a stark reality of bush life on the continent.

About 30 meters from his position, John spotted what looked like a large fallen tree. He summoned all the energy and raced to the area. The tall thick grass like brush was coarse and sharp, and their tentacles tugged at the fabric of his baggy camouflage. John could not worry about a few minor scrapes and bruises—he just wanted to get to that fallen log. When he got there finally, the spot appeared to be perfect. The tree must have been dislodged from its moorings a few years ago by one of the seasonal torrents which drench the Caribbean Coastlands of Colombia on a perennial basis. Termites and the natural weathering of the elements created a rather soft and spongy mass right through the middle of the log. Bradley had found a bed; he quickly flung the luggage bag over the log, made another check of the surrounding area and then rolled into the makeshift bed.

The retired navy man placed a smoke canister strategically around the makeshift sleeping quarters. This should act as an insect repellant and ward off other potential predators. Despite the exhaustion, Bradley did not fall asleep immediately. He just kept thinking about the days ahead and the potential obstacles to find the missing American student. Her father wants her back badly and he has entrusted him with the task of bringing her back alive and well. The former soldier, had some distinct advantages. He had visited Colombia several times before and is very familiar with the people, and their culture. Most importantly though, he has maintained contact with some sections of the Armed Forces. There are guys currently serving who were on many training exercises with him—when the time is right John knows that he can always count on them.

Bradley rested on the log for about half an hour, and his thoughts were focused momentarily on Preston—the man who hired him. The wealthy Texan is the reason and purpose for him being so far from home; so deep in Colombian terrain. Previously, he vowed to stay away from this kind of high risk and adventure, but when he got the call for help from a desperate father—a man who loved his daughter beyond measure, he felt a deep and compelling urge to respond. Mike Preston is an old friend as well—a friend now backed into a corner of hopelessness and despair. A man, despite the vast array of resources at his disposal who now finds himself in a powerless situation. Thugs and bandits are threatening to unravel his life. The strong outward appearances and stubborn machismo were just a kind of coping mechanism—Mike Preston had to stay focused no matter what. Crumbling and hurting from the inside, the affluent Texan vowed not to rest until his beloved Christina is back home.

Those were his final thoughts before falling asleep. The long trek had taken its toll, and not even the giant jungle bats and screeching owls, scouring the cool and dark night sky were capable of disrupting his deep slumber.

Chapter 8

Mike Preston deliberated over and over again before finally placing the call to the Chairman of the Joint Chiefs of Staff. They were old college buddies and did all the kinds of stuff kids their age did. Mike and Mark grew up in the suburbs on the outer fringes of Houston, Texas. They were so close to each other, many thought they were twins. Growing up, the guys were notorious for their pranks especially around Halloween and April fool's day. Mike remembers this one so very well. On a hot summer day, Mark and Mike decided to stretch their creative genius, they experimented with some basic homemade ingredients and came up with a concoction they thought would be a blockbuster. Both youths had visions of creating a patent for their wonder product. Dubbed, "Youthful Bliss" these, pseudo scientist listed an impressive array of benefits to be derived from the use of their wonder formula—find the girl of your dreams and keep her coming back, say goodbye to pimples, grow new hair . . . . And the list goes on!

Business was booming, and the two homegrown wizards were gaining fame and notoriety. One of their first clients was Joe, the neighborhood bully. Youthful Bliss was right up his ally—Joe's face was heavily scarred by festering pimples and he began losing his hair at a very early age. Anxious to find relief, he bought several sachets of the purported miracle powder. After six weeks, Joe did not see any of the results the young chemists had promised. He got into a mad frenzy and decided to take matters into his own hands.

On a scorching hot day, Joe confronted Mike and Mark in a narrow deserted alley. "Sleazy fucking bastards, yo' all promised me new hair, but instead the few fucking strands I had just disappeared! Yes, whatever is in that powder did a number on my dick as well—I lost all my hair down there too!"

With that angry introduction, Joe lunged at both youths; his big brawny right arm striking Mark a crushing blow in the left rib cage. Winded and dazed from the jarring impact, Mark fell over, landing heavily on his mate. Joe did not waste any time. He pinned both of them firmly to the ground by interlocking their arms. Impaled against the hard and abrasive surface, Joe punched them relentlessly with his free right hand. To complete the onslaught, Joe stomped and kicked the placebo peddlers with his heavy size 11 Bruno Magli boots. Mark sustained a broken nose as well as a concussion, while Mike had several lacerations to the face and bled profusely from his mouth and ears.

They were spared further agony and battering only when an off duty policeman heard the commotion in the deserted alley way and intervened. After the fracas, both youths took a very low profile and never attempted any other experiments.

Mike managed to force a smile as remembered the fun times. As for the science experiment—that's just one he would prefer to forget anyway. As he reminisced, his lips parted involuntarily and he realized that he was actually smiling. He actually smiled! This is something he had not done since Christina's abduction in Colombia.

He picked up the telephone and dialed area code 301 556 7543. The voice at the other end sounded strong and assertive: "Hey

Mike, it's been quite a while, as a matter of fact we haven't seen since Anna died, how you doing buddy?"

"Just hanging in there mate."

"You sound a bit under the weather though—not like my old guy," said the Chairman of the Joint Chiefs of Staff, Reuben.

"Sure, you're quite right" Mike answered.

"What's the trouble—anything I can do?" interjected Mark.

"Christina has been abducted in Bogotá, Colombia by a group of thugs and I need all the help I can get; it has been such a difficult time for me Mark, words just can't explain. I have not eaten a decent meal since this nightmare. Christina went there to conduct research, study and help improve the environment and those crazy bastards did this terrible thing—my God!"

"Oh Mike I hate to see you like this, I'm so sorry to hear of this tragedy; what can I do to help?"

"Whatever you can buddy, I just want my daughter back, that's all that matters to me now."

"I've got a meeting at 10: 30 in the morning with General Dumas, Director of the CIA, and although we have a very packed agenda—this Iranian Nuclear stuff and troop withdrawal from Baghdad. The insurgency in Libya would take up the greater part of our meeting—but don't worry, I know how committed you are to the family; your daughter's kidnapping would be included. You have my word."

Preston stretched and felt like extending a hand to thank his boyhood buddy for the support and commitment. He felt a great sense of relief after listening to the Chairman of the Joint Chiefs of Staff. He managed a smile as Mark continued.

"Additionally, sometime tomorrow I would call my Colombian counterpart—General Castenadas to get a feel of what's happening on the ground down there. We've got an excellent relationship with the Government. Our troops train there regularly and conduct joint naval and inland training exercises to help with narco trafficking. By the way, have you heard anything from the kidnappers, or initiated any plans for a possible rescue or the payment of a ransom?"

"No, nothing from those fucking bastards, anyway I've been talking with a former Navy Seal and Special Forces man—John Bradley." Preston slammed his fist angrily on the side table as he answered the Chairman of the Joint Chiefs of Staff.

"That's great! You've got a good man on your side; he is a highly decorated veteran with a lot of experience. I know him personally, he's got a purple heart and several citations for bravery and heroism."

"Oh yes; that's right and he is already on the ground—over a week now, he should be getting in touch with me again. I am so anxious to hear from him!"

"Alright Mike, I think you should try to get some sleep; I know that this is an extremely difficult time for you, but I give you my firm commitment to do everything possible to ensure your daughter's safe return."

"Thanks Mark, you've always been a good friend," said Mike as he hung up.

Chapter 9

The morning sky became a bit clearer, and fragrant sweet scents emanated from the amazing array of colorful jungle plants. Mother nature had already sent out a subtle reminder to her numerous species. At this time of the day, the air seems to have an extra measure of freshness. Already, the birds were chirping in the trees as they herald the birth of a new day.

The pristine beauty of nature enveloped the entire area, and the sky started to clear up as the creatures of the wild were all positioning themselves to greet the new day. Dawn is just around the corner and with impeccable precision the ritual had started. The species of the animal kingdom are about to begin the hunt for food and fight for their survival. Surely, it's a fight where only the fittest survive.

Somewhere in the distance, a large Boa Constrictor is slithering ominously close to a tangled mass of rotten twigs. It moved gracefully among the dead foliage while sniffing the air with a flickering tongue. The snake seemed to pause and then make a sharp turn, it raised its head and in a flash, like a coiled spring, lashed out with lethal and pin-point accuracy. It all happened so quickly; the rabbit had no time to react. The snake's large

him as my point man on the ground here. Something about him tells me that a lead is possible with his help. He knows the area almost like the palm of his hand. You know that gut feeling."

"Hope you're right on that one; I've been in touch with my sources in Washington—the Chairman of the Joint Chiefs of Staff to be precise. I expect a call soon."

"That's great news, we need all the help we can get; maybe you should ask your source in Washington to contact the Colombian Authorities. I would need special permission to move around with all that military stuff."

"Sure, that's not a problem—would take care of it," said Preston with a flair of authority.

"Great, would wait to hear from you then," replied the former Navy Seal.

Bradley laid out his plan to Mike Preston in clear and simple detail. His first task is intelligence gathering. He wanted every bit of information on the kidnapping and most importantly, an interview or meeting with the local Police Chief. He would need unlimited access to the case file from local authorities including pictures of the crime scene and footage from any surveillance cameras operating at the time of the incident. Mike felt a sense of peace and calm after speaking with John—the soldier was so supportive and reassuring.

John ended the discussion with Mike by giving him a commitment to bring Christina home.

"This is a pretty vast country, much bigger than Texas with a population of around forty-seven million people. She could be anywhere between Puerto Bolivar and Buenaventura; but you have my word—I'll find her and make those mother fuckers who did this pay a heavy price. You have my word!"

By now the sun pierced its warm rays through the thick canopy of trees, Bradley had covered quite a bit of ground since he came ashore nearly five hours ago. He deliberately chose some high ground overlooking the Bay of Santa Marta to set up his base camp. The area provided an excellent vantage point. Bradley placed the pair of binoculars to his eyes and trained it on the cluster of buildings which formed the main commercial center of Santa Marta. From his vantage point, he could see the modern skyline of the city.

Before making his clandestine entry into Colombia, Bradley took some time to look at the country's history. He learnt about Colombia's rich and diverse culture and had a distinct fascination with Santa Marta—the Capital of the Department of Magdalena said to be the oldest city in the Americas. The history and cultural diversity is not the only reason he had for being in this city though. He had done some preliminary research earlier and based on the information gathered, John had a gut feeling that he landed in the right place. He just had to do all the legwork—gather the intelligence, establish contact with the right people—and most importantly, be patient.

John, completed his cursory scan of the Santa Marta coast and the city skyline from the vantage point he now occupied, and then picked up a notepad from his side pocket. He looked at the picture of Christina again as he made some rough notes on her case: Abducted, October 2009 about three kilometers from Pontificia Universidad Javeriana, Carrera 7, Bogata. Number of kidnappers: Six—all male, between the ages of 19 and 30. Fatalities during the assault on the tour bus: One, Ernesto Abrillo, driver. The rebels were heavily armed with Kalashnikov assault rifles, Rocket propelled grenades (Soviet era RPG-29's), Uzi Sub-Machine guns and several hand grenades. Bradley, worked hard to create a profile of the group holding Christina.

While at home in Houston Texas, he prepared a shortlist of four potential suspects. At the top stood the National Front for the Liberation of Colombia. Followed by Martyrs and Patriots for

Change. Number three—the National Resistance and Peasant Advocacy Group for National Heritage. The final group on Bradley's list is the Colombian Black Devils.

One by one he carefully analyzed each group, NFLC, historically has not accepted kidnapping as part of its strategy to bring about change and has often been criticized for being too cozy with the ruling administration. Additionally, they've been campaigning for democracy and electoral reform. Their actions suggest that they would be vying for political office.

The former marine and navy seal drew a red line to strike out the National Front. Martyrs and Patriots and National Resistance shared a similar ideology. They were powerful and strong advocates for land reform. Soil conversation and land usage are always at the forefront of their activities. In June 2006 they were able to mobilize over one hundred and fifty thousand peasant landowners and other persons concerned about environmental degradation to joint rallies in Santa Marta and Bogota. Both groups had military wings, but they were ruled out as well.

John focused his attention on the last group—The Colombian Black Devils. Of all the guerrillas, they are the most militant and radical. They make vast fortunes from the drug trade; piracy and arms trafficking off Colombia's Caribbean and Pacific coasts. Kidnapping is also another fundamental part of their modus operandi. They are led by the notorious Carlos Del Monte alias El Capitan and their base is deep in the highlands of the Sierra Nevada. Bradley would focus all his attention on El Capitan and his group of murderous thugs.

They have developed a kind of notoriety, which even by Colombian standards is considered extreme. The Black Devils reverted to very extreme methods to instill fear and intimidate their enemies—real or imaginary. Earlier in the year they beheaded five farmers who accidentally stumbled on one of their Cocaine facilities. To reinforce their power and gross brutality, El Capitan and his henchmen located the fields of the beheaded farmers and burnt all their crops, killed their livestock—and as a final insult raped the women and young girls. They were a mean, cold and ruthless bunch! Any encroachment on their turf, inadvertent or otherwise is certainly one way of hastening your demise. The villagers who fled the horrific scenes near Riohacha on that day can surely attest to this.

The former American Special Forces Man, looked at his watch; time seemed to be moving at a faster pace on the South American Continent. He lifted the heavy bag and started to move in a southwesterly direction. John spent almost an entire day in the highlands above the city. Bradley felt that the time is right for an incursion into the city; finding a place for his gear is the immediate priority though. Travelling into the heart of Santa Marta with a huge military style bag would certainly make him a target. He removed his travel documents, wallet, cash and credit cards first. Bradley would not venture into town unarmed. He quickly retrieved the 9mm Semi-Automatic and tucked it into his baggy side pocket. His knife and ankle holster completed the arsenal for the trek down to the city center. The remaining gear was buried under a thick canopy of dried leaves, close to a cactus-strewn rocky outcropping.

Without his full and heavy duffle bag, Bradley moved down the slope rather quickly; at this pace he should be in the city well before nightfall.

Chapter 10

The Chairman of the Joint Chiefs of Staff walked briskly into the meeting room. It's not normal for him to be late. Something had kept him up late last night and it caused him to be ten minutes late for his meeting with the Head of the CIA. His college buddy and lifelong friend, Mike Preston needed help urgently. Reuben heard and felt the pain in his voice and really wanted to find a way to help him.

Preston started to unravel emotionally and Reuben knew it; he knew that something had to be done quickly. Reuben couldn't say exactly what course of action he'd suggest, but he certainly won't sit and watch his boyhood buddy wither away in grief and hopelessness. Reuben thought about Christina and the hell and torment those bastards have inflicted on her. Mark felt obligated and knew that he just had to find a way to present Preston's cause to CIA Director Dumas—but he had to be tactful.

There were so many issues and trouble spots around the world to be discussed. Finding a way to help Peston is paramount; his lifelong buddy really needs his support now. He already had so much to deal with. The fucking insurgents in Libya were running all over Benghazi with AK 47's and rocket propelled grenades.

Tripoli, Sirte or even Bani Waled may be overrun in a matter of days. Latest reports from authenticated CIA sources and satellite imagery, indicate that the Strongman is moving heavy armor into Tripoli. We think this is in anticipation of a major rebel offensive on the city within the next forty eight hours. Then we have Tunis and Tahrir Square—so many damn hot spots around the world!

The Chairman of the Joint Chiefs of Staff also had some concerns about the Iranian Nuclear proliferation and the real possibility that Tel Aviv would launch a pre-emptive strike on Tehran. The US had more than its fair share of trouble around the world. Washington had to find a way to address other pressing world issues. The timeline for the withdrawal of American troops from Iraq and Afghanistan had to feature prominently in today's meeting with the CIA Chief. These matters weighed heavily on Mark Reuben's mind as he walked into the spacious meeting room.

There was some preliminary chatter among the seated officials; a computer technician made some minor adjustments to the Power Point slide show for presentation during the course of the meeting. The Defense Secretary fidgeted with his tie, his appearance suggested that he dressed in a great rush. To begin, the blue polka dot tie seemed oddly out of place and did not match the plaid shirt with the wrinkled creamy-white collar. To further compound his misery, on the way into the meeting he clumsily elbowed the stainless steel milk jug, spilling the milk all over his tweed jacket and trousers. Secretary of defense Montague felt like kicking himself.

On the contrary, Mark Reuben is immaculately dressed. He wore light blue cotton shirt with a matching dark blue tie. His well fitted dark gray suit matched perfectly, and the mirror-like sheen on his fine black leather shoes simply accentuated his impeccable appearance. The Chairman of the Joint Chiefs of Staff looked sharp and ready for the meeting.

Everything else seemed to be in place; the Chairman walked right past the Secretary of Defense and took his seat next to CIA director, Dumas.

"Good Morning gentlemen, this meeting is called to discuss several issues of importance to the United States National Security."

Mark Reuben lifted a glass of water to his dry lips and allowed the cool soothing drink to slowly trickle into his system, as he finished his opening remarks.

"Gentlemen I would now hand over proceedings to CIA director, Dumas. With all this rebellion and militancy in North Africa, trouble brewing in Egypt and the Arabian Peninsula, I am pretty damn certain that he has a whole lot to share with us—General Dumas, the floor is yours."

"Thanks Mark. Let me begin by putting things into perspective. How many of you—and I know you're attending the almost fortnightly White House briefings, and also through the ubiquitous social media have been able to keep abreast with the plethora of world events? These unusual events—the Arab Spring I think they call it, was started rather innocuously by a fruit vendor in Tunisia. Yes, a simple market vendor in one defiant act of self-immolation ignited such nationalistic fervor as never seen before. This tiny spark provided the catalyst and fuel for all the major uprisings—it has affected close allies, moderates and even regimes hostile to the United States."

"Gentlemen, this is our real challenge; we must devise a new approach to deal with the situation. Each one is unique and has a different level of volatility and special set of circumstances. There is no one answer—no panacea, no magic bullet! Critical in all of this is the security of the United States—our homeland security and the safety of our embassies on foreign soil is of paramount importance."

The CIA director completed his briefing with a PowerPoint presentation giving graphic detail and statistics on the unfolding world events. Defense Secretary, Dave Montague quizzed the CIA Chief on the wisdom of a complete and unconditional withdrawal of US troops from Iraq in light of the tumultuous events. Chairman Reuben replied that a final decision has not been reached. This matter is slated for discussion at the next Congressional Meeting, scheduled for early in the New Year.

Secretary of State Price stood in support of General Montague on the question of troop withdrawal and asked the CIA chief to prepare a draft contingency plan for all United States embassies in the areas of concern around the world.

As the meeting was about to be concluded, Mark Reuben, Chairman of the Joint Chiefs of Staff requested permission to raise a matter which was not included on the agenda.

"How many of you are familiar with the name, Mike Preston—an outstanding American citizen and wealthy businessman."

General Montague lifted his hand in acknowledgement. "Of course, he's a real patriot and philanthropist—an exceptional son of the soil."

"Good, yes he's really a wonderful guy," replied Reuben with a nod of approval.

"Anyway, to get directly to the point; his only daughter Christina was kidnapped by Colombian rebels about a week ago."

"What the fuck was she doing down there?" interjected Secretary of State Price.

"Does it really matter? She is a fucking American citizen and that's the important point here! Let's get that straight, ok smart-ass. Whether she is there screwing every dick-head in Bogota or Cartagena it's totally irrelevant. Her safe repatriation to the

United States is all that matters," Mark blurted out angrily as he banged his clenched fist on the table. The impact heavy enough to knock over a partially filled glass of water.

"Sorry man, didn't mean it that way," replied Price, apologetically.

"Tell me something, Mr. Secretary of State—just put yourself in Preston's position. Would you've just sat back and done nothing to gain your daughter's fucking freedom! Tell me man! Tell me!"

The CIA Chief stood up and walked over to where Mark was standing and placed his arm around the rather livid and infuriated Chairman.

"Take it easy man, don't get too heated up, let's get some details on the situation."

"Thanks, Chief I'd love to do that," said Reuben as he returned to his chair.

Mark briefed the meeting on Christina's case, using the information he got from Mike Preston. The tone in the CIA Director's voice indicated some level of seriousness and real urgency. Mark already knew that his mission has been accomplished.

The meeting at Langley, Virginia then concluded at around 11:45 and at 12:15pm Washington time, 11:15 pm in Bogota, General Dumas picked up the telephone to speak with his opposite number—General Castenadas.

Chapter 11

Bradley sprinted the last hundred and fifty meters of the way. From his position he could see the lights of the City. Santa Marta is even more beautiful by night; he really wanted to experience some nightlife. A soft bed and a warm cozy dinner, and yes—some female company. Life in the bush is not so difficult for John, but sometimes the natural cravings would kick in. Just then he thought about Christina and the hell she must be going through somewhere out there in this vast wilderness. As he approached the city he made a silent affirmation: "Christina, I am here to find you and take you home to your dad. Just stay alive—I am not leaving without you."

John walked briskly past a 4 meter high perimeter fence, he could see the very large shipping containers and knew straight away that he was in the vicinity of the Santa Marta Port complex. He pulled the map from the small knapsack to find the nearest hotel. Based on the distance he had travelled, it became clear that the city center is not very far away. He heard the rumbling of some type of heavy locomotive—a train perhaps. Bradley learnt from a tourist information brochure of a freight train service operated by the Santa Marta Ports Authority, *Sociedad Porturia de Santa Marta SA.*

The rumbling got louder and louder; he even started feeling the vibration of the ground beneath him—and oh yes—right over there. Like a gigantic metallic snake, the silver-gray train came rocketing down the railway with its cargo. The port of Santa Marta is an important hub for the transshipment of manufactured products, construction material and other commercial goods.

John Bradley now felt a sense of euphoria as he got closer to the heart of the city; the thought of a warm bath, a decent meal and all the other comforts he has been deprived of, made him chuckle with excitement. The former Navy Seal and Special Forces man quickly reminded himself though of his mission: The safe return of Mike Preston's daughter—Christina Preston. He would enjoy a little leisure, experience the night life and the cuisine eventually; but the core and fundamental purpose of his trip takes precedence over everything else at the moment.

By this time the night sky above Santa Marta became illuminated with a dazzling array of fluorescent and neon lights. John stopped near to a building with a very unique architectural design. He got close enough to see the white and blue shield of the court of Arms—John Bradley had finally arrived in Downtown Santa Marta, the Capital of the Department of Magdalena. He looked at his watch; It read 7:05 pm local time and 6:05 am in Langley Virginia, United States of America. The former Navy Seal walked briskly for another 25 minutes before he found what he was looking for.

The building appeared quite impressive with an immaculate and appealing façade. He had barely completed his final strides to the lobby when the polished glass door was held open for him by a hotel butler in a bright maroon blazer: "Buenas noches; bienvenido a la hermosa Estelar Santamar Hotel y centro de convenciones."

Bradley reciprocated with a bright smile." No tengo una reserva, pero necesito una habitación; Yo he estado viajando to-do El día." The butler confirmed the availability of range of suites at the hotel; relieved John handed the man his rucksack as he escorted him to the reservations desk.

The American visitor already felt at home; what an awesome introduction and welcome. Impressed is definitely an understatement. This employee is the perfect example of a great first impression; he used his experience and expertise gracefully. If this is the expectations benchmark—then Bradley knew what to expect later. The attendant's almost involuntary response to the inquiry of the newly arrived guest is worthy of commendation and praise. Estelar Santamar would be very high on the ex-soldier's list of hotels when next he is in Santa Marta.

The entire process of checking in was completed in about 25 minutes—and without a reservation. Wow! John just couldn't believe the excellent customer service, and already he felt like a king. When Bradley got to his room all he wanted was a warm bath. The previous thrill and adventure of diving into a bubbling jungle waterfall, and the experience of the high velocity blasts from the cascading water, is now a distant and quickly fading memory.

Bradley plugged in his Laptop and mobile Phone into the electrical outlet. The computer would need a bit more time to be powered up before John got connected to the Local access Network. The receptionist had indicated previously that Estelar Santamar had great Internet service. The battery in his mobile phone still had some power—John managed to maintain it through the use of his solar power pack.

When he got out of the shower, he ordered room service; the attendant was at the door with his dinner in record time, expertly balanced on a large tray draped with a white towel accentuated colorfully by a solid embroidery trim. The smell of food permeated the room as she walked in.

"Good evening sir, please enjoy your dinner." The words uttered from her mouth with charm and great sincerity.

"Thank you very much my dear," replied the rather hungry guest.

John wasted no time digging into the delectable entrée servings—lobster in tangy Banana-Tamarind sauce; grilled vegetables, steamed cassava in mildly peppered coconut milk. Sweet Corn on the cob and a colorful garden salad completed the meal. The dessert consisted of a silky banana ice cream and Coconut cake. There were generous portions of tropical fruit—papaya and mangoes. John ate voraciously, then flung himself horizontally on the king size bed. His alarm was set for 10:30 pm, at that time he would place a call to Mike Preston for an update on his progress thus far. Mike should also appraise him on developments in Washington and Langley.

Chapter 12

Captain Alvarez awoke just before the first streak of morning sunlight came over the exquisitely beautiful Taganga Bay. This is a picture he had seen so many times and every day the beauty of the bay grows more and more breathtaking. Taganga my home! I will never leave or forsake you, the old seaman made a silent admonition as he got up from the bed. Marabel is already up, cleaning and preparing for the day. This marvelous homemaker loves creating those tasty dishes and keeping the house impeccably neat and clean. She also kept a lovely rose garden and grew a wide array of herbs and vegetables for the family.

Alvarez rushed to the kitchen, the old teapot whistled to indicate that the water is ready for the fresh home grown coffee. Marabel always made a strong brew for her husband before he goes out to sea. Manuel extended both arms and embraced her—it was an unusually long and strong and robust hug. His darling wife and inspiration sensed that something was amiss. In twenty years, he had not given his queen such an embrace—he squeezed so hard and strong, her breathing became partially impaired.

"Good morning Bella baby, I have some good news," The fisherman used his love bird name for Marabel, as she stared at him in shock and utter amazement. She tried to wriggle out of the constricting grip to expand her lungs and breathe normally, her husband oblivious of the discomfort.

"Manuel! You start to drink tequila again, I don't want you drinking that stuff before you go out fishing."

"Darling it's nothing to do with that, I had a good catch last night—the best in almost five years. I met a man from America; he gave me a job—yes darling. This man hired my boat, I had to take him a few kilometers up the bay. And for that he paid me two thousand five hundred American Dollars. Come Bella, come! Feel it, touch it—smell it!" Exclaimed Manuel, as he spilled out the content of his prized envelope on the pitch pine table.

"Oh my God! Manuel! Manuel! I don't want any 'narcontraficante' to chop off your head and feed it to the sharks. I'll prefer to remain dirt poor and at least have you around."

Marabel found a way out of her husband's embrace and caressed his face lovingly; her fingers lingered over the jagged scar on his left cheek. "Manuel, you see this—it brings back bad memories. When that evil demon slashed your face, I had to nurse you like a baby for almost two months. Do you remember that Manuel; do you?" inquired Marabel passionately.

"Darling I know, but there is no need to worry, how can I ever forget?" Replied Manuel with a broad smile.

Marabel shrugged her shoulders vigorously as she replied. "Fue un mal momento para nosotros" (It was such a bad time for us)

The Captain spoke to reassure his wife that the money was indeed clean. "You have no need to worry darling, the visitor is here in Santa Marta for a special assignment, and I may be working with him again before he travels back to his home in

America." Marabel appeared to be a bit calmer now as she moved away from Manuel to turn off the flame under the kettle. She picked up the sizzling hot water, removed the lid from the coffee pot and poured until the rich dark brew trickled from the top and spilled onto the table. The old seaman has been drinking Marabel's delectable aroma—filled coffee for the last twenty-five years and it seemed to get better with every sip.

The sun sprayed its beautiful rays all over Taganga Bay, so Marabel and Captain Alvarez really wanted to make this a very special occasion. They have good reason to celebrate; the family has been struggling so much over the last few years. On a cool cloudy morning just a few short weeks ago, something good happened. The old seaman still reminisces on the chance encounter with a stranger from America. As the family prepared for the journey up the coast, the indelible impact this visitor had on his life seemed so surreal. Alvarez threw a portion of food and drink across the gentle waves to pay homage to the spirit of his ancestors, to whom he attributes his exceptional fortune.

Although Marabel had her own apprehensions about the entire episode, she quickly convinced herself that Manuel's recent good luck had some kind of supernatural connection. She too will pay homage by casting a bouquet of bright tropical flowers and some of the goodies into the water. As she packed the baskets with all the delectable treats—spicy corn bread, cassava pudding and Manuel's favorite—roasted chicken laced with herb and ginger sauce, Marabel said a silent prayer. She watched from the kitchen window as Manuel prepared the boat for the day's journey.

By then Mrs Alvarez had already figured out how the money is going to be spent. While they would splurge on a few things—buy some new furniture—Marabel had other plans for that money. She had a *date* with *Banco de Occidente, Avenidad Del Libertador in* Downtown Santa Marta early on Monday.

Captain Alvarez continued to prepare the boat for the trip. He glanced over his shoulder at the weather beaten house overlooking Taganga Bay. By now, Marabel should have the family ready. His eldest son Pedro got the good news before the other children and was busy helping with the chores. The old seaman completed his preparation and started walking back towards the house. Through the back door, he saw little Miranda, jumping and running around in her bright floral dress and a floppy white hat. His cute and sassy little princess was up and ready to go!

Manuel climbed the old wooden steps. As he entered the kitchen, the aroma of good home-cooked food filled the air. The rugged pitch pine table, draped in a brightly colored cloth was brimming over with several delicacies. Marabel is busy cleaning up and packing away her pots and pans, while Young Pedro packed the picnic baskets.

"My love, how long do we have again? It's almost time to go," said Captain Alvarez as he lifted up Miranda.

"I am ready Manuel, let' take the baskets down to the boat," replied Marabel as she threw the damp kitchen cloth on the wooden rack.

When Captain Alvarez and his family left Taganga Bay, it was around 10:45 am. The lush green hillside overlooking the bay appeared so regal and majestic. Alvarez recounted the many trips he made from this charming and exotic spot. However, today's trip and the circumstances which made it possible would be forever etched in his mind.

Chapter 13

Christina woke up a bit earlier than usual. She was still energized and invigorated from last night's really special experience. The inspiration sparked by the memory of her late mother was indeed sensational. Christina turned on her side while making another entry in her Journal.

"Day 27 in captivity—found renewed strength and courage; every day is a day closer to freedom, don't give up now."

The regular morning routine did not appear to be the same today. Christina had good reason to be curious. Why so much activity in and around the compound? There were definitely more rebels on the base; what's really happening today? Even the night guards were already being replaced, and a lot of boxes were being shifted around. Normally, the guards would change over around 8.00 am; Christina looked at her watch and it was just 5:45 am. What were the reasons for this sudden change and the flurry of activity around the camp?

Christina signaled to the short burly guard walking casually nearby. "I would like to go to the bathroom and I don't have much time, hurry please!"

He nodded in approval and instinctively adjusted the strap on the AK 47 slung diagonally across his chest and shoulder. He looked like a fairly new conscript who hadn't yet completed the basics. He seemed so awkward and ungainly. For a moment Christina entertained the thought of whacking him with a drop kick, grabbing his Kalashnikov and make a run for the heavily wooded forests.

Actually, it is not the first time such thoughts came to her mind— thoughts of escaping from the guerrillas are always with her. Certainly, this is one way of keeping hope and her spirit alive. Christina dismissed the idea of escaping for the time being. She would focus on maintaining her fitness—mental as well as physical and wait for the right moment. Christina is quite confident of her ability to outwit her captors, but timing and patience are the key components of her plan.

She thought of another reason why she must remain focused and alive, as the awkward and rather clumsy sentry escorted her to the small enclosure which served as a toilet and personal hygiene bay.

Her dad would most certainly use the enormous resources at his disposal to secure her freedom. His love and dedication to her is beyond measure. Christina had absolutely no doubt about that.

Christina made a desperate effort to be out as quickly as possible. Yesterday a centipede wriggled up her calf as she relieved her bowels. The early biology lessons paid off quite well here. Christina remained as still as possible and calmly slapped the crawling insect with her bare hand. She finished it off with a swift stomp using the studded sole of her sneakers.

The rough makeshift toilet provided a sanctuary for a host of tropical bugs and other crawling insects. Despite this however, her captors made a fairly good effort to maintain good sanitation and at least minimum hygiene standards.

Captivity, and yes the anger and frustration—even feelings of abandonment is slowly permeating through her mind. Last night however, was quite an inspiration though. She refocussed her thoughts again on her late mother and the inner strength which seemed to radiate and invigorate her. Christina quickly splashed the water all over her body, a few soap suds clung lazily to her skin as she wiped with the slightly damp towel. Christina slipped on her underwear, quickly pulled on a pair of Old Navy Jeans—the same one she wore on the day of the kidnapping, and headed out of the little chamber.

Christina covered the fairly short distance from the crudely built washroom with no more than twenty strides. At age 22 and 1. 75 meters tall, she is extremely fit and agile. As she entered her place of confinement, Christina observed something quite unusual; a female guard had already gone inside the cabin. She was actually removing some of Christina's personal belongings. Christina went berserk! "Fucking bitch! What are you looking for!" And with that she swiveled on her left foot and landed a perfect kick to the woman's head. It was a lightening fast motion and Christina had no intentions of letting up. The female guard got a rather crude introduction from this cagey American with the mentality of a street fighter. She certainly did not anticipate such a battering, and Christina showed her no mercy.

The blow to the head had jaded her quite a bit but the guerrilla fighter did not fall over. Her weapon was slung over a wooden peg near the only widow in the log cabin. She turned towards the direction of the Israeli made Uzi Submachine gun, and rued the earlier decision to part with the lead spewing death machine. Christina would have had second thoughts if the fighter was armed. At close range those rounds are extremely lethal.

The rebel fighter realized that Christina had seen the Uzi as well. Slightly shorter than the American, the Colombian knew that she doesn't stand a chance in a sprint with the American. So the thought of making a run for the weapon soon faded from her mind. Instead, she charged forward at Christina in a series of wild 180 degree turns. She caught Christina by surprise; one swirling rotation hitting the American smack on her left temple.

Christina lost her balance momentarily, and the heavier adversary came slamming down hard on her torso. The woman was now all over her, clawing wildly at her hair and face while screaming: "You fucking American bitch I will feed your fat pussy to the crocodiles."

Christina tensed her abdominal muscle and with all her strength heaved the attacker into the air; she landed heavily on her back and had no time to recover. She quickly followed up with a hard knee to the rib cage. Miranda buckled up like a rag doll on the hard dirt floor, her body writhing in pain and anguish. Christina picked up the Uzi Submachine gun just as three other guerrilla fighters stormed into the room.

They quickly wrestled the weapon from Christina, duct taped her hands behind her back and tossed her on the old bed. The other woman was mumbling something barely audible; the guards helped her to her feet and then she was taken out of the room. The sloppy looking sentry remained in Christina's cabin while the two men helped Miranda walk to the command center. Once inside, a tall man with a mustache, dark glasses and a Cuban Cigar shouted at the bruised and battered woman.

"So the broad kicked your ass—she almost got away. You are lucky, fat bitch—I would have slit your fucking throat and carved your pussy with my knife, he snarled at the sobbing guard. This prisoner is the big fish we've caught and any of you fuck things up—expect no mercy! Now, get your sloppy ass out of here before I lose my temper. Get out of here now!"

Chapter 14

General Castenadas sat in his padded mahogany chair and sucked hard on the cigarette. His last physical was not bad at all for his age. At 64, he is not doing badly. His career in the military is on the right trajectory and in just a few more years he'll be ready to retire. He had his eyes on a prize piece of real state on San Andres Island on the scenic Caribbean coast. A yacht and private jet perhaps and some other luxuries. Two more years and its time to kick back and enjoy the benefits; he had worked his butt off to make it up the hierarchy and nothing must stand in his way now.

His entry into the Colombian military at the age of 23 came as a surprise too. He did not have any outstanding physical qualities. Perhaps it had to do with his uncanny ability to solve problems. In fact Alvario Garcia Castenadas failed his physical. He was only accepted because one of the commanding officers had a great liking for the way he performed in the survival skills test. New recruit Alvario acquitted himself admirably in that component of the entry examination.

The General reached for the brown manila envelope with the official Colombian Government Seal and slit through the flap with the sliver souvenir letter opener. He poured out the contents quickly on the solid glass square which covered the desktop. General Castenadas stood momentarily to stretch his legs as the antique rotary dial phone rang rather loudly.

He reached for the receiver and placed the black telephone to his ear. "Buenos Dias Senor Reuben, how are you? It's been quite a while."

"Excellent, a lot of stuff is happening these days, but we are keeping the bad guys in check." The Chairman of the Joint Chiefs of Staff, cleared his throat as he responded to General Castenadas.

"General, tell me—how are things down there? I heard that the insurgents are stepping up their activity."

"Yeah, they are certainly giving me some extra gray hairs and sleepless nights."

"It's just a matter of time before you guys kick their fucking ass anyway."

"I've got no doubt about that, the last shipment of Apache attack helicopters is already making a difference. We blasted several of their camps to smithereens in a series of raids three days ago. I heard that the cannon fire from the new birds cut them up into tiny bits."

"Yeah that's good, we supply only top of the line hardware to our allies—we are in this war together, buddy."

General Castenadas pulled back the dark mahogany chair and sat in a semi upright position as the Chairman of the Joint Chiefs of Staff continued.

"Enough of that stuff anyway; I want to discuss a very important matter—nothing to do with national security or so."

"Don't worry my friend, you can always count on me!" Replied the Colombian Defense Minister.

"I'm sure you've heard about the American exchange student kidnapped near Quinta de San Pedro Alejandrino about four weeks ago?"

"Of course, incidentally I got a report only this morning from the Division Commander on the case—the victim is a Christina Presto?"

"Christina Preston!" Interjected CJCS, Reuben.

"The men have been working almost round the clock to find her. Pontificia Universidad Javeriana has thousands of flyers posted all over the country. They are offering a huge reward for anyone providing information on the American girl. Their official website and Facebook pages have also been inundated with queries and suggestions since the abduction, but so far there have been no real leads."

"I need you to put some heat on your people man, this is not just any girl. Her dad is a very successful Texas businessman, and a close and dear friend—these folks are like family."

"Mike Preston, really?"

"You've met him before, haven't you?"

"Yes. Of Course, a really nice guy—owned a Petro Chemical and natural gas company down here in the late eighties."

General Alvario Castenadas spun around in his chair and picked up the letter opener again; he tapped lightly on the desk.

"Mark, before the end of today, I am authorizing the Department of Magdalena to utilize all assets in the search for Christina. I would also be requesting weekly reports on the progress of the efforts to locate and rescue her."

"Thanks mate, I'm really counting on you."

"By the way, we already have a man on the ground. He is a former Special Forces and Navy Seal—a guy by the name of John Bradley."

"How long he's been on the ground?" General Castenadas asked with an air of authority.

"Just a little less than a week," replied the Chairman of the Joint Chiefs of staff.

"OK, please give him my number, I'm sure we can work together on this one."

The Chairman thanked the Colombian General, hung up the telephone and walked towards the door.

Bradley woke up feeling quite refreshed and invigorated. Dinner was great and the soft bed really made him feel like cuddling up for a while longer. He quickly dismissed the thought and decided that it is a good time to call Christina's dad—Mike Preston.

He reached for the mobile phone but the battery power was not at its optimal level. Instead, he picked up the bedside phone and dialed.

The voice at the other end of the line seemed faint and rather distant.

"Hello, Preston."

"Hi Mike, how you are doing?"

"Just hanging in there man. You've made any progress since our last discussion?"

"No breaking news, but I've moved down to the city center for a couple days. Just want to establish contact—never know where a clue might come from."

"Want to hang around the clubs and other entertainment spots; at this point what we need is a break—a tiny opening and some luck."

"John, it's almost a month since those cowardly bastards stole my angel. Who knows what on earth they are doing to her!"

"This bothers me a whole lot," Bradley replied while flipping the pages of his yellow notepad; "I am hitting the road tonight for a couple hours."

"Got to find something man—a start at least, some clue."

"Yes, yes! I really need you to get a lead; John this is driving me crazy," said Preston as he banged his clenched fist on the side of his bed.

The old soldier felt Preston's exasperation, he heard the labored heavy breathing of a desperate father. A man who would do anything to get his daughter back. Bradley showed great empathy and emotion as he listened to Preston's passionate plea. He quickly realized though that getting emotionally attached would certainly do more harm than good anyway.

To find Christina, Bradley knew that all his soldier instincts and traits—cunning, guile, stealth and the element of surprise must be tapped.

Mike Preston heard the land line ringing as he continued to speak. "John, I've got to take another call, let's chat again in the morning. Good luck tonight."

"Thanks, would certainly need That."

Preston ended the call and John pulled his black jacket then headed for the doorway. Before leaving, he briefly opened the door, pulled it inward and smeared the outer handle with a transparent layer of odorless gel. This is a simple trick he had learnt many years ago. As a Navy man, he had travelled extensively and stayed in numerous hotels the world over. He heard stories of strange goings on in rooms temporarily vacated by guest. So his simple security measure forms part of of his travel routine every time he checks into a hotel.

Bradley walked briskly through the carpeted lobby; the décor was quite appealing. Beautiful planters lined the hallway. This was complimented by large murals depicting the rich colorful history, culture and tenacity of the indigenous Tayrona Indians. Bradley paused, momentarily absorbing the magnificence of Hotel Estelar Santamar.

He entered the elevator cubicle. There were four other persons; the couple standing in the corner appeared to be honeymooners. They were openly petting and necking and oblivious of the other occupants, they showed no restraint. At one point they got so carried away John felt as though the guy wanted to do a root canal on his mate. "Whatever became of privacy?" John asked himself this question over and over again long after the couple alighted on the seventh floor.

At the front desk, he inquired from the receptionist about night life in the city center. He soon found out that Santa Marta is a fun lover's paradise—limitless pleasure, girls and parties galore! Tonight he would go out and have some fun. Three days in the Colombian bush—he really deserves an adrenaline rush tonight.

The cab pulled up close to the curb outside of the hotel. Earlier, the receptionist recommended La Escollera, a trendy disco and bar just off the northern tip of El Rodadero Beach. John made mental notes of the route from the hotel to the night club. It's a fairly short drive—just about 20 minutes.

He strolled through the security checkpoint and was soon on the inside. At the bar he ordered a martini, sat on the metal stool with the foam and leather top. The music had a rhythmic Latin beat and soon a rather cute female started moving gracefully towards him.

She paused for a moment and John caught a glimpse of her shapely body. The medium built beauty wore a sexy tight fitting black denim skirt complimented with a white cotton top. Gabriella's shoes were of fine Italian leather and as she lengthened her strides towards Bradley, he felt a slight flutter in his heart.

"Would you like to dance?" John was quite impressed with the fluency of her English.

"Yes, would love to," replied the American as he extended his hand.

John held her gently as he settled into a groove. He sniffed her exotic fragrance while stroking her silky black hair. Gabriella moved with the grace and guile of a ballerina and matched all of John's moves.

"You're quite good you know," John commented as he broke into a waltz.

"Did Latin dance—you're not bad as well," said Gabriella with a broad grin.

"You speak English quite fluently."

"Thanks." I studied in the States—Midwestern University."

"Really, what did you do?", Bradley asked.

"Marketing and Information Technology," Gabriella replied with a shy smile.

Bradley held Gabriella during a brief musical interlude and asked her to accompany him to the far left hand corner of the club. There he chose a a secluded seating area with options for additional privacy.

The sign centrally posted read: patrons requesting folding cubicles should contact any available attendant. Gabriella and Bradley were soon seated in a cordoned off area chatting leisurely and awaiting their drinks order.

"Can I call you Brad?"

"That's cool with me, some of my old buddies call me that anyway."

"So what brings you to Santa Marta?" Gabriella rolled her eyes as she inquired.

The musical rhythms changed again as the waiter returned with their drinks. After a short interlude, the Disc Jocky broke into some contemporary American soft pop and many of the patrons used this time to cool down a bit. Previously, the DJ had the party crowd swaying to some pulsating salsa mixes; they went really wild and everyone swayed and rocked and gyrated.

A few other patrons opted for a break and soon moved away from the flashing neons of the discotheque. For them, a cool romantic walk on the exotic tropical grounds is much more therapeutic. Bradley sipped another martini as he gazed at the woman next to him; there is something about her that causes his heart to flutter. For now he'll try to curb his primal instincts and stick to the task at hand—finding Christina Preston.

Gabriella took a tissue from her purse and gently repaired her lipstick. She had already drank half of the Pina Colada and felt that it's an ideal time to start engaging the tall handsome stranger in some conversation.

"Still waiting on you to tell me what brings you to Santa Marta?"

"Seems like you're quite keen on finding out—anyway, I'm here on important business." Replied Bradley.

"That's kinda vague; You certainly haven't got the look of a businessman, what business you're in?"

"Your opinion and I won't try to change that anyway."

"Good, at least you've made an accurate assessment of me—that's really cool, yeah like that."

Bradley gulped the last portion of his martini and signaled to the waiter.

"Need another Pina Colada?"

"Yeah and that's cool—the final one; I measure my drinks carefully and besides, it's Wednesday—got a heavy schedule at work tomorrow."

"Work! A beautiful girl like you? One would think that some knight in shinning armor would see to it that you don't work. At least I would!"

Gabriella opened her Gucci purse and flashed a laminated ID card. Bradley's Jaw dropped and his eyes opened wide and bulged with shock and disbelief. The name was printed in bold black lettering: Seargant Gabriella Carmelita Hernandez, Santa Marta Police Department.

As he stared at his dancing partner in disbelief, Bradley remembered the feeling he got when he left the hotel. Actually, he told Preston that he would be lucky tonight and a break is coming.

"You're reacting like all the other Machiavellian pricks I work with every day. I do the same work the fuckers do—and more. Yet they treat me with such indifference."

For the first time John heard and felt the exasperation in Gabriella's voice as he instinctively leaned closer to give her a long reassuring hug.

"Don't let that upset you my dear, just stay positive and believe in yourself. Pressure on the job is another way of measuring your resilience and tenacity."

Bradley unwrapped his arms around Gabriella and looked at his watch. It's now 11:53 am.

I think it's a good time to for me to call a taxi."

"Sure you want to do that?"

"Well, I'm thinking more about you; surely you will need to get some rest for your hectic workday tomorrow."

"Very thoughtful," replied Gabriella. "Where are you staying while in Santa Marta?"

"Estelar Santamar Hotel and Centro Convenciones," replied Bradley.

"Oh yeah, quite a lovely place, it's just a few kilometers from El Rodadero Beach; I spent a few days there last year."

"Don't bother to call a cab, I would drive back to Estelar."

"Great! But before we leave, I want to tell you why I am really in Santa Marta"

Gabriella sucked on the tip of her plastic drinking straw as she extracted the remainder of the drink.

A live band had taken center stage and the patrons were partying wildly again. This reminded her of the good old college days when staying up all night was the in thing. Oh how times have changed she reminisced. It seemed only like yesterday. The past was a distant memory anyway so Sergeant Hernandez won't be too preoccupied with it.

Bradley took her hand as they strode towards the entrance. I am here to find a missing American student. Her name is Christina Preston and she was kidnapped during a visit to a historic site near Quinta San Pedro de Alejandrino about a month ago.

Gabriella involuntarily jerked her hand, temporarily releasing John's left hand. "This is so incredible; I am working with the lead investigator on that case, we got a call from the High Command today asking for an urgent report on the case. I think they got a call from Washington also, everybody is on edge. When there is a call from Bogota we all know it's serious stuff. This General Alvario Castenadas is a no nonsense guy; If he does not get answers some heads will roll."

Bradley could not contain his excitement. He thought about entertaining some romantic thoughts towards Gabriella but this soon dissipated. By the look of things, he would be working on Christina's case with the female cop.

John has never been much of a religious person but he firmly believes in a higher power, and the immeasurable and limitless value of positive thinking. He could not stop thinking about his earlier dialogue with Mike Preston, Christina's dad. He just got the gut feeling that getting out of the hotel would have provided a vital lead in the search for Christina.

He got into the car; his mind racing, still trying to absorb fully what just transpired as he fastened his seat belt. Gabriella sped down the three lane highway while Bradley gave her some more details of himself.

"You just got the look of a military man, I sensed that from the moment you held me."

"Tell me Gabriella, what has your sector done so far to gather information on Christina's kidnapping?"

"Follow up on a few leads, bits and pieces on our website— nothing significant."

"The army has been cooperating to some degree; a few helicopter patrols and an intensive search of suspected rebel territory, but so far—no trace. She seemed to have vanished into thin air."

"This could be similar to looking for a needle in a field of hay; your country is so vast with several porous borders."

John saw the lights of his hotel in the distance and asked Gabriella to slow down a bit.

The silver sedan was now doing 55 kilometers per hour as they passed a cluster of incandescent street lights.

"I would certainly arrange for you to visit the Station sometime later today, the commanding officer, I am sure would want to chat with you."

"Yes of course, that's good for starters."

"Call my mobile anytime. How difficult is it to get to your Precint?"

"It's about 45 minutes; anyway don't worry about getting there, we'll come and get you."

"Thanks that's perfect, I'll really appreciate it," replied Bradley.

Gabriella pulled up onto the parking lot at exactly 12.39 am. John got out of the car and walked over to the driver's side. He thought about inviting the female cop up to his room but quickly discarded the idea. Instead, he bent over and thanked her for a rather lovely and interesting evening.

At this time his thoughts were on Christina Preston again and tonight he felt an immense surge of confidence. He felt as though a lead—a tiny ray of hope is now within his grasp. The next 24 hours would be extremely important.

John extended his hand to Gabriella and wished her a safe journey home. There is no need for him to worry anyway. The female cop carried her service pistol at all times, in addition to a can of mace and pepper spray. Bradley watched her lights fade in the distance before entering the hotel compound.

Chapter 15

Christina started to eat her breakfast and was a bit perplexed. It's not normal for her to be given the morning meal so early; something appears to be amiss here. She did notice an unusual amount of activity at the camp, and generally the men appeared to be quite animated. By now she had cleared her mind. After the skirmish with the female guard Christina was feeling so empowered. She felt very confident that whatever her captors did—her renewed vigor and commitment to be free again would never be daunted. The confidence and belief in her dad is also another factor in her determination to make it out of this jungle captivity.

As the wooden door swung inwards, Christina saw three men armed with AK 47's approaching. The man wearing a black beret held a cigar to his lips. Christina sneezed as the pungent smoke wafted around the makeshift prison.

"Shit! This smoke is really making me nauseous." Christina cursed beneath her breath while covering her face with both hands.

The man wearing the black beret spoke. "American! Pack your stuff, we are moving to another location." Christina looked at him and wondered what the hell is going on. At first, she felt like screaming out. But then she remembered her goal—getting out of captivity alive and well. Step one in this process—cooperate with her captors and do not show any resentment.

Christina slid down the side of the bed and reached for her canvas knapsack hanging on a small rail near the only widow in the 8x9 ft cabin. Of course, she doesn't have a whole lot of stuff to pack. Just the items she had taken with her on that fateful day to Quinta de San Pedro Alejandrino. A tourist brochure, her Blackberry and diary, together with some other items of clothing and the thick gray blanket supplied by the guerrillas.

The sun's rays were streaking through the tall thick canopy of trees as the five man party moved out. Although Christina remained blindfolded, she paid great attention to her surroundings. They were travelling for about an hour before the commander ordered the group to take a break. Christina knew that they were out of the dense forest now—why? She felt the sunlight more intensely and this is certainly an indication that they were in a less shaded area now; Christina knew that even with the blindfold on.

They were definitely approaching a river. Could this be the Magdalena River? Christina had a gut feeling they are heading towards this major waterway. They were definitely heading towards a mighty river. Christina kept hearing the rushing waters clashing against the natural vegetation and other objects in its path.

Before giving the order to resume, the man wearing the black beret pulled out a cellular phone from his military camouflage jacket and spoke with a loud voice.

"El Capitan, we are on the way with your trophy, you've got the money? I want to know right now; this is cash on delivery only, no fucking up please!"

Christina heard the conversation and wondered what the hell this man is talking about. What trophy are they talking about?

She, assumed that the person at the other end had responded in the affirmative as the group were soon on their way. They travelled for another twenty-five minutes before the journey changed from a foot hike to a boat ride. Christina could hear the commander negotiating with some locals for a better price for a trip up river. Shortly afterwards, the party were on their way again.

Christina dreaded any kind of river travel especially as she knew of all the predatory creatures lurking in the Colombian rainforest and rivers. From the fearsome giant Anaconda and venomous Pythons to the deadly crocodiles; she heard of the scary and near-death encounters.

Along the way, Christina reminded herself that to make it out alive she had to be tough mentally, and being fearful is not an option!

They were heading inland to a landing area. The men spoke about selecting a safe shallow point to berth the small craft. A rope, looped around a sturdy mangrove root provided a secure mooring. The men pulled hard on the wet heavy rope to get the small wooden craft close enough to the water's edge. They then helped Christina disembark. She missed a step and her left foot kicked hard against the murky water as they landed.

She was beginning to tire now. They were travelling for close to two hours, and this phase of the journey turned out to be quite a steep climb. Still blindfolded, Christina's breathing became labored and heavy. Despite feeling very tired, Christina made a desperate effort to stay abreast with her captors. They soon came to a large clearing in the forest—a kind of a grassy meadow. Christina knew this because the sharp prickly grass caused many abrasions on her neck and hands. She pulled a napkin from her knapsack and pressed it against the small gash on her left thumb. Christina continued to apply pressure on the small wound as the party moved forward at a steady pace.

Christina knew that showing visible signs of this would not help her cause. No matter what, I must persevere she thought as the pathway narrowed slightly. They continued along that course for about another half hour. Later, the captive American observed that she no longer felt the sharp tall grass scrapping against her bare cheeks. The vegetation appeared to be much shorter—actually in some areas it was cut quite low. Christina used her sense of touch to make this assessment and indeed she was quite accurate.

As the party advanced, Pablo, the tall heavy set guerrilla fighter clad in fatigues and a black beret, held Christina and quickly removed her blindfold. Christina by now had developed a rather keen sense of smell and touch. As her captors continued along the path, Pablo reached for his mobile phone and dialed a number; he spoke rapidly into the mouthpiece.

"We are less than 15 minutes away, you have all the paperwork in place for the money?"

"I keep my word comrade—it's not the first time we're doing business," El Capitan retorted in a rather exasperated tone.

"Good, your package is in order then," replied Pablo.

The business El Capitan spoke about had to do with the many drug deals the Black Devils and Pablo's men had brokered over the years. The two groups did not have any signed pact, however they cooperated extensively. Actually, It was the little known group of rag—tag insurgents called fighters for freedom and the rights of the people who staged Christina's kidnapping. Prior to this, no one heard about them. Bradley did not even have them on his list. Their leader Commander Pablo immediately saw an opportunity for fame and notoriety. Following this, negotiations started between Pablo's group and the more established anti government outfits. After two weeks of talking, El Capitan's offer of five million US Dollars was accepted by Pablo.

One stunning revelation of this whole episode was the intricate international support network operating covertly with the insurgents. No physical cash changed hands during the exchange between the guerrilla groups.

El Capitan's had an offshore shell company operating under the trade name Unicon Investment Services. This company is really a placebo. They appear to be quite legitimate; the Certificate of Incorporation and registration documents confirm that they are registered in Monrovia, in the West African State of Liberia. Their primary business activities are listed as oil and gas exploration and logging.

The company operated a subsidiary in Santa Marta, Colombia called "Renacimento Petrleo. This company is actually owned by Carlos Del Monte-El Capitan. Renacimento Petrleo has already issued the necessary instructions to transfer 4.2 million United States Dollars to an account operated in the name of Las Rosas. The true owner of Las Rosas is Commandante Pablo; the business was registered previously with falsified documents and other forged paperwork.

Once all the requisite paperwork is completed, Pablo and his men would toast to their success. They can no longer be considered neophytes in this business, but rather influential power brokers. The one slight disagreement both leaders shared—high processing fees, had a quick and amicable resolution. Carlos Del Monte, leader of the Colombian Black Devils gave a rather eloquent explanation of the charges. Agents must be paid, bribes and kickbacks and other forms of "keep quiet fees" must be guaranteed before any funds are transferred. And of course, the unsuspecting local banks would apply their own charges.

The party arrived at the Camp around 5:50 pm, and late autumn darkness had already crept its way into the dense jungle foliage. Camp Diaz is a very large facility—the actual operational area inclusive of the strategically positioned perimeter guard towers, exceeds twenty-five hectares. All other buildings and structures were immaculately maintained. Del Monte certainly did an excellent job—at least with the appearance of the camp. The entire area is not fenced but the tall pine trees were strategically planted and some huge logs were placed selectively to create an almost perfect illusion of an enclosure.

Christina quickly accessed the surroundings, but something immediately caught her eye. The log cabin in the far left hand corner of the compound. There were other buildings—the guard towers ascended a mammoth 75 meters and were placed along the perimeter at intervals. The tower directly facing the entrance of the path through which they entered previously was manned by a sentry armed with a 50 caliber machine gun. Affixed to the thick heavy wooden outer log beams were two gigantic spotlamps. Impressive, Christina thought!

None of this however deserved more attention than the large log cabin located near the far right hand corner of the compound. It stood out among all the other structures and looked more like a fine work of art.

Christina looked on rather attentively as the two men continued their conversation. She saw the young commander remove two legal size sheets of paper from a brown manila envelope. Pablo looked at the papers, nodded his head and signed on the line in the lower left hand corner.

Carlos, Del Monte looked at the signed document. He confirmed that Pablo fully understood all the terms and conditions before the FFRC leader left Camp Diaz. The review of the documents now completed, it's time for Pablo and his men to begin the trek from the foothills of the Sierra Nevada. In a few days they would have access to 4.2 million dollars. More money than most people would ever see in their entire lifetime.

Pablo felt so good about his accomplishment. This previously unknown guerrilla fighter now commands the respect of the more established anti-government insurgents. Quite impressive! For the moment though, his main focus is to make it safely down the narrow and dangerous mountain path.

Despite Pablo's overt bravado, he had a closely guarded secret and as they trekked down the foothills, the engulfing darkness magnified those fears. Snakes! Pablo had a pathological fear of these slithering creatures. It's really quite amazing to see how quickly the area became immersed in pitch-black darkness. They had only travelled for about twenty minutes; the trip back to base is about two hours, and includes a thirty minute canoe ride. Pablo did not want to dwell too much on this, but it is the very genesis of the fear tearing him apart.

In the early evening, giant crocodiles lay in wait at the water's edge and have brought down many unsuspecting prey. And as the threat from stealthy creepy Serpants looms in the impending darkness all of Pablo's fears were magnified. As they made their way closer to the river, Pablo lit two phosphorous flares and launched them into the sky. He crossed himself as the canoe pulled up alongside the makeshift ramp. The flares provided great illumination and as the little boat swayed in the murky swirling water, Commander Pablo's fears were beginning to subside. The most difficult part of the homeward journey had started.

Del Monte walked with an extra bounce after the conclusion of the deal. He now had a major trump card—a really big prize. His sources within the Colombian Military had confirmed that Christina was the daughter of a rich American gringo. The source also indicated the man prepared to pay any a huge ransom to gain her release. Carlos could barely contain the feeling of exuberance which overwhelmed him.

Since the formation of his group of rebel guerilla fighters about seven years ago, he has never felt so powerful. He now has the potential to access even more power! Carlos is a shrewd tactician and savvy businessman. Even before one dime in ransom money has been exchanged, he struck a deal with conspirators within the upper echelons of the Marine Armada. In addition to the usual early warning and tip-off on any impending raid or counter narcotics surveillance and eradication activities. Carlos had already secured a commitment from the collaborators for five hundred M16's equipped with M79 Grenade Launchers, and an unspecified quantity of night vision goggles and other military paraphernalia.

Now if these allegations turn out to be true, another furor between Washington and Bogota would be inevitable. The matter of sophisticated US military hardware and supplies making its way into the hands of rebel insurgents caused a major diplomatic uproar last Spring. The Colombian ambassador at the time, Amarillo Lopez-Martinez was summoned rather hastily to a meeting at the State Department to explain how an entire shipment of US Army fatigues, boots and two hundred and fifty Israeli made Uzi Submachine guns vanished without a trace.

The then Minister of the Interior and Defense resigned, and two top generals were sent packing rather unceremoniously. The president had given an unwavering commitment to Washington to act decisively on any allegations of corruption within the military. At one point, the rumbling within the various sections of the Military establishment on the issue of trust and integrity were so loud; Washington threatened to withhold the 150 million military and economic assistance package, earmarked for Colombia.

Carlos became aware of the high level of mistrust within the Armed Forces, and quite interestingly, used it as an advantage when negotiating any deal with his sources inside the military. The son of unknown peasant farmers could not begin to comprehend the immense power and leverage he now has at his disposal. As he walked briskly back to his quarters, Del Monte made brief eye contact with the young sassy American whose fate dangles delicately on a string. He actually felt a bit of emotion watching her graceful and elegant strides as she made her way to the specially built cabin.

He saw the face of defiance and determination—a face not dissimilar to Juanita's, his last sister. It was the same defiant look she displayed when they were confronted by tear canisters and live gunfire while attempting to save the family farm, a few years ago. Carlos looked at Christina again and this time the close resemblance to Juanita seemed even more distinct.

How would the young commander handle this situation? Since becoming the leader of the Colombian Black Devils, he had acquitted himself admirably. He made decisions quickly, showed great tenacity, wisdom and other leadership characteristics, far greater than his age.

Carlos threw the small piece of the unfinished cigar to the ground and smothered the last ember with the heavy combat boots he wore. The day was long and quite eventful—tonight he would celebrate! There was no shortage of wine in his cellar and it's been quite a long time since he touched Francia. Tonight he would make up for all of the neglect.

They would have a good long romantic romp after a warm bath in the tub Del Monte had designed. Carlos and Francia have been romantically involved for quite a while. She has long black hair, slanted eyes and a sleek well-proportioned waistline.

Extremely proud of her Tayrona Indian roots, Francia knew every herb in the vast jungle. She has concocted several lifesaving remedies for sick or wounded insurgents. Her ability was tested not so long ago when one of the fighters slipped and fell heavily while on a training exercise on the shooting range.

The poor guy had to be taken by stretcher to the camp infirmary. His left ankle, bruised and swollen caused him excruciating pain. Del Monte summoned Francia and she kicked into action immediately. Rushing to her backyard garden, the young herbal queen plucked a pungent smelling plant out of the ground. She washed the dirt off the finger like roots and placed them in a small stone mortar. Several swift blows with a hard wooden pestle resulted in a dark yellowish paste. Francia immersed the injured man's ankle in a sack filled with the mixture. Two days later, the patient is back on his feet and running all around Camp Diaz.

Tonight, Francia would be mixing a love portion though; all the sweet flowers of the forest skillfully concocted for maximum potency. She kept a wide variety of these herbs dried and many oil extracts were also produced. When Carlos walked into the room, Francia only had a colorful wrap draped around her sexy shapely body. As he came closer towards her with open arms, Francia saw that look in the eyes of her man—a lustful erotic and hungry look she did not get from him in quite a long time.

When Christina got to the door of the large cabin, the effects of the long trek up the steep hill had taken its full toll. As the guard swung the heavy wooden door inward, her eyes were fixed on the far left hand corner—the sleeping area. Travelling from her original place of captivity to this new location obviously created some stress and discomfort. But at first glance, the accommodation was of a superior quality.

Christina completed a quick visual assessment of her new living quarters and remembered the words of the man with the cigar and the dark military fatigues, to the guards.

"Please ensure that American blonde is comfortable and well fed."

The guard showed her around; pointing out areas like the bathroom and other necessities. Whoever built this deserves special commendation, thought Christina as she placed her few belongings on the small bedside table.

The two guards were soon replaced by a female conscript. This has always been the pattern throughout the six weeks of her captivity. A plastic tray was placed on the wooden table in the middle of the room and the soldier asked Christina to have her meal.

Christina broke the lid on the box of orange juice, peeled the plastic wrap off the small block of cheese and quickly made a sandwich. She finished with the banana as the dessert. It's about three hours since her arrival at Camp Diaz. The creatures of the night were already making the rounds, and by now Christina had become somewhat of an expert at deciphering the night sounds. The owls had a distinctive screech; then there were the crickets, followed by a plethora of scary bats flapping their colossal wings. They all played in harmony, an amazing cacophony of sounds so unique, only a trained ear could decode or understand their nocturnal melodies.

Christina certainly did, and used nature to her fullest advantage. After all, her major is in the field of environmental studies. Her eyelids were beginning to become heavy and she knew that it's time for a good long sleep. The cool forest breeze had the effect of a natural anesthetic and soon the American hostage fell into a deep sleep.

Chapter 16

Bradley woke up as the warm sun broke through a rather hazy morning sky. From his ninth floor hotel room at the Hotel Esteler Santamar, he glanced down at the magnificent surroundings of the City of Santa Marta and continued to marvel at breathtaking beauty. Bradley couldn't help but wonder why so much of the negative publicity regarding Colombia reaches the international press and not a great deal is heard about its culture, indigenous people and other natural wonders.

John quickly showered, got dressed and headed down to the lobby. The early morning buffet has started. Bradley pulled a plate from the neatly stacked bundle positioned on the long cloth-draped table just to the front. He picked up a pair of wooden handle tweezers and plucked out four steaming hot sausages from the stainless steel receptacle. A few slices of toast complimented with an omelette, topped with colorful peppers and roasted onion rings completed John's breakfast.

Bradley took a table facing the large doors. This is an old habit the ex-Navy Seal maintains wherever he goes; it had actually saved his life on two occasions before.

The line up for breakfast continued to grow as John ate; he really enjoyed the combination selected and for a moment got the urge to grab a ripe banana and some of the lavender—colored grapes from the fruit bar. He decided against it just as the mobile phone holstered on his belt started to ring.

"Good Morning my American friend, had a good rest?" Gabriella's sounded rather lively as she greeted Bradley.

"Sure, what did you expect after such a great party last night; I've been waiting for your call for well over an hour now."

"Really? You military men—so fucking impatient!"

"Anything new on the case?" Asked Bradley inquisitively.

"Yeah, got a whole lot to talk about; actually my division commander wants you to come down to Head Quarters right away."

"Great! Where exactly are you in downtown Santa Marta?"

"We are on Carrera 4, about 25 minutes drive from Estelar Santamar."

"I can arrange for one of our patrol cars to pick you up shortly."

"Ok then; just finished breakfast, would be ready in ten minutes."

"That's fine, see you in a while then."

Gabriella, walked back to her desk after speaking with the commanding officer—a burly sergeant named Alberto Nunez. Nunez is a perfect example of what happens when a cop moves up the ranks and becomes lazy. He carried a pot belly and smoked cigars almost uncontrollably. Other officers jokingly call him pregnant Nunu in an almost comical reprimand for the man who just a mere seven years ago held the title of divisional boxing champion.

The American Special forces man placed the mobile device back into the black leather case, swiped his credit card, signed the printed receipt and then headed towards the front door.

John stood outside for just about 15 minutes, he soon saw flashing lights and heard the whaling police sirens. He walked a little closer towards the curb as the vehicle approached and waved frantically to attract Gabriella's attention. The squad car came to a complete stop and Bradley entered the back seat.

"Manuel, this is a retired United States Special Forces man and Navy Seal, John Bradley; he is here to help in the search for the kidnapped American student."

The squad car driver eased a little bit on the accelerator as he negotiated a tight turn and greeted the ex soldier.

"Welcome to Santa Marta."

"Thanks mate, I am really looking forward to working with you guys."

Gabriella asked Manuel to take an alternative route back to the Police Head Quarters as the early morning traffic began to build up. It was approaching 9: 00 am local time and already the long queues of vehicles—brightly colored taxis and other *commercial vehicles were making their way to the bustling city center.*

John couldn't help but enjoy the Santa Marta skyline and magnificent urban scenery. In the foreground the towering mountains stood majestically above the city. The cloud caped ranges spoke silently a thousand words of welcome to every visitor. Lush green verdant valleys give life to a myriad of flora and fauna beckoning to be enjoyed by those seeking adventure and the thrill of the outdoors.

This natural beauty manifests itself also in the miles of pristine white sand beaches along the gem like coastal plains. Bradley's immersion in the scintillating beauty of the city got a brief jolting as Gabriella spoke.

"OK, American soldier, we are almost there"

"Good, I am really enjoying your lovely homeland. I hope we can solve this case quickly so that I can start my vacation."

"Sure, sounds like you've got plans; I would always recommend San Andres Island."

"Yeah, we'll talk about that when my job is done."

Bradley thought about the subtle invitation he extended to Gabriella but quickly remembered that they were not alone. At least for the time being, he would focus on the main reason for him being in Santa Marta - Christina Preston. Gabriella's voluptuous bust, shapely waistline and succulent lips must not distract him; finding Christina requires his full and unequivocal attention. John had no intention of reneging on his commitment to her father, Mike Preston. The car pulled into the curb leading to the Santa Marta Police Head Quarters and Gabriella led the American through the main entrance.

Mike Preston just kept on walking around the office. Sally, his secretary and personal assistant for the past nine years saw the pain and anguish in her boss's eyes. The last few weeks had really taken a toll on him—his eyes were now hallow and sunken. Even the shirts which fitted so snugly around his neck and shoulders about a month ago now appeared loose and tacky. Preston was feeling the effects of the stress caused by Christina's kidnapping; the calm and tranquil world he knew just a few short weeks ago had suddenly spun out of control.

Sally now started to show some empathy for her boss. Preston is a kind and caring boss so she prays fervently that his beloved Christina would return safely to the United States.

It's Tuesday morning and as the early Texas sun shone over the Houston Skyline, Sally decided that it is time to get her boss a cup coffee. She strode across to the kitchenette, plugged in the coffee maker and soon the delectable aroma filled the room. She placed the sizzling hot brew in his special mug and walked towards the door. Sally tapped lightly on the glass panel and entered Preston's spacious office.

"Mr. Preston, I brought you a cup of your favorite coffee; hope it helps to brighten your day."

"You've not been yourself these days, but be strong and just hang in there—everything's going to be just fine."

"Thanks Sally, you're so thoughtful as always."

"I wish I could do much more to ease your pain"

"I know you mean well my dear—you've been of great help in this difficult and traumatic time"

"Thanks Mr. Preston."

"Please, Mr. Preston; you've got to be strong for Christina—she is counting on you!"

"You're so right Sally."

"Have you looked at the notes I left on your desk."

"Thanks, haven't done so as yet."

"Anything important?"

"Sure—the meeting tomorrow with Mr. Kuroskey, from Kazakistan."

"What time is that again?" Asked Preston as he glanced at the highlighted notes on his glass covered desk."

"It's at 10:30, and I've already pulled the files."

"Excellent work Sally, I know I can always depend on you."

"Also, remember to call the gentleman from Washington—I think his name is Reuben."

"Mark Reuben?" Interjected Preston.

"Yes Sir, that's right!"

"OK, maybe he has news from Colombia, I'll call him straight away."

Mike Preston sipped the last few drops of coffee from the mug, wiped his rather dry lips with the extra soft napkin. His desk was positioned to capture the amazing city skyline and he decided to enjoy every moment of it today. He was gradually beginning to find himself again. Sally is quite right, he had to find the inner strength to hang in there—at least for Christina!

The Chairman of the Joint Chief of Staff took a few short steps just as the phone rang. Mark Reuben picked up the receiver and heard the unmistakable voice of his longtime friend.

"Hello, Mike; how are you?"

"You sound a lot better; more like my good old buddy."

"Don't have much of a choice, I want to see my daughter return safely—she's all I've got!"

"Something's happening on the ground down there."

"Good! Good!" Preston exclaimed.

"Yes, that's right."

"Had a long chat with my Colombian counterpart, General Castenadas; he gave me the assurance that the Police and Army are doing all in their power to find Christina."

Preston leaned back in his leather reclining chair as Mark continued to provide more details on the search for his kidnapped daughter.

"Your guy, Bradley has been quite busy as well. General Castenadas indicated earlier that a meeting is scheduled for later this morning between the ex Special Forces man and the Chief of the Santa Marta Police."

"That's wonderful! Shouted Preston. Seems like we are finally making some progress."

"Mark, I can't find words to say thank you for all that you've done; it's really nice to have someone as caring and thoughtful as you on my side."

"Mike, don't even mention it; we go back a very long way and you would have done the same thing for me—that much I know, old buddy."

For a moment, Preston became teary eyed and he struggled to keep a firm hold on the receiver as sweat oozed from his slippery palm and fingers. Mike was really touched by the sentiments of his boyhood friend. Their friendship has always been special and bonding, but Christina's situation has certainly given it more meaning, strength and an enduring purpose.

"Don't worry Mike, everything's going to be fine. Christina would be back on US soil soon and I want to be there with you on the tarmac to welcome her home."

"What can I say—friends like you and my strong faith and trust in Almighty God gives me hope; thanks mate—thanks a million!

"Ok Mike, got to run now—just remember I am only a phone call away. I intend to chat with General Castenadas for another update by noon tomorrow—would keep in touch."

"Take care old pal, hope to hear from you soon."

Chapter 17

Carlos Del Monte didn't expect to hear from his contact inside the Colombian military. There were no outstanding financial matters; the relevant transfers were already completed. Cash payments were done via the pre arranged drop off spots. So why did Esmiralda—the pseudonym used by the mole within the Colombian Armed Forces, left this urgent text message on his mobile phone: "American special agent meeting with Santa Marta Police High Command today; we must talk urgently!"

Del Monte looked at the message again; still perplexed, he frowned then dialed the number. For security reasons, he never uses the same cellular phone. He carries about a dozen or so devices—all registered under fake identities. This makes tracing his calls quite a challenge. His contact on the other side does the same. So far, their methods of evading surveillance and eavesdropping have been quite effective.

The voice at the other end was quite soft and muffled—almost like an eerie ghostly whisper.

"New developments on the ground which could disrupt overall plans for the American girl."

Esmiralda raised his voice a bit to convey a level of urgency and seriousness.

"This Special Forces/Navy Seal man is here to get the girl; I met him a few years ago on a training exercise! He is a mean killing machine and an expert jungle warrior—man, this guy is fearless!"

Carlos swung his heavy boot across the wooden table top almost spilling the brew from the large pot.

"What the fuck are you saying!"

"How long has this gringo been in our country?"

"Not too sure, only got the details last night." "I tell you man, this could really fuck up things for us."

Esmiralda made a desperate effort to stay calm and control his emotions. He has been in the military for the better part of three decades and he wants his legacy to be memorable. So this alliance with Del Monte had to be watertight; there must be no room for errors!

His whole future is at stake here. Retirement looms on the horizon—a luxury villa off the coast of Panama or even a resort on one of the magnificent Islands of the Grenadines. Actually, one of buddies already has a private Island down there. What else can you desire—a sleek catamaran and a platoon of sexy, scantily clad girls to do whatever you ask.

Esmiralda soon returned from his brief moment of bliss to focus on the immediate realities.

"So what are you suggesting comrade?" asked Del Monte as he poured another cup of coffee.

"You must mount an operation on the Santa Marta Police Head Quarters today and kill the fucking American! I want him dead!"

"This operation must begin at thirteen hundred hours local time," commanded Esmiralda.

"We would need time to plan such a mission—it's going to be risky, can't afford to lose any of my men."

"Leave that up to me, I know just what has to be done; you have some assets already in downtown Santa Marta?"

"Yes, of course; Comandante Guiteriez and a few other guys got a few days off to be with their families in the area."

"I want no fucking excuses, just get moving! Send a message to the men down there and leave the rest to me. Don't worry about anything, I would arrange the weapons, ammunition and logistics."

"Chief! You're the best," replied Del Monte as he headed towards the doorway.

"Get moving, hurry! The element of surprise is in our favor; fuck this one up man and you know it's going to be a disaster for all of us. If you don't deliver the head of this American mercenary, our entire network comes crashing down!"

Bradley walked briskly into the office of Police Chief Alberto Nunez. Gabriella did the formal introduction then went back to her desk. Nunez swiveled gingerly in the chair and bumped his belly on the edge of the large cluttered desk as he extended a hand to the American.

"Hello my friend, how are you?" "Welcome to Santa Marta Police Department, make yourself comfortable—be my guest."

Nunez pointed to the black leather chair. John pulled it back slowly with his left hand and sat in a slightly diagonal position. The high rise building afforded quite a commanding view of the city. Being a military man, security is always a concern. Bradley made a quick assessment of the third floor office of Commander Nunez. He couldn't understand why the chief sat with his back towards the large glass panels. Maybe it's just a matter of style or taste. He would make his comments and observation at the appropriate time anyway.

He is in Santa Marta to gather *information* on the whereabouts of Christina—and eventually rescue her from the insurgents.

"John Bradley, former US Special Forces and Navy Seal, it's a pleasure. So tell me chief what's been happening with the young American student—it's about two months since she was snatched in broad daylight."

"Yes, that's right!" "It's a rather unusual situation; this is the first time I can recall a glaring daylight kidnapping and the perpetrators have not been caught!"

"You have some footage of the scene captured by a television news crew working in the area at the time of the incident."

"I think forensic has something"

"Can we arrange to have a look? Maybe some seemingly insignificant detail was missed—a second peek won't hurt."

"Sure, no problem,"

Commander Nunez picked up the phone and dialed extension 29 to request the DVD.

"Ok they'll send it up shortly"

Bradley looked at the clock on the wall; he's been in the Police Head Quarters for almost an hour now. He didn't have to worry about time especially if at the end of the day he had good news for Mike Preston. If it meant spending the entire day at the Police Head Quarters—John did not mind. This is actually his second week in Colombia and already it felt like an eternity.

"Have you been able to get any clues as to where Christina would be? I know this is a huge country."

"Nothing of any real value; we got a call about nine days ago from a villager in a remote district. It did not yield anything really. A small group of campers was spotted near the east side of the Magdalena river as they prepared for a trek up the Tayrona National Park. The villagers saw a female among the hikers and alerted the local authorities."

"Some of our sources suggest that the guerillas actually holding the American girl did not take part in the actual kidnapping. The word is that a small almost unknown band of insurgents staged the kidnapping and later struck a deal with one of the more established guerilla groups."

"Anybody on your short list of suspects?"

"Well, your guess is as good as mine; there's one particular set of fighters we have an interest in though—the Colombian Black Devils."

"Yeah, I've got them at the very top of the list of possible suspects!"

"Of course, they are well organized militarily and also have the capacity to exert political influence. In terms of manpower, the Colombian Black Devils have more men and women in a state of combat readiness than all the other anti government guerrillas combined. They are definitely a force to be reckoned with."

The police chief removed his cap revealing a thick black cushion of curly hair. Nunez ran his fingers through his scalp briskly as he made a rather feeble attempt to sit upright. Bradley interpreted this as a measure of uncertainty and indecisiveness.

"How long do I have to wait before the DVD gets to your office?"

"Let me check with the department again." Nunez nodded impatiently as he called the head of Forensics.

"What! Somebody's got to be crazy, this had better be a bloody joke—there is no DVD in the file? Who the fuck is responsible for this—I need some answers right now!"

John heard the exasperation in the commander's voice and quickly offered an alternative solution.

"Ok Chief. Let's not worry about the DVD; where is the bullet riddled tour bus?"

"Last time I checked, it was in the holding bay—a massive garage; that big brick building just to our left."

"Great! When we're done I would like to have a look around."

"Sure, would be glad to show you the work of those cowardly bandits," said the burly police chief.

Bradley had barely finished his statement when he heard a loud explosion; the building shook violently and rounds from a high powered rifle whizzed across the room.

"Get down! Get down! Hit the fucking ground!" Shouted the retired Navy Seal as more rounds peppered the walls. Splinters, bits of masonry, shell casings and choking dust flew across the room. This was a swift and audacious attack; whoever planned it knew what they were about.

The sniper was positioned directly across the street and obviously had one objective—killing the occupants of the building. Bullets continued to ricochet; Bradley laid flat on the floor. Nunez too was sprawled out on his fat belly with an H&K Semi Automatic Pistol drawn from the holster.

Nunez pointed to the elevator door but John did not recommend that route. As they headed towards the stairway, another massive explosion rocked the building. Bradley got a quick glimpse of the entrance to the police compound and saw the devastation. A gray Land Rover fitted with a 50 caliber machine gun rammed through the heavy metal gate. Part of the gate was catapulted some fifty meters, landing on an unused concrete structure. The force of the impact completely dislodged a large slab causing it to crash against two large metal containers with a deafening boom!

Bradley saw the chaos from the vantage point as he followed Nunez down the stairway. Before reaching the ground floor Nunez directed Bradley to the Armory. The police commander quickly opened the heavy duty double lock. John grabbed an M16 and an ammo belt with extra magazines and four hand grenades. Nunez pulled a .223 Bush Master, a helmet and two flak jackets.

"Go! Go! Go!" Shouted Bradley as they ran down toward the ground floor while bullets continued to whiz through the air.

The attackers had already killed the three guards posted at the compound post entry and checkpoint. From the ground floor more evidence of the carnage became much clearer.

The insurgents brazen assault troubled John immensely. To begin with, how did the rebels know of his meeting with the Santa Marta Police Chief. And to launch such an audacious attack in broad daylight gives an indication of some level of conspiracy and or corruption. John Bradley just had a gut feeling—something's not making sense here. Somebody high up in the military is passing information to the rebels and that person wanted him dead—that's the harsh reality. Who could it be?

His main purpose in Santa Marta is to find Christina; but certainly he would answer this troubling question before returning to the United States. After leaving the military, he heard the rumors and allegations of complicity between the local Authorities, and some drug dealers and anti government fighters.

Bradley dismissed those thoughts momentarily and flung a thick wooden bench to the ground and took up a firing position. He told Nunez to knock over the other one and hold an offensive position to the far right.

The man firing the heavy machine gun from the land rover continued to blast a deadly hail of lead into the building. Two other insurgents dismounted and also sprayed a murderous cocktail onto the compound. Bradley knew he had to move quickly. The Glass and metal facade which formed the greater portion of the entrance now had the appearance of mangled fragments. The rebels had poured a lot of fire power onto the Police compound and the area looked like a war zone.

By this time other police men had taken up firing positions and the sniper in the adjacent building was taken out. Santa Marta Police Department still had a few very good marksmen. Bradley quickened the pace and trained his weapon on the careening Land Rover. His first volley shot out the left front tire as the vehicle got closer; he then leveled the rifle and fired directly at the guerrilla who was still spraying bullets from the machine gun. The first blast struck him in the back of the neck and pole vaulted him into the air. While still in midair, Bradley fired again; this time the rounds went straight through the head. "Mother fucker, see you in hell!" Exclaimed the American as the man slammed onto the rough concrete surface.

On the east side of the ground floor, Police Chief Nunez was holding his own as well. The two fighters who had dismounted from the vehicle previously, now took positions behind a thick chunk of broken concrete. One fighter brandished a rocket propelled grenade and was preparing to fire the weapon.

"American! American! Cover me." Shouted Nunez as he rolled across the floor to take up a new firing position. Bradley inserted a fresh magazine then rained a hot carpet of lead in the direction of the two men. While Bradley's fire distracted them, the Police Chief maneuvered himself into a vantage point. This placed him slightly above the attackers barricaded by the concrete. Nunez signaled Bradley who responded with oiled precision. He lobbed the grenade swiftly in the direction of the insurgents. The explosion was deafening and in the dust and confusion the man with the RPG tried to reposition himself. Nunes took careful aim and squeezed the trigger; the heavy slugs from the Bush Master ripped off the attacker's face and he fell over pinning the RPG against his chest.

In the mayhem, his partner decided to make a run for the vehicle now moving at a snail's pace with only three of its tires functioning. He started sprinting but did not get very far. Chief Nunez steadied himself and fired again; this time he was careful to take aim at the legs. The guerrilla felt a sharp zipping pain in his right thigh before he buckled and fell over. Warm blood oozed from his molten green fatigues as he screamed in agony.

There were three other occupants in the marooned vehicle and they were definitely cornered. At the moment, the Land Rover provided a fair amount of cover. Bradley wanted to capture at least one of them. That's one sure way of finding out who wanted him dead.

Moments later, there was a loud blast followed by a massive orange ball of fire. The guerrillas had pre arranged detonation devices on their vehicle. A huge plume of smoke enveloped the compound; the insurgents also detonated several smoke bombs as they donned gas masks moments before. Bradley, Nunez and the other officers had done a good job in repelling the attack. Four of the attackers were killed and one sustained a serious leg injury. Three of them were about to escape but Bradley had other ideas.

The smoke started to subside a bit but the fire from the cocktail of gasoline, explosives and burning tires raged on. Bradley wore a helmet and flak jacket out in the yard. He did a quick calculation. There is no way the attackers could exit the compound using their original point of entry.

It meant that they had to find a way out via the back. The compound is secured by a 2.5 meter high wall ringed with concertina wire. They'll have to scale that wall or blast their way through. Bradley called Nunez on the radio.

"Ask your men to hold their fire; I am going to get these guys."

Bradley ran in a zigzag pattern until he was close to the perimeter. The three men obviously made their way from the burning vehicle and would be looking for a way out.

A fire engine sprayed fire repellant foam on the burnt out vehicle and the acrid smell of smoke filled the air. Bradley continued running—and there they were all three of them hastily trying to string a rope ladder. While retreating, the leader of the group Alberto Guiteriez had stumbled upon some discarded industrial string. He quickly fashioned a grappling hook and was ready to make the escape a reality.

One of the insurgents had made it to the top already but had great difficulty negotiating the concertina wire. He tried desperately to swing his right leg over the wall only to be snarled by the sharp razor wire. To further complicate things, there were sharp metal spikes implanted at a forty-five degree angle along the entire length of the wall. The rebel fighter continued to kick and struggle as the soft metal hook attached to the rope strained under his weight. His frantic movements only making the situation much worse.

"Going somewhere!" Shouted Bradley as he fired the M16 into the air. He then leveled the weapon, pointing it directly at Gutierez.

"Hit the ground hard and stay down asshole!"

The guerrilla fighter did not appear be carrying a weapon but Bradley took no chances. The man was partially over the fence when he lost control and fell heavily back onto the compound. In all the commotion, the retreating rebel dislocated his hip joint and sustained multiple fractures to the Tibia.

Bradley then ordered all the men to lay flat with their arms wide apart before calling Nunez on the radio.

"Send two officers outside; I am at the back close to the large shipping containers. I've captured all three bastards." "May also need a stretcher, one of them has a damaged hip and severe leg injuries."

"American soldier! You are a hero and a good man to have around; don't worry I'll take care of that."

Bradley kept the rifle trained on the three men; he moved a bit closer and directed a question at the medium-built guy with the torn camouflage jacket.

"Who is your commanding officer?" "Open up your goddamn mouth, speak up before I blow your fucking head off!"

The rebel fighter pushed himself slightly off the ground, turned his head and looked at Bradley and saw the rifle muzzle pointed at him. The American hand a rather menacing look on his face as he slid his left index finger from the trigger guard. Del Monte's lieutenant is certainly not prepared to have his brains splattered all over the pavement. He looked at the man holding the rifle over him, and decided not to take anymore chances with his life. The captured rebel fighter screamed in fear as he shouted out his name to the Special Forces man.

"Alberto! Alberto!" he yelled, not daring to take his eyes off the imposing figure of the man holding the M16 rifle with the fixed bayonet.

John retrained the weapon on the insurgent with the thick mustache and the molten green army uniform. The ex navy man was so correct in his prior assessment when he cornered the retreating trio. Alberto was the one directing the first fighter as he attempted to scale the perimeter wall using the grappling hook made from scrap metal.

Bradley took three quick strides towards Alberto Guiteriez as he attempted to stand up.

"Fuck you American! Imperialist pig—go to hell!" The captured man grabbed a broken concrete brick as he blurted out more obscenities at the Special Forces man. John saw his aggressive intent, but this did not disturb him as much.

It's been quite a long while since someone had called him imperialist and this really infuriated the ex marine. He quickly flipped the rifle, gripping the muzzle with both hands while pivoting in one smooth arch-like motion. As the jagged metallic stock came crashing down on the base of Alberto's skull, he winced and groaned. The barrage did not stop there; a hard bruising kick to the stomach impaled the hapless screaming man to the ground. John pointed the gun at him again, and dropped to one knee as a mixture of blood and mucus drained from the corner of his mouth.

"Mother fucker! Ready to talk now. Come-on! Come-on!"

Alberto continued to moan and make other inaudible sounds. By this time, Commander Nunez and his men came down to where Bradley had cornered the guerrillas. They lifted the injured man onto the stretcher; Alberto Guitirez was helped by another officer while the other rebel fighter walked on his own.

"I want these prisoners taken to a maximum security facility away from this station. After today's incident; I have serious concerns about the safety of this whole area," lamented Bradley as he walked back towards the battle scarred ground floor entrance with Nunez and the other men.

"Are you implying that we have conspirators among our ranks."

"Just look at it this way—I had an unscheduled meeting with you in your downtown office, and out of the blue a sniper opens up with a high powered rifle, peppering the room with gunfire. We had to duck and roll to escape the ferocious onslaught. If you think that's just a coincidence, you're dead wrong!"

Nunez had a rather perplexed look on his face as he walked alongside his American guest. If the man is right, then the credibility of the Police and Military could be in for a serious battering. The police Chief would not want to believe that some elements within the Armed Forces, or his own officers are in collusion with the insurgents. Such an unholy alliance could have very far reaching implications.

"Did you speak to anyone outside of Santa Marta about our meeting?" Bradley asked, sounding rather agitated.

"I referred the matter to the Central Command in Bogata earlier this morning—that's the standard protocol."

"Well, somewhere in the network there are conspirators, traitors—it may be just a small group but I am absolutely certain that the insurgents had prior knowledge of my presence in Santa Marta."

"American! What you are saying makes a lot of sense; these bastards—when their true identity is revealed they would be tried for treason and executed by firing squad"

The Police Chief struggled to control the anger he felt as they walked through the debris strewn entrance. Three of his men are dead, the Santa Marta Police Head Quarters is the nerve center for all operations in the Department of Magdalena—the security of this facility should never be in doubt. Another troubling thought for Nunez is the physiological impact of this daring attack. What would the ordinary citizens of Santa Marta think?

If the police cannot provide a measure of safety and security for their own, then how can they protect the city's 1.2 million residents? The repercussions of this could be felt throughout the entire country and possibly all over Latin America. It may take a very long time for the civilians to regain confidence in the police and military, in whose hands their security has been entrusted.

The Police Chief had his thoughts interrupted briefly as Bradley tripped over a twisted piece of metal pipe strewn among the rubble. The American quickly regained his balance as he supported himself by pushing hard on the rifle stock.

"Have the prisoners cleaned up and put in a safe place until all the arrangements are made to move them. I also want you to make plans for their interrogation once they are in a secure location." Bradley instructed Nunez as they started to walk up the stairway leading to the office where both men were sitting just about forty five minutes ago.

They were in the middle of discussing the whereabouts of the kidnapped American student, Christina Preston when the shooting began. John would always remember his introductory visit—he certainly got more than a warm welcome, it was blazing hot!

Minister of Defense and the Interior, General Castenadas got the news of the attack at about 2:45 pm local time. He could barely hold back his shock and anger. The fact that these rebels were able to launch such a defiant and daring raid in the heart of the city, really infuriated the General. To further complicate matters, the attack appeared to have been targeted at a visiting former American Serviceman, on a special assignment in Santa Marta.

Despite his feelings of exasperation, the General believes that this attack could signal the beginning of the demise of the insurgency. About 18 months ago, he formulated a plan which gave explicit details on how to eliminate the rebels. The draft presented by the General first called for the identification and subsequent liquidation of the leadership of the insurgency. Once this objective has been achieved, another phase would focus on disrupting and eventually choking off their supply routes. No material assets would be able to enter the camps and with all exits sealed, their demise would then be inevitable.

General Castenadas did not see this as a problem since the country already had a military cooperation pact with the United States. Both countries participate in an annual training exercise aimed primarily at demobilizing and eradicating the massive and intricate drug networks.

One controversial aspect of the plan however, was the use of American drones to kill guerrilla leaders. The Americans have been extremely successful with this technology in their "war on terror." Castenadas also knew how effective they were in neutralizing Al Qaeda and some of its affiliates like Ansar al Shariah. There are also speculations that the Israeli Defense Force may be deploying drones to annihilate enemies of the State.

As he paced the floor, thinking about the brazen attack on the very nerve center of Santa Marta security—the police Head Quarters, General Castenadas knew he had to find a way to succeed this time around. He would advocate forcefully for its implementation—and if necessary turn it into a political issue. All over the country people are clamoring for a more radical and aggressive approach in dealing with the rebels. The General never entertained any thoughts of challenging the current President, but at this point he is prepared to do anything for his beloved motherland, Colombia.

When the draft proposal was first presented, it failed by a mere seven votes. Three members of the top Military Brass abstained and two were out of the country on official government business. The General felt that the President, Rafael Espinosa-Mendez should have exercised is executive powers to ensure the approval of the plan.

The General decided that the time was right to call the president. He would inform him about the attack on the Santa Marta Police Compound while making a subtle attempt to present the case for the re submission of his draft counterinsurgency plan. General Castenadas firmly believed that President Rafael Espinosa-Mendez would use his authority this time around in support of his master plan aimed towards ridding the motherland of this menace.

General Castenadas crossed his arms and walked towards the large rectangular desk. He picked up the telephone and dialed the President's number.

"Hola! Buenos tardes mi amigo.Como esta?"

"Buenos tardes senor Presidente. Mui Bien gracias!"

General Castenadas decided to cut most of the introductory chit chat and tell the President what happened earlier today.

"Mr. President, I have very bad news to report. At around 12:40 pm local time, a group of armed insurgents stormed their way onto the Police Head Quarters in downtown Santa Marta."

"They were heavily armed and blasted their way through the barricaded checkpoint; there were casualties, I am afraid."

"Wait a minute General, what are you saying?" Armed rebels in broad daylight attacked our Police Headquarters?"

"Yes Mr. President, they were eventually repelled but we lost three of our officers in the process."

"Oh My God! This is unbelievable, we've got to do something definitive about these ruthless infidels."

The General felt his heart racing as he listened to President Espinosa-Mendez. Now is the perfect time to make his move. He pushed the chair slightly backwards and stood up momentarily.

"Mr. President, we are on the same page; I want us to have a second look at the draft counter insurgency and anti terrorist proposal—I am asking for your support, we cannot allow this situation to escalate. If we don't act quickly and decisively another rebel group could be empowered—and before we realize what's happening, they are marching into Bogota."

"I quite agree, we must stop them by using all the resources at our disposal—the Army, Police, our Navy and Air Force.

"So I have your blessings to get things started? Time is certainly not on our side, Mr. President!"

"General Castenadas, the last time you presented the recommendations, I had a few concerns especially on the issue of the drones. I am sure we would be able to get the necessary cooperation and assistance from the United States."

"You've got my full and unequivocal support General."

"Thanks Mr. President! If we fail to act, our legacy will be mired in shame and infamy, and I am absolutely sure that we both want to leave an untarnished legacy."

"You are so correct, General—we have no other choice."

The Interior Minister could hardly restrain his emotion after getting the President's commitment. He now sat on the edge of the desk, and crossed his legs before hanging up the phone. He must now begin to prepare for the next national executive meeting. This is normally convened on the final Thursday in November, during which all Divisional Commanders present their reports and recommendations. At this meeting a date is then set for another Grand Session of the Top Military Brass. That's when General Castenadas will present his draft proposal. In the meantime, the Interior Ministry Chief knew that there are some other important calls to be made, including one to the Chairman of the Joint Chiefs of Staff, Mark Reuben.

Chapter 18

Christina took some time to become familiarized with her new surroundings; she rubbed her eyes and stretched before getting up. At least the bed did not hurt her back; she really had a very restful night. Even though she remained in captivity the new facility made her situation much more bearable.

Yesterday's trek up the rugged mountain path had taken a heavy toll on her physically, but the comfortable rest has certainly energized her this morning. Christina had developed her own survival plans; she was no longer grumpy and lethargic. Instead, her mood remained upbeat and vivacious. Exercise became a part of her daily routine—yoga, taekwondo combinations, together with rigorous calisthenics were all part of Christina's training discipline.

The 22 year old American prisoner couldn't wait to experience the feeling of freedom again. By now, Christina had even started rehearsing some of the old Judo moves she learnt as a college student. Actually, she used some of the same techniques to defend herself against a female guard only a week ago. Christiana had a gut feeling that her dad had already hatched a plan to get her out of captivity. That's why she had to remain focused, and her fitness plays such an extremely critical part in the process. As she peered through a small opening, Christina could see the men going through their morning drills. They looked quite impressive doing several rope climbing stunts, carrying heavy logs and quickly moving into mock firing positions. Christina estimated their number to be around five to six hundred, and they appeared to be a highly motivated and disciplined outfit. There was something about their leader which caught Christina's eye though. She had been close enough to hear him during yesterday's transaction with her former captors.

He sounded rather articulate and intelligent—it was quite evident that he wielded great power and respect. Christina felt that he had some kind of tertiary or even university education. As she continued her own morning workout, Christina wondered what were the contributing factors which may have driven this man to become a guerrilla leader. Whatever the cause, one thing became clear to her—he holds her fate his rather youthful hands!

Christina dropped to the floor to begin some pushups on the incline. A small wooden bench served as a perfect buttress for her feet. The height of the bench placed her body at a forty-five degree angle to the floor and she felt the intensity of the repetitions. This lasted for about 15 minutes before she ended with a final burst. Sweat poured from her torso as Christina pulled the towel off the side of the bed; she dried her face and made a few strides around the cabin for the perfect warm down.

Del Monte placed the cup of coffee against his lips, took a sip of the hot brew, but he just could not swallow. He did not like the gut feeling he had. So much time has passed since yesterday's attack on the Santa Marta Police Compound and up to this point he has not received any word on the outcome. Did something go wrong? Were they able to kill the visiting American Special Forces man? Why the lack of communication? These were some of the troubling questions weighing down on Carlos Del Monte's mind as he watched the men training so diligently.

He had a major bargaining chip—the American girl, and sometime this week a message would be sent out to both the United States and Colombian Authorities. Del Monte already had the draft which reads: We are holding Christina Preston an American citizen in a safe location at one of our bases. She is in good health and all measures are in place to ensure that she remains well. Please note however, that we would accept no responsibility for any harm which may come to her in any rescue attempt. Our demands for her release are as follows:

The immediate and unconditional release of Commander Martinez.

An end to the wholesale giving away of peasant lands to foreign investors and other forms of exploitation of our natural resources.

The repatriation of all lands and other assets previously given to the imperialists. In cases where there are legal and other restrictions—we demand full financial compensation.

PAYMENT OF USD TEN MILLION AS A RANSOM. The terms and conditions to be arranged at the appropriate time.

Once these conditions have been met, the kidnapped American would be released to the relevant authority. The various other guerrilla groups would begin a process leading to disarmament, subject to the government agreeing to integrate them into the police and the Armed Forces.

Del Monte strode briskly out into the compound where the troops were just about to complete the morning's training. He was so proud of these men and women; for a moment he wondered what it would be like if he no longer has to lead them. In reality, he knew that's a distinct possibility—and the final outcome is inextricable linked to the young university student now in his custody. Carlos would take it one day at a time; at the moment there are more pressing concerns and challenges.

He walked directly towards the center of the parade square. It was the standard practice for him to address his fighters after such sessions. The patriotic speech is heavily punctuated with quotes from the legendary freedom fighters of Latin America and the wider world. As Del Monte prepared to speak a man came running out of the woods, he appeared to be tired and worn out.

Del Monte and a few of his troops grabbed their weapons and ran towards the gasping man. When they were close enough, the visitor crouched, bent over slightly and placed both hands on his wobbly knees. He spoke in a muffled and tired voice.

"Terrible news, Commander! The attack on the Santa Marta police compound ended in failure—all our men were captured or killed; the American mercenary escaped unharmed!

"You got to be out of your fucking mind!" Carlos Del Monte yelled, as he stomped and kicked the course hard dirt. The other rebels looked on in shock as their leader continued shouting; previous experiences have taught them how to deal with the man they call, El Capitan. None of the men spoke, instead they helped the battered man to his feet and headed towards the main building.

Carlos touched his face and took a slow deep breath after he regained his composure. His transformation was almost instant. The lively, usually buoyant guerrilla leader looked pale and deflated and almost lost for words as he entered the large hallway. Is this the beginning of the unraveling of the intricate web Del Monte had spun? Does this new development signal a threat to his power and control? These were some of the issues playing on his mind. The next twenty-four hours would be crucial. Commander Del Monte lit one of his favorite Cuban cigars as he paced back and forth, pondering what the future holds.

It was about 6:15 pm when Bradley started to interrogate Alberto Guiteriez. Although it was a long eventful and tiring day, the results were phenomenal. The captured man provided a treasure trove of information—and most importantly Bradley got clear details on Christina's whereabouts. Getting Guiteriez to talk presented quite a challenge though.

John had to obtain authorization for the use of special interrogation techniques to ensure that the prisoner spoke. He experienced some frustration due to legislative and other hurdles before finally getting the approval to proceed. At first, some of the top men of the Colombian Armed Forces were reluctant to sign an order agreeing to the use of the highly controversial procedure.

The Americans have used it extensively in the fight against terrorism from Khandhar, Afghanistan to Guantanamo Bay, Cuba with astounding results.

Bradley quickly constructed a sturdy wooden bench which was then placed on a thirty-five degree incline. The captured insurgent had his hands and feet strapped to the structure, a thick cotton hood covered his tilted head. Two large plastic buckets filled with water were placed on a nearby stand. Bradley picked up a smaller container filled it with water and then began to pour it over the restrained man's face. The prisoner coughed and sneezed, spraying a fine nasal mist into the air.

The four Colombian Generals who witnessed the interrogation, got a first hand lesson on Waterboarding. Guiteriez continued to cough and push hard against the heavy straps securing him to the bench; this continued for another twenty-five minutes. Bradley took his time, deliberate, cold and methodical as he poured more water over the insurgent's covered face.

When the exercise was over, Bradley thought about accepting the invitation to spend the night at the remote military compound. The American had other plans however, and still felt a bit uncomfortable especially after the experience with Police Chief Nunez earlier today. Of course, he would need their full cooperation if he is to mount a successful operation to free Christina. There's no other choice—he must have the military and police on his side.

The Colombians, had already agreed to give him special permission to use any of their facilities with access to appropriate military assets. Bradley can also carry a concealed weapon under this agreement.

The focus now is to plan and execute the rescue mission. He would need maps, logistical and other support to first, locate Christina. Colombia has a vast expanse of tropical jungle terrain; some of the most venomous snakes are known to be present in their rain forest. Finding Christina, would certainly present some challenges.

The retired Special Forces and Navy Seal, had great confidence that despite potential hurdles he would live up to the commitment given to Mike Preston, about two and a half weeks ago.

As the jeep pulled out of the army compound, Bradley waved goodbye to the officers. They all cooperated fully and shared with the visiting American many tips on how to get Christina to safety and freedom. Many of them had spent several years working as hostage negotiators and were quite eager to give advice. The soldier indicated that it would be another thirty or so minutes before they arrive at the Estelar Santamar Hotel. After the day's grueling activities—the blistering attack in Santa Marta, John struggled to keep his eyes wide open. An occasional bump on the roadway jolted the American as the driver navigated through the oncoming traffic.

They were travelling through an area called Quinta Carerra which reminded Bradley of his early entry into Santa Marta as Antonio eased up a bit on the accelerator.

"Man, can you go a little faster." said Bradley as he felt the army jeep slowing down.

"Take it easy man, we're going to be there in about 15 minutes." replied Antoino as he swerved to get away from another vehicle.

"Crazy drunk bastard, want to get my ass killed!" shouted Antonio angrily as the car travelling in the opposite direction, veered precariously into his lane.

"Hey buddy, you're the military—don't let that frigging asshole run you off the road, just step on the gas and sideswipe the mother fucker! You guys don't know anything about hard offensive driving down here." Bradley banged his fist against the torn upholstery as he interjected angrily.

Antonio gripped the steering wheel firmly, the muscles in his face became hard and tense. While he narrowly escaped the speeding driver going the other way, the split second maneuver had him on a potentially dangerous course. Momentarily, he lost control and was about to crash into the rear of the taxi just ahead. Bradley sat upright as he yelled. "Gear down! Gear down! Now step on the brakes slightly, just a touch. Yes—That's it!"

Antonio's first thought was to slam hard on the brake—but this could have been even more catastrophic.

The line of vehicles travelling well over 90 kilometers per hour may not have anticipated the sudden stop. A major smash-up or collision on the highway was certainly averted by the navyman's quick thinking.

Antonio quickly regained his composure and thanked the American for getting him out of trouble. He thought about the long report an accident would have warranted and the possibility of a reprimand.

The remainder of the journey back to Estelar Santarmar Hotel was uneventful. Bradley saw the neon lights in the distance and felt a sudden desire for a warm bath and some great food. As the Colombian soldier drove up the well lit path, John already had his belongings slung over the shoulder.

He slammed the door of the army jeep, extended a rather tired and bruised right hand to Antonio, and yawned loudly as he finished his parting words.

"Buenas noches mi amigo, mantendría en contacto. Tómatelo con calma en el camino de regreso a la base."

John rushed through the elevator door. He couldn't wait to get to his seventh floor room; hunger and fatigue already taken a toll on him. The former Navy Seal had plans for a great meal tonight—he pushed himself to the limit today so there's no need to feel guilty. He remembered the scrumptious and delectable dinner last night and instinctively felt a gnawing in his stomach. It was 8:15 pm when John Bradley swiped his keycard and entered the room.

A combination of exhaustion and euphoria gripped the American. He felt tired from the unrelenting all-day drama which unfolded in downtown Santa Marta. And absolutely thrilled, because for the very first time since his clandestine entry onto the Colombian Mainland—he had good news for the man who sent him on this mission. "Finally, I know where those bastards are holding Christina," Bradley shouted as he clenched his fist defiantly.

The former US Marine could hardly control his emotions as he slid the glass and aluminum bathroom door open. John quickly turned the water on. The warm misty spray felt so soothing and therapeutic but he had to hurry. He could not wait to dig into the buffet dinner already in progress, and there is another very important person to contact—Christina's father, Mike Preston.

The director of the CIA heard of the attack during a meeting with the Chairman of the Joint Chiefs of Staff, held at his office in Langley, Virginia

"You're telling me that a meeting between the American sent down there to rescue the girl and the Police Chief turned out to be a firefight?"

"That's correct," replied the Chairman of the Joint Chiefs of Staff, Mark Reuben as he nodded repeatedly.

"Our man is fine, I hope? These damn assholes must pay for their cowardly actions!"

"Sure! Sure! He's OK; John actually fought alongside the Colombian officers in repelling the insurgents."

"When I spoke with General Alvario Castanedas about an hour ago, he raised some serious concerns about what transpired in Santa Marta."

"What did he say specifically? Concerns—give me some details, we put a lot of resources there—training and equipment you know."

"Do you remember about two years ago, there was talk about complicity between the insurgents and some key military and government figures?"

"Of course; we had a lot of discussion on the subject—and at one point, Congress was putting the Government under real pressure to relinquish its agreement to provide training, technical support and other sophisticated military hardware."

"That's true; some of our stuff somehow ended up in the hands of the rebels—night vision equipment, flak jackets, phosphorous grenades and M16's, fitted with M79 Grenade launchers."

"General Castanedas couldn't quite understand how the rebels knew the exact time and place of Bradley's meeting with the Santa Marta Police?

The CIA Director bolted out of his chair and banged his fist on the hard oak desk. "Those fuckers are up to tricks again! They're leaking information which could endanger American lives. Mark, I give you my word—they're not getting away with this!"

"I quite agree with you. Castanedas wants to solicit the help of our man down there to conduct a probe into the matter."

"Don't see a problem with that." said Dumas as he sat down again on his black upholstered chair.

Mark Reuben too was somewhat emotional about the allegations of collusion between one of America's staunchest allies and the rebels. If these allegations prove to be true, there could be serious implications for both countries.

He got up for a moment, walked across the carpeted floor to the water cooler and filled a large glass. The first few sips felt so good and refreshing as Mark loosened his dark blue necktie allowing the clear cool liquid to trickle down his throat.

The Chairman of the Joint Chiefs of Staff started turning slowly and began to walk back to where he sat previously. Somehow the distance seemed longer—or was it his legs? They seem to be moving much slower, and he felt as though they were about to buckle under his weight. Yet, he continued to make strides—albeit shorter ones.

"No, oh no." Mark said to himself as the glass slipped from his now wet and slippery palm. He was sweating profusely and he felt a numbness in his left arm and fingers. His vision became quite blurry as he tried to make it back. He knew that something was terribly wrong—but what could it be?

His annual physical revealed nothing to worry about; the physician recommended that he spent some more time doing physical activities. All labs and other blood work where fine—at age sixty, the career diplomat and former secret service man had no known health issues.

The CIA Chief saw Mark's distress and rushed across the room as he stuttered and struggled to stay upright.

"Mark! Mark! Are you all right? Come, come, take my hand, let me help you; talk to me Mark!"

The CIA Director peeled off his tweed jacket hurriedly and extended a right hand to the stricken Chairman of the Joint Chiefs of Staff. He got just close enough to partially cushion Mark as he fell to the floor with a foamy froth spewing from the corner of his mouth.

Dumas darted to his desk and hit the panic button covertly positioned under the upper right hand corner. Alarm bells sounded simultaneously in all the emergency centers on the CIA compound. An alarm coming from the Director's office is highly unusual. It signals a grave and dire emergency and requires an appropriate response.

As he ran back to Reuben, lying face down on the floor, a team of paramedics and four Special Forces units in full combat gear rushed into the room. "Chief! Chief! Oh my God what's wrong?" The lead paramedic screamed as he knelt beside the ailing man to check his vital signs.

"He's got a low pulse and shallow breathing – come-on guys! We must get him to the emergency room quickly!" The burly doctor removed the stethoscope from Mark Reuben's chest as he instructed the team.

CIA Chief Dumas watched anxiously as the semi-conscious career diplomat—his longtime friend was strapped to the gurney and whisked into the waiting ambulance. As the sirens blared, Chief Dumas picked up the tweed jacket from where he had thrown it, and packed up his desk.

He is taking the rest of the day off—Mary would be shocked to see him home so early. Today's experience had an indelible impact on the nation's top spy. His new mantra—Cherish every moment!

Chapter 19

The guard took Christina outside; this is the very first time she got to have a good look around. As the stocky built rebel pointed to the laundry area—a partially enclosed section about 10 ft by 12 ft., Christina spoke.

"Buenas dias, it's a really beautiful day, isn't it? Great scenery, so nice, and—look at all these magnificent trees."

"Si si Senorita, mui bien gracias," replied the guard as they kept on walking.

He looked really surprised and rolled his rather bulging eyes in disbelief. Christina's current captors had no idea that she spoke fluent Spanish.

"Como si Yama?" Christina quipped as she entered the washing room.

"Alfredo, senoraita—Alfredo Riaz," replied the guard somewhat sheepishly.

"How long have you been a guerrilla fighter?"

"Since ah—"The man paused involuntarily as if to recollect his thoughts to remember how long he's been in the guerrilla army.

Alfredo stuttered slightly; his thin lips parted, curling as he spoke. "Two thousand and seven, October would be exactly three years."

Christina placed three pairs of cotton socks, a few polo shirts and a towel into the plastic bucket then sprinkled a half cup of detergent and opened the tap. The water gushed out and quickly spilled over.

"American, we save every drop of water in this place, shut it off quickly," the guard instructed Christina.

She leaned forward and turned the galvanized fitting counter clockwise to stop the running water.

"Tell me something, Alfredo. Where did you grow up—in a town or village?"

Christina was thinking ahead. She once read a book on how people in captivity survived and eventually escaped from their captors.

One critical factor was their relationship with the people holding them. In the story, Christina learnt that the captive befriended a particular guard, and even flirted a bit with him—and before long got vital information. The prisoner successfully transmitted logistics and other details out to agents and a daring commando raid resulted in her rescue.

Christina showed how savvy she can be; she just got a gut feeling that Alfredo had a soft spot for her. The way he looked upon entering the room—his eyes were literally glued to her entire body. At first she pretended not to notice it, but Christina could almost feel those prying eyes.

The guerrilla fighter shifted the AK 47 assault rifle to a more comfortable position as he answered Christina.

"Why ask, does it matter to you anyway?" Alferdo shrugged his shoulders as he replied.

"Just curious—knowing won't do any harm," said Christina as she looked directly into the man's eyes.

"I grew up near a small town on the coast." The Guard saw her playful taunt as he answered with a broad grin.

"Coastal town?" Christina added with an equally teasing smile; she now knew that her question must be more pointed. The water started to spill out of the laundry bucket again, this time though she turned it off before Alfredo noticed. She really wanted to test the Colombian.

"Your country is so beautiful—and quite large; which side of the coast your town is situated?" This could be a test for Alfredo—maybe not. Christina knew from her studies at university that Colombia shared two coastal gateways—and that's somewhat of a phenomenon in the Latin American continent.

Alfredo looked at the captive American as she bent over to squeeze the water from the thick cotton towel. Her silky long hair cascaded down firm and shapely shoulders. Oh how he wished he could run his fingers through the magnificent flowing mane, thought Alfredo.

He struggled to keep his eyes off her. Gosh! Those long well-shaped legs—the way she walked striding so elegantly in her well fitted jeans.

Alfredo really wanted to impress, he quickly remembered his geography. "I was born in Puerto Diaz, but at an early age my family moved to El Raderdero close to Santa Marta. So I grew up on the Caribbean side," replied Alfredo with a broad smile.

His clean white teeth catching Christina's attention causing her to blush a little.

"Oh, I see and which Department is that?" inquired Christina as she nodded her head approvingly.

"I see you are testing me again, but that's fine—I'm very happy to help you."

"Not really soldier boy; I am just so lonely and want someone to talk to."

Alfredo felt a surge of excitement; he lost his balance momentarily and felt his knees buckle. He sweated and his heart raced. He steadied himself and slung the rifle over the other shoulder using the heavy synthetic strap as he replied.

"Magdalena, and in case you want to know, it's capital is called Santa Marta—one of the oldest cities in the Americas."

"Wow! Alfredo, I see you know quite a lot about your country, very well; that's really nice."

"You see, we fighters are not just a bunch of misfits or delinquents. I know the impression people have out there. That's so far from the truth—among our ranks, we have professionals, university graduates, teachers and trained medics. Our Commander in Chief has a degree in civil engineering, and once ran a good business."

"Great Alfredo, you're fantastic! One other question; how is this area called?"

"Hey, American—you're playing with my head now—I will only tell you that we're in a certain mountain range."

"Please Alfredo! Please, you've got to tell me, I am getting very comfortable with you—and I think I may even—"

Christina barely finished her passionate plea when a loud burst of gunfire erupted from the southern perimeter guard tower. The gunner manning the 50 caliber machine gun emplacement seemed to have spotted some unexpected or suspicious movement near the outer fringes of Camp Diaz.

Alfredo grabbed Christina and pulled her to the ground then leveled his weapon. "Stay down! Stay down!" he screamed. Christina pressed her body hard against the coarse surface; she felt the rough gravel squeezing her breast, but dared not lift her torso a millimeter. The gunfire seemed so close; Christina placed both hands against her earlobes to muffle the shattering blasts.

Her heart pounded as she kept her head glued to the ground. Christina's mind went back to the day of her kidnapping and the bloody scenes of that fateful Saturday morning. Would this be another traumatic experience for her? No! No! Not again, thought Christina as the gunfire intensified. She had the horrific experience of seeing a man shot through the head during the attack near Quinta de San Pedro Alejandrino. This gruesome image would be forever etched in her memory.

Alfredo had re-positioned himself about three meters from where Christina took cover. The gunfire coming from the southern end seemed so close but he did not fire his weapon. This would have been useless anyway as the attackers were some distance away—well out of the 3oo meter range of his Kalashnikov. Alfredo had another reason for not firing—the attackers may train their guns in his direction and put Christina in great danger.

The Colombian guerrilla fighter had other plans and would do anything to protect the young beautiful American student.

Another guard tower opened up with a burst from a Soviet made ZSU Shilka cannon. This heavy four muzzled beast modified by the insurgents had no match. This version could either be fitted on a Jeep or mounted otherwise. The Shilka is really an anti aircraft gun—the Chechnyan rebels felt its devastating effects during the fight against their Russian neighbors.

The insurgents were now using this monster as a heavy machine gun by simply changing the trajectory of firing. During the construction of the towers, Del Monte had given the men special instructions on how to construct the platform. The additional reinforcement ensured that the cannon had a proper and solid base; the gunner with a 360 degree field of vision could fire at will.

As the huge slugs tore up parts of the forest canopy the group attacking from the north were in a serious predicament. They were bandits from another region looking for arms and other supplies to bolster their own stocks. Certainly they did not anticipate such an onslaught. One man was impaled against a large tree by rounds from the ZSU Shilka; his left arm completely severed just above the shoulder and a gaping crater replaced his skull. In the heat of the battle two of the attackers for no apparent reason jumped out from behind the protective mound. One of them had a grenade launcher and tried to take aim at the gunner raining down slugs on their position.

This was a kamikaze maneuver and the result inevitable. The man in the guard tower, tilted the weapon and fired a murderous burst, the big bullets tearing into the hapless man's torso.

Their leader started to shout frantically. "Run! Run! Let's get to fuck out of here!" They dodged several rounds ducking behind the trees as they raced towards the slope. This skirmish left them bruised and battered—four dead and no supplies to take back to their jungle redoubt.

Meanwhile, Carlos Del Monte took charge of men defending the southern side. He maintained radio contact with the guard manning the tower as they took up defensive positions. Several thoughts raced through his mind but the most worrying question—was this attack in any way related to the botched raid on the Santa Marta police compound? And is the American Special Forces man involved in an operation to free the girl?

The firing from the north tower ceased, so Alfredo decided to move from his position and head towards Christina. She was visibly shaken but unhurt. He grabbed her by the hand and pointed towards the log cabin some 50 meters away. They sprinted across the dirt and gravel outfield; the distance looked much longer, Christina thought as Alfredo pushed open the heavy door. She asked Alfredo to look after the abandoned laundry and thanked him for taking care of her.

"I hope you're going to be fine—sorry for all the trouble," Alfredo said just as he started to slide the metal latch on the cabin door.

"That's alright, you've been so helpful—I will always remember you Alfredo," said Christina using the soft inflection in her voice to show her sincerity. The Colombian rebel nodded and made his way out to the compound. Christina had experienced another harrowing ordeal and needed to rest for a while.

In the meantime, Del Monte and the other fighters were looking at a dark plume of smoke coming from an area close to the ridge. It appeared as though the retreating attackers had set off some explosive charges as a diversionary tactic. The jungle forest provides a rich source of combustible material—felled trees, decaying foliage and even uncut saplings. Many of them have natural oils and resins so a fire here could have a devastating effect.

The smoke soon turned into a raging inferno as the wind blew over the forest. Carlos Del Monte started screaming at the top of his voice: "Hold your fire! No more firing, stop the shooting." He had to get the men to cease firing. By now the flames had engulfed a good portion of surrounding forest and the Colombian Black Devils Chief feared that more gun or rocket fire would worsen the situation. The gang of bandits by this time had disappeared deep into the jungle undergrowth. Carlos instructed

Geoffrey Gilbert

his men to go back to the main store room. Inside they quickly unfurled the thick industrial grade nylon hoses and rushed to the pump house. There they hastily made the connections using brass couplings; they loaded the huge bundle onto the old jeep and bolted across the open ground to the hydrant closest to the now raging fire.

Del Monte had used his engineering skills in designing the compound. In this lush tropical rainforest water sources were abundant. There is no shortage of rainfall, and the rivers, springs and giant cascading waterfalls made water harvesting very easy for the rebels. As they sprayed the flaming trees from two separate points, many of them remembered the long grueling hours in the sweltering tropical heat building their water storage.

They continued the blasts of water on the flaming trees for about an hour before the blaze subsided. Later, as they watched the last glowing embers succumb to the gushing onslaught; the crew felt proud of the work they had done. Once again their leader—Carlos Del Monte, alias El Capitan had led them to another victory.

The band of roving bandits was repelled; they had tested the group's defense capability and they passed the test with flying colors. The defiant rebels gathered their equipment as they chanted lustily - victory or death! Unaware that another battle for their camp is looming, they continued to chant and dance—the insurgents just couldn't contain their jubilation at this time.

Del Monte joined in as the men celebrated with more chanting. They had a great day on the battlefield today and the celebrations and party would continue later tonight.

His young lover Francia, made a magical romantic concoction of herbal aphrodisiacs, and El Capitan is prepared to give his sassy and voluptuous beauty a night of wild erotic excitement. " I would certainly give her the fuck of her lifetime tonight," said Del Monte he strode across the open yard.

134

Chapter 20

Mike Preston had retired for the night. Today went quite well; his devoted assistant had done an excellent Job. Mike was honest enough to admit that the pressure from Christina's kidnapping had him on the ropes. After the meeting today with the visiting executive from Kazakhstan he observed something rather unusual.

When Burkhoskiev left his office, Sally kept looking at her boss in a way she had never done before. At first he thought his eyes were playing tricks on him. But it continued—She had a rather seductive look today. The tight snugly fitted black skirt revealed her rather shapely butt and pale blue inner top trimmed with a tinge of light lacy frill, showed her voluptuous and sexy figure.

Since the passing of his wife Anna, Preston deliberately chose to keep women at bay. He is filthy rich and could sleep with a different woman every night if he wanted to. At sixty he just wasn't in the mood for gold diggers.

But tonight, Sally just kept playing on his mind. He took another sip of the coffee and placed his cup on the bedside table. Turning slightly on his side, Preston adjusted the shaded lamp and glanced at the silver clock positioned just over the Television stand. It was such a marvelous time piece—well over twenty years old and still very accurate. He picked up his cell phone, scrolled through the contacts to find Sally's number. He found it just as the land line started to ring. This had better be important he whispered beneath his breath while reaching for the receiver.

"Hello, Mike Preston," he recognized Bradley's strong and assertive voice instantly.

"Mike, how you doing—sounding very upbeat tonight; you're hanging in there man?

"Well, what else can I do; it's been almost seven weeks and I still don't know where my daughter is—that's quite painful. Can you imagine the torment and pain I feel, I've got no appetite and I'm unable to sleep. My life is a living hell Bradley!"

"You should start sleeping well again." John reduced the volume on the TV set before giving Mike the good news.

"What do you mean—what! Are you onto something?—A clue, a tip or ransom note—anything! Anything at all!" Preston sounded rather angry, he really wanted some answers fast.

Bradley took a slow deep breath, moved to a more comfortable position before replying to Mike Preston.

"Mike, there are some interesting developments and I now have vital information on Christina"

"Oh my God—let me get the details; is she alright Bradley—is she?

"Of course, she is alive and well; around midday today, a group of rebels launched an audacious attack on a police compound while I met with the chief. I fought alongside the Colombian Police to defeat them."

"But Christina—where is Christina?" Are you trying to tell me that she is with the police."

"No, no, we were able to gather information from one of the captured men—clear and precise details on her whereabouts." Bradley got up from the bed to turn off the mini fluorescent lamp on the night stand while responding to Preston.

"So Bradley, you're saying that you know where they're holding her? I want to be clear—is that what you're telling me?"

"Definitely, I got the sucker to spill his guts; at first he resisted but in the end he gave in."

"So where is she Bradley? Tell me man—tell me something! Is Christina alright?"

"I have no doubt Mike. You see, the guerrillas know that your daughter is worth much more alive and healthy. They're actually treating her quite well. One of the captured insurgents is pretty close to the leader of the group holding Christina"

"Don't want to sound pessimistic, but tell me something Bradley—what makes you think that the captured rebel spoke the truth. He could well be giving you the information to save his ass. Or worse yet—he could have fed you an elaborate ruse."

"No way—I took charge of the interrogation—got no doubt about the intelligence and other details obtained. Mike, I've been in this business for more than twenty-five years. I am confident, so stop worrying man."

"Wow! That's great." Preston bolted up from the bed and exclaimed enthusiastically; he could hardly contain himself when he heard what Bradley said.

"So what's the next move man, when are you going to kick some ass?"

"The rescue plan—I've already started working on something. But Mike, it appears that the rebels are getting intelligence from a source within the Military—some form of collusion I suspect. I have no confirmation of this, but certain activities just cause my suspicion to grow.

"You're not serious! That's crazy man—this could have serious implications for Christina, Preston shouted out angrily!

"Calm down Mike, calm down; these are just allegations. I've been working with the Colombian Military for several years; they are brave and committed men. I have great respect for them, so let's not rush to any hasty conclusions!"

"I trust your judgement John, after all you're the professional—you've got the experience; that's why I hired you anyway." Preston rubbed his eyes and tried to muffle the yawn as his head rolled involuntarily. The sleep signals were prodding him, but he had to stay awake—this is not about him, certainly not. Christina's safe return is paramount and he is prepared to do whatever it takes to make this a reality.

Bradley heard the tone in Preston's voice; he did not realize that he's been chatting for more than a half hour. He needed to get some sleep; tomorrow is going to be an extremely important day.

"Mike, this is a critical period. By midday I should complete the logistical and tactical details of the rescue plan. The Military has already given me full access to any assets required for such an operation. I had a very long day, but at least there were some positive developments to report. I've got a meeting with General Castenedas sometime tomorrow to discuss my rescue plan. We'll be chatting again soon; go get some rest, take care now.

Preston hung up then pulled the light blue cotton bedspread to partially cover himself. His eyes got heavier but he managed to keep them open a bit longer. Finally, he had some news from the man he sent to Colombia—a retired US Navy Seal who made a promise to rescue Christina and take her back to the United States.

He certainly did not mind the long chat with Bradley, so many things were going through his head at this point. Mike Preston looked at the clock again and he remembered the number he was about to call earlier, just as Bradley's call came in. He picked up his mobile phone and dialed the number.

Sally still had her colorful bath wrap partially covering her beautiful shapely body. She almost didn't hear the rather faint chiming of her mobile phone nestled inside the cluttered work bag. This had better be important. Who could be calling at this time—certainly her ex-boyfriend Marco doesn't have her new number. Who the hell could it be thought Sally as she pressed the answer button.

"Hello, this is Sally" Preston loved the softness in her voice and licked his lips in anticipation.

"Hey, how you are doing my Sweet Chocolate? Just dialed your number by chance." He took a slow deep breath as he felt a slight palpitation brought on by the lie told. Of course, Sally never knew that her boss had a pet name for her.

"Nothing really just fooling around a little. My girlfriend came over earlier—had a couple martinis, she played with my pussy a little bit and that's about it. You know the kind of fun stuff girls do when they're lonely. And baby, I just want to let you know that I've shaved it all off just for you."

Preston swayed and lost his balance temporarily, his lips became rather dry and his heart was pounding.

"Ah, I see, you're quite a naughty girl, didn't realize you did girls too. Tell me Sally, how do you guys do it?" Preston asked in a rather surprised tone of voice.

"You're kidding right, sure you want to know that; we've got so much more good stuff to talk about—you know. Anyway, don't worry about that girl pussy talk—it's only a temporary fix until I can find a real man!"

"Well, look no further baby!" Preston reflected on what he just said and wondered if he did not cross the line.

By now, he felt a sudden rush of blood go straight through his groin as he formed a picture of a nude and sexy Sally sprawled out on his bed. Freddy had not fired off in quite a while, but Mike had the confidence that he could give Sally the fuck of her life tonight.

"How about coming over for a while? Could do with some company."

Sally stood up; momentarily dropping the floral wrap onto the floor. Her nipples became taunt as though she had taken an instant aphrodisiac. Wow! Finally her boss wanted to fuck her; the seductive outfit she wore in the office today must have done something to him.

"You really want me to come over Mike? Sally asked, as she pulled open the wardrobe drawer. Tonight she would look for the sexiest pieces in her Victoria Secrets collection. Something really erotic and wild! Sally pulled the drawer completely out of the metal track and tossed the contents onto her bed. Sally quickly made her pick. A wicked lacy frilled bright red, size seven lingerie piece with matching open crotch panties, and now this hot seductive diva was ready to hit the road.

"Sure, I really do. You know all this stuff I've been dealing with— Christina—so much is on my mind," Preston said passionately and sighed as he anticipated Sally's response.

"Don't worry, I've been waiting for you to ask me, yeah for a while now. Let me get dressed—should be there in about a half hour, depending on traffic."

Sally, picked up the keys for the Tribeca, grabbed her purse and headed for the back door, She pulled the outer metal grill gate and made her way quickly down the metal steps. As she stepped from the final threader, the thin leather strap on the black Guchi purse caught a sharp barb on the gate causing it to be tangled. Sally cursed under her breath as she tugged the string, causing the contents to spill onto the driveway. "What the fuck, got no time for this—shit, why now?"

Preston's assistant quickly composed herself, picked up a small canister of mace, her credit cards and the other spilled items, then got into the vehicle. She slammed the door to show her exasperation and started the engine.

Sally quickly backed out of the driveway onto Highway 16. It's about a thirty-five minute drive to Preston's place, but tonight she could easily save some time and get there much quicker. Sally pressed hard on the accelerator, and soon she navigated her way onto Washington Avenue then headed south to the Memorial Park area; the speedometer dial eased passed the 75 km mark as she revved up the engine.

The rows of neon lights appear to be much brighter as Sally made a left turn and away from highway 16. Another ten minutes or so and she'll be in Preston's sprawling mansion. As she got closer, Sally felt her nipples tingle and an exciting pre orgasmic anticipation slightly distracted her attention from the oncoming traffic. Before long, Sally calmed herself—the last thing she wanted was an accident on her way to her boss's mansion where a session of hot erotic pleasure awaited her.

"Freaking jackass, want to run me off the frigging road!" Sally screamed as another driver made a crazy maneuver barely missing her rear bumper.

She held the steering wheel firmly, and kept on driving at a steady pace until the lights of Preston's glitzy mansion appeared in the distance. Sally's heart raced as she got closer.

The property, perched on a gentle incline was ringed by towering trees and the perimeter lights were strategically placed—Other signs of the great wealth and opulence of Mike Preston—the high brick wall and gated entrance were quite evident as Sally approached.

Preston looked at the time again; wearing just a white cotton shirt and pajama pants he reached for the phone. This should be Sally, he thought while lifting up the receiver.

"Hi, can't believe you're here already. Drive right up to the gate—not to close and I would let you in."

Sally pulled into the driveway, triggering a flood of warm incandescent light on both sides of the pathway. The large metal gate swung open almost silently—a manifestation of the excellent maintenance. Preston leaned against the metal balustrade and directed Sally to the open garage.

"Pull a little bit to the left, then straighten up—yeah, that's right—just a little, well, OK that's fine."

She stepped out of the car and sprinted up the flight of stairs into the open arms of the eagerly awaiting Preston.

"How about to drink?" Preston asked, barely able to control his excitement excercabeted by the erotic fragrance of the woman he now embraced.

"Sure—would like a Pinacolada or a glass of red wine—whatever is easy for you."

"I've got a bottle of the finest French wine—Le Cabinet, already chilled so come on pretty angel"

Preston took Sally by the hand and led her into the spacious living room. "Oh my God," Sally couldn't contain her excitement.

"This is awesome, said Sally as she stared at the exquisite furnishings and rare collections adorning the magnificently painted walls.

Mike returned with two glasses and handed one to Sally.

"Come my love, let me show you around; Preston placed his left arm around her waist, pinching the light fabric of the soft cotton mini skirt. As they were about to enter the doorway, he placed his unfinished glass on a nearby table. He then slid his fingers gingerly under the fabric and began to gently massage her firm and shapely butt.

Sally started to moan softly. "What are you waiting for baby, my pussy is on fire for you. C'mon, C'mon give it to me baby."

Preston continued to run his fingers all over Sally's body. By now the little cotton dress had found itself strewn over a sofa in the far corner of the room. He glided his fingers along her silky smooth legs while pulling on the stringed thong fitted snugly around her bottom. Sally helped Mike by reaching for the tiny bow holding the laced underwear onto her hips. As the thong fell to the floor, Preston placed his mouth against her nipples and licked them like a sweet succulent tropical fruit.

Sally wasted no time too. She placed both hands around his waist and peeled off the pajamas and white cotton boxers right down to Mike's knees, then bent over and placed his erect penis in her mouth. Preston winced and clenched his teeth making some strange inaudible guttural sounds. "Sa . . . . Sal . . . you're killing me! Oh my darling, oh! Oh! Oh! Please don't stop it now; baby please—oh yes! It feels so fucking good!"

He groped her ass with one hand and caressed the soft supple vaginal cavity while screaming in wild erotic ecstasy as Sally continued to roll her slithering tongue over his rock hard dick.

Mike seemed to be in a trance-like state as he moaned uncontrollably "Sally, Sally oh gosh—um, uh."

She took her wet lips away from Mike's penis and pointed towards the open bedroom. Mike released her temporarily and kicked out the rolled up pajamas.

"Mike I am on fire for you darling. Come baby I can't wait any longer. Let me feel your dick; come on my sweet love. I've been waiting for this moment since the very first day I stepped into your office.

He lifted Sally off her feet and carried her straight to the king size bed. The room had the smell of spicy fragrant candles and the aura of an erotic spa. A swirling bubble bath and fountain, all made the atmosphere more alluring.

Preston laid her down gently on the multi colored blanket, his heart pounding in anticipation as he climbed in beside the beautiful brunette. Sally had a wild passionate look in her eyes and as he stroked and caressed her silky smooth body, the sighing and moaning only got louder.

"Oh! Oh! Ah! Baby, let's enjoy each other; come on honey lets make love all night! Yes honey, I love the way you do it. Oh yes Mike darling! Make love to me all night baby! Come my lover boy, give me all you've got."

Chapter 21

Bradley woke up so energized; this had a lot to do with yesterday's events. He felt really good speaking with Mike Preston. At least he gave him the breaking news—and today the strategy to rescue Christina begins. He had already spoken with General Castenadas, Colombia's Minister of Defense and National Security. John did not intend to take any chances. After the episode at the Police Compound in Santa Marta, he had good reasons to put a question mark on some elements within the military establishment.

John sat in the lobby of the Estelar Santamar Hotel and stared at the clock located on the wall at the back of the receptionist's desk. He had a delectable breakfast once again and somehow he felt that his stay at this great resort is about to end. Bradley had no regrets and would certainly recommend the facility to all his friends. He had already posted some comments on trip advisor—this he anticipates would help to spread the good news and further promote Colombia's excellent hospitality and cuisine.

As he waited for the military transport, the retired US Special Forces man reviewed the notes he had written on the yellow note pad. The first action item is the aerial reconnaissance of the area where Christina is held by her captors. Del Monte's man captured during the firefight in Santa Marta really spilled his guts—even providing some rough sketches on the site where the American hostage was holed up for the last couple of weeks.

During and after the interrogation, Alberto Gutirez told Bradley and the team of the trade off negotiated between Del Monte's Colombian Black Devils and a smaller and less important group of insurgents. He gave chilling details of the transfer of money to complete the process and the intricate and clandestine methods used to disguise and launder these funds.

Bradley continued to look at the notes and the sketches; the area appeared to be heavily forested and steep with narrow and treacherous precipices. The site appeared to have a huge plateau and Christina's kidnappers seemed to have done some elaborate construction. A Colombian officer told Bradley afterwards that Gutirez's description resembles an area near the foothills of the Sierra Nevada mountains—a place the indigenous Tayrona Indians called "Tierra de Valles oscuros y sin retorno."

John looked at the clock on the wall again. The transport seemed to be taking a bit longer—the General told him that all the arrangements were made to take him to an undisclosed destination. Since the troubling events at the Santa Marta Police Head Quarters, all matters relating to Christina's kidnapping are considered top secret. Bradley attributed the delay to this. Castenadas did tell him that it won't be business as usual. He picked up the morning paper and strolled through the large arched doorway to enjoy the beautiful shrubbery and magnificent gardens which adorned the hotel entrance.

Pausing briefly near a curbside lamppost, Bradley removed his mobile phone and called General Alvario Castenadas.

"Good Morning General, I've been waiting for close to twenty minutes—no sign of the military transport."

"Sorry, the guys ran a bit late, but they're on their way. We are using an unmarked vehicle to avoid any undue attention. Martinez, the Corporal who worked with you during the interrogation is driving."

"Good, I'll be on the look out," said Bradley as he walked towards the street already bustling with traffic. Shortly afterwards a black bullet proof sedan pulled up and he immediately recognized the powerfully built Martinez. He got into the back seat quickly and was greeted by the driver and the other occupant.

"Thanks guys, how long is the ride back?" asked Bradley as he leaned slightly sideways.

"We'll get there in about thirty five minutes or less, the traffic is not too bad this morning. Don't worry anyway, I can always take another route if it builds up."

Bradley pulled out his notepad again and started to make some additional notes. His list of supplies included updated maps of the Sierra Nevada Range, flares, nylon rope fitted with grappling hooks and two sets of Colombian Army fatigues, a helmet and a machete. Before the attack on Del Monte's compound, Bradley would retrieve his duffel bag hidden away in the hills above the city and most importantly—make contact with Captain Alvarez. The old seaman knew the coastal waters and the highlands of Santa Marta perhaps better than the Military men.

The driver took a left turn off the main highway and headed for a nearby intersection. He accelerated and then made a right turn, this time branching out onto a dirt and gravel road. This area looked a bit familiar to Bradley; it reminded him of the route the interrogation team had taken a few days earlier.

Bradley looked through the window as the vehicle swerved and bumped along the rugged coarse unpaved road; he thought about the details obtained from Guiteriez, Del Monte's lieutenant, now in the custody of the Colombian military. He had great faith in the intelligence gathered and couldn't wait to implement it. Mike Preston wanted his daughter back home and Bradley knew that the key to a successful rescue is a quick surgical strike on the compound, deep in the Colombian highlands.

As the driver peered in the rearview mirror, he saw the impatient look in the eyes of the retired American soldier. Bradley made brief eye contact and gave a rather terse retort.

"Seems like we're going to the South Pole buddy, sure you're on the right path?"

Martinez tapped on the brake slightly as he approached another bump in the road while responding to the American.

"No need to worry man. We're almost there. Just look to the right of the ridge, we have less than a mile to go now."

John rolled the window down and focused his attention on the wooded incline a short distance away. He couldn't wait to get to the remote destination for the meeting with a select group of military men.

The level of secrecy for this meeting meant that only General Alvario Castenadas, President Rafael Espinosa-Mendez and a hand full of senior officers had prior knowledge of it. After the fiasco at the Police Command center in Downtown Santa Marta, Bradley and his team were not taking any chances.

The unmarked sedan lurched and bumped as they got closer. Bradley could see the high perimeter fence crowned with multiple layers of razor wire, and a large metal gate marking the main point of entry. There were two machine gun emplacements on opposite sides of the fence as well as guard towers positioned strategically atop three gigantic metal silos.

Martinez spoke on the car radio as he brought the vehicle slowly to a halt at the top of the ridge, a short distance from the main entrance. A guard emerged from a concealed dug-out and removed the thick heavy steel bar to open the gate. Bradley felt a great sense of relief as the vehicle came to a halt and all three occupants got out.

The building was covered with a colossal concrete slab and looked very much like a bomb shelter. Martinez led the American down a dimly lit passageway; the windowless wall and rather bland interior made the environment claustrophobic. Finally, they got to a spacious hallway with a long rectangular table in the middle. Bradley breathed a sigh of relief when the Colombian escort showed him where to sit at the table. Martinez saluted and left the room.

There were four high ranking officers around the table. Bradley only knew one of them and wondered if that's the reason why the previously empty chair was positioned next to him. His name is General Ernesto Augusto Gustav, and both men had worked previously on joint US and Colombian military exercises. John felt quite relieved to see the General after so many years. Bradley thought that Gustav looked quite good for his age.

The General celebrated his sixtieth birthday earlier in the year and is in excellent shape. Unlike Nunez, the chubby Santa Marta Police Chief, Gustav remained passionate about his fitness. The visiting American couldn't let this go unnoticed as he extended his hand to greet his fellow soldier.

"Hey, my good old buddy—never thought I would be back on Colombian soil again; how has it been with you?"

Gustav extended a hand to the soldier and smiled broadly while greeting his old American friend.

"Life's unpredictable man, I intend to retire in a couple years but you never know—still love my work but we'll see what happens."

The General introduced Bradley to the rest of the team, and the men went straight into the discussion of the plan to rescue Christina.

Bradley filled the tall glass with water and placed it on the quilted paper napkin before laying out the rescue plan. He took a few sips as he unfolded the wrinkled map and placed it carefully beside the small pouch he carried.

"Gentlemen, let me first say thanks to all of you. I have been in your awesome country for just a little over two weeks, I feel so much at home and I am really thrilled. However, I am not here on vacation or just sightseeing. I am here because a young American University student has been kidnapped, and her dream of becoming a research scientist shattered by a group of thugs. Her dad hired me for this special assignment to bring her back safely to the United States."

General Gustav leaned back in his chair and touched his thick curly mustache as he responded to the visiting American.

"Yes, that's right, these murdering bastards snatched her in broad daylight, but we'll teach them a lesson soon. My American friend, we would make all our military assets available to you; our troops would provide logistical, tactical or any other form of support. Just ask for whatever you need!"

"Thanks General. Again, I must say that you guys have been so helpful and I know that in the remaining days I'll be depending on you a whole lot more. I've got the plan nicely laid out for this special assignment, and I am extremely confident that the mission would succeed."

Bradley got up and walked over to the flip chart stand and pinned the large map over it. "Alright gentlemen, this is an area about the size of Texas." He zeroed in on the Sierra Nevada Mountains with the thin pointed rod as he spoke.

"The gigantic ridges and gullies, impregnable forests and massive plateaus make accessing somewhat of a challenge, but I am confident. The intelligence we've got from the captured insurgent indicates that Christina is held in this lower quadrant. The terrain is rough and extremely rugged, that's why only elite commandos would accompany me on the mission; failure is not an option!"

The tall lanky officer sitting next to General Gustav nodded and asked Bradley about the raging rivers flowing all over this treacherous and difficult landscape.

"A few years ago we lost four of our best troops in a training exercise close to that region. I remember the day quite well. We were dropped off near the landing zone by a Black Hawk Helicopter; the gear seemed heavier that morning and when we landed the whole place was covered in mist. Our mission simulated the rescue of a squad of soldiers marooned at the top of a high ridge. The river was about eighty meters wide, so a thick sisal rope was tied to a large tree on the western side. One man volunteered to swim across the rolling waters to secure the rope on the other side of the river. When we were finished, the remaining troops started to wade across. We were about two thirds of the way when calamity struck. A huge piece of a rock from a nearby hill just broke off and slammed into the water; the displacement creating a massive wave and surge. The impact was devastating, breaking the rope and forcibly catapulting four of the troopers into the air. They landed hard; the heavy gear adding deadly momentum and lethal force. The guys didn't have a chance! We were too far from them to offer any help. We looked on in shock and horror as our mortally wounded comrades were swept away by the rushing water."

The riveting account of the tragedy really touched Bradley; he felt the passion in the man's voice as he gave details of the events on that fateful day. Certainly, there were very important lessons for consideration in the rescue plan the American had drafted.

"That's the main reason why I am here; this is your country and all of you, I am sure know much more than I do about the terrain, weather and the culture. I have no doubt about that, and I am so glad you spoke about your experience even though it brought back painful emotions." Bradley walked over to the tall Colombian and tapped him on the shoulder to show his appreciation.

"These sketches I've done are based on the details obtained from the captured insurgent a few days ago; I tried to be as accurate as possible because I know that one minor miscalculation could be costly, both in terms of time and human lives.

"So you think the girl is kept in that log cabin; there are other buildings on the premises you know—what happens if she's moved from time to time?" Gustav continued as he zoomed in on the sketches Bradley presented to them.

"The man was quite specific in his details—the building to the right of Christina's Cabin, about one hundred and fifty meters is a general assembly hall. To the north west or left, there is the main barracks and according to Guiteriez about four to five hundred insurgents are housed there at any given time."

He went on to show them the guard towers and the other secluded cabin from where El Capitan commanded his many loyal troops. Bradley also shared with the men some startling statistics pried from the interrogated prisoner: The Colombian Black Devils have an impressive arsenal of weapons and military supplies. They are well equipped with enough arms and ammunition to hold out for a good six months. This is a formidable group of highly organized fighters with a great passion for unconventional warfare and guerilla tactics.

"This may well work to our benefit, we would give the impression that a major assault is on his way; but the operation would comprise one or two commando units for a quick surgical extraction of the kidnapped American."

The retired American Marine and Navy Seal continued to lay out his plan: "General Gustav, before the operation is launched, I want to make a special request for a reconnaissance flight over the Sierra Nevada at least two days before the actual operation. I would also need accurate weather forecasts for the next seven days. One of my local contacts has a great knowledge and experience of the mountains speaks about unpredictable weather patterns in that region."

"That's right," said the Colombian Army General. "Sometimes it gets extremely cold and windy, but I am certain you would carry the appropriate gear—wouldn't you Bradley?"

"Of course, you know the way I operate buddy, once I commit to a mission I take full responsibility for every aspect of it; nothing is left to chance."

"You have not changed one bit my friend, and I have no doubt that you'll kick these bastards so damn hard, they won't even know what the hell hit them."

Bradley picked up his sketch pad and pointed to the cabin where he believed Christina was held and continued to explain how the plan is to be executed.

"As we speak, the USS Antartica is on its way to Colombia via the Caribbean coast. Your Defense Ministry through General Castenadas made all the arrangements. The Antartica is in Colombia ostensibly for joint naval patrols with their Colombian counterparts."

To the unsuspecting observer though, the presence of the US warship is nothing but another routine call on a friendly state. At least, that's the impression the military wanted to create. The Antartica would be in Santa Marta to support Bradley and the elite group of commandos spearheading the operation to rescue the captured American Student.

"We would land the team close to the South Eastern end of the ridge, on the side facing the Magdalena River. There will be no river crossing; two Black Hawk helicopters would land the extraction team at the foot of the ridge the night before the raid. We'll set up base camp check supplies and equipment before advancing up the rugged mountain. The team would consist of nine men but the actual assault party would be made up of no more than five commandos. Four men would remain at the base for guard duty and backup support. We're not taking any chances and failure is not an option!" Bradley slammed his fist on the hard wooden table top to stress the seriousness of the mission, causing the water from the glass mug to spill over.

General Gustav quickly contained the spill by folding the end of the bright floral cloth to make a temporary barrier." Take it easy my good old American friend, you don't have to worry—we are with you all the way; everything is going to be just fine. I would give the order for the reconnaissance flight as soon as we are finished here and you should have your aerial photos by thirteen hundred hours tomorrow."

"I have no doubt about the support from you guys—it's just that when you're planning and executing such a mission some variables and unknown factors can determine success or failure. But what the heck! Special forces are trained to think and react quickly; in every adversity we see opportunity—that's our mantra, so General you're quite right."

Bradley thanked the General and his men again as one final rehearsal of the assault was done. The American had already decided that only two men under General Gustav's command would be part of the assault team. The rest would from other sectors of the Colombian military subject to his approval.

The meeting lasted for well over two hours, and Bradley knew that he had another very important call to make. It's been quite a while since he had spoken to his old friend—Captain Alverez, the veritable sailor from Tangaga Bay. Bradley just had a gut feeling that the sea fearing Colombian would have quite a lot to tell about the seemingly mystical, Sierra Nevada Mountains.

As Bradley and the men left the highly fortified room, images of the rescue plan kept flashing through his mind. He's been on Colombian soil for the well over a month and something kept telling him that victory was within his sight. They kept on walking at a brisk pace until the courtyard was in full view.

General Gustav reminded Bradley that the flight over the designated area would proceed as planned and the findings made available shortly thereafter. Bradley smiled at the General as they cross the gravel courtyard. The vehicle to take him back to his hotel was parked to the right of the main gate, and Bradley recognized it was the same driver who had picked him up earlier this morning. He entered the unmarked car from the left side door as Martinez turned the key in the ignition, and they were soon on the way back.

Christina finished the meal rather hurriedly; she did not sleep very well last night. Her thoughts were at the family mansion back in Texas and more so on her dad. This ordeal has already thrown a monkey wrench in her plans for a better education, but that's minor. For Christina, it's more about missing home, family and close friends. The weekend movies and burgers with pals, all the fun; somehow captivity seemed a bit more painful last night but Christina knew that she's got to hold on.

She wiped away the tears streaming down her cheeks and tried hard to maintain her composure. Christina knew that drifting back into depression mode only leads to more emotional trauma and diminishes her chances of getting out of the jungle alive and well. It's been quite a while since she had seen her soldier friend and this was quite odd. Christina started to connect with him—the way he shielded her when the camp came under enemy fire, plus the other acts of kindness did not go unnoticed.

Christina had been around the leader of the insurgency long enough to figure out his many moods and even anticipate some of his actions. She had an eerie feeling about the soldier she had become friendly with. The last time they spoke, Alfredo told her about his disillusionment with the guerilla movement. He mentioned the many excesses and abuses sanctioned by Carlos and his closest henchmen. He also told Christina that Del Monte enjoys summary execution and in some cases the victim is shot without even a blindfold. There is no such thing as a trial, and many men were killed on the basis of circumstantial evidence or just flimsy suspicion.

The American prisoner prayed that her friend did not suffer a similar fate and that he would be assigned to do guard duty at her cabin soon. Whatever personal interest the insurgent fighter may harbor did not really matter to Christina. She certainly intended to use this as an advantage—at this point escaping from this jungle confinement is her main focus.

Christina peeked through the tiny crack in the log cabin and just started to make some rough sketches of the surroundings. She noted the position of all the buildings, the distances which separated them as well as the positions of the guard tower. The last time Alfredo did guard duty, he told her of the American agent and the failed attempt on his life. She had no reason to doubt the Colombian and certainly, this information gave her renewed hope. The only problem now is being unable to hear from Alfredo; but Christina had no intentions of giving up on her freedom. She would do whatever is necessary to keep her dreams alive.

The young hostage started to hatch her own escape plans and Alfredo had a critical role to play. Somehow Christina felt that her freedom day is coming. This sense of renewed optimism resonated through her entire persona today. Christina walked back towards the bed and continued to transfer her mental notes onto the paper. Stepping across to the wooden rack, she pulled the rucksack off the stand to retrieve her tattered notebook. During moments like these, Christina found solace and comfort in writing. She looked at her initial entry marking the date insurgents raided the tour bus en route to Quinta de San Pedro de Alejandrino. Next Saturday would be exactly two months since her incarceration and it seemed like an eternity.

As she reviewed her rough drawings, Christina remembered something she had observed while the men were out on the compound last Monday morning. One of the fighters fed a pigeon from his hand before wrapping a thin sheet of paper around the feet of the bird. Fully fed and energized, the bird swirled into the air and soon faded in the distance. Quite impressive thought Christina; from that day she began to toy with the idea of getting a message out. She thought about the plan to use the pigeon courier to contact anybody on the outside. But the key here is Alfredo—he is critical for the success of this plan, and until Christina hears from him the task seems rather daunting.

For the moment, she'll remain positive and upbeat; nothing at this point would dampen her indomitable quest for freedom. Christina finished the sketches, folded her notes neatly and slipped the notebook back into the backpack. She pushed hard on the heavy wooden door to alert the guard; it is time to do her weekly laundry. Christina quickly gathered her small bundle of clothes as the guard unlatched the door. The day had an aura of calmness about it, and she certainly walked out into the yard feeling a strange kind of excitement.

Christina moved briskly towards the laundry area, the guard following closely behind her, and walking at a steady pace just to keep abreast with the extremely fit American. When Christina got close enough to the rough cut entrance, her eyes made contact with a familiar figure. There's something about the way he carried that Kalasnikov. As the man got closer and closer,

Christina realized that his features were so familiar. The slight swagger in his step and that jerky elongated stride; the captive American paused, focusing all her attention on the man. "Oh my God, it's him, it's him!" said Christina as she placed her right hand over her trembling lips to muffle the emotion in her voice.

Her escort, following a short distance behind heard the excitement in her voice, and broke into a quick sprint to position himself directly beside her and asked inquiringly: "Are you alright, seen a ghost or something?"

Chapter 22

El Capitan sat on the long wooden bench and sipped from the simmering hot cup; this is not unusual in any way as Del Monte enjoys sharing a meal with his men. This keeps them motivated and enthused—after all how many bosses really make time to mix and mingle with their regular foot soldiers? Carlos is one such leader, he is never afraid to give a firm reprimand when necessary, but on the other hand he is always there to support and encourage the men.

Since the fiasco in Santa Marta and the raid on Camp Diaz, the leader of the Colombian Black Devils had a very uneasy feeling. This is quite unusual, Esmirlda did not call since the day of the failed attack on the Santa Marta Police Head Quarters, and this is having a very negative effect on El Capitan. Last evening, he confided in the man closest to him, the plan to relocate the captured American girl. This would be more of a pre-emptive measure; Del Monte had a gut feeling that the American agent on the ground in Santa Marta might be up to something, and it was his intention to outwit Bradley every step of the way.

Esmiralda his main contact within the military was quite reliable and accurate. He had provided very credible intelligence ahead of time on many anti insurgency operations planned by the Government forces. Since they spoke about two weeks ago, his source simply went cold, and El Capitan did not like the feeling. For once, he felt vulnerable and not in control of the situation.

He finished the coffee, draining the last few drops and then striding rather briskly to his command post. Once inside, he summoned two of his top aides. He would discuss these concerns and plans to move the American hostage to another location.

The two men climbed up the heavy wooden planks leading to Del Monte's Command Post. The bunker like structure was heavily fortified. Huge double rows of sand bags reinforced the thick logs which gave the compound a rather daunting and impregnable fortress-like appearance. There is an opening in the sandbagged roof to access the seventy-five meter high guard tower, fitted with an M60 E3 heavy machine gun. A sentry stationed at this emplacement, commands a 360 degree field of vision and can inundate the surrounding area with a deadly barrage of gunfire. An assault on Camp Diaz would be bloody to say the least, and that's exactly what Carlos Del Del Monte wanted it to be. When his epitaph is written the words should be quite symbolic: "The resting place of Carlos Del Monte-El Capitan, fearless and indomitable freedom fighter who defended the Motherland from this mountain bastion with his last drop of blood"

"Good Morning Comrades." Del Monte greeted the two men as he directed them to the large meeting table.

"Thanks chief we are glad to be here," lied the taller of the two as they sat to begin the meeting with their leader. In fact they were trying desperately to contain their well founded fears; prior experiences have taught them that whenever such a meeting is called by the Chief, something bad has happened or is about to happen. Nevertheless, they tried to remain calm and did everything possible to ensure that their demeanor did not give away their true inner feelings.

"Alright men, let me come straight to the point," said Carlos as he stood at the head of the table. We are facing a difficult period of uncertainty; during the last few weeks things did not go well for us. We lost some men in the assault on the Police Headquarters and that's not the worst—Guitirez, and a few other men were captured."

"Yes Chief, that's not good at all; so what's the next move?" asked the guerilla fighter named Ricco.

The Colombian Black Devils commander placed the stub of his cigar and crushed it under the sole of heavy black boots and snuffed out any semblance of a sparking ember.

"Well, I have reason to believe that the American agent who should have been killed in the assault is planning a raid on our camp. It's strange that neither the Government nor the Colombian military has made any attempts to negotiate the release or even talk about a ransom. This could only mean one thing—an assault to free the hostage. I am sure that by now, they have the intelligence of the captured men and some kind of plan is already drafted; we must act swiftly to disrupt their plans."

Both men showed their approval by punching the air with clenched fists; the guerrilla leader acknowledged this and lit another of his Cuban Cigars. The strong pungent smoke quickly wafting through the room, its effects inducing a sneeze from Ricco, the guerrilla sitting closest to the Chief. The man whizzed a muted cough, Del Monte acknowledged his discomfort and moved a bit further away.

"Of course, and that's the main reason for our meeting," said Del Monte as he pushed the unfinished cigar into the bronze colored ashtray."

"At sunset on Friday, that's three days from today we would move the American girl to another location; this would require some really quick work. The area chosen is called Serpants Gorge known for the large snakes and other venomous reptiles prevalent in the surrounding valleys. Ernesto, your assignment is to immediately lead the advance party to repair the old structures. You should focus mainly on the accommodation for the hostage. The quarters for the fighters could always be spruced up once we secure the American. Ricco, your job is to ensure that all supplies and hardware are on hand to make this happen; If you need anything, now is the time to open up your fucking mouth! This is a do or die mission!"

The men heard the firmness in Del Monte's voice and realized that quite a great amount of responsibility rested on their shoulders. They knew that in this mission there is no room for errors or failure. Their commander has absolute confidence in them. It's going to be tough grueling work, but the men had the resources, and most importantly—the resolve and commitment to make it happen.

Del Monte thanked his loyal soldiers and led them out of the room; he watched with a sense of pride as they made their way past the parade square then into the general barracks. The next couple of days would perhaps be the most important in the life of El Capitan and for the very first time, Carlos Del Monte felt extremely uneasy—even unsure of himself and the future.

General Alvario Castenadas wanted to be the first foreign dignitary to visit Mark Reuben, Chairman of the Joint Chiefs of Staff. His early morning flight from Colombia's Simon Bolivar International was uneventful save for the occasional turbulence on board the Boeing 737 jetliner.

Castenadas, landed at New York's JFK International at 12:15 pm and went through the diplomatic protocol. There are certainly some benefits of being a high ranking diplomat—no long lines, preferential treatment at airports and a bullet proof limousine to whisk you away to a five star hotel.

The Colombian Minister of Defense and the Interior had boarded another plane, this time to Ronald Reagan National Airport. The complementary United States Air Force flight had an estimated flying time of just about an hour and forty five minutes. General Castenadas couldn't wait to see his American compatriot and longtime friend.

His trip to the United States underscores the deep bond of friendship between both men. General Castenadas and Mark Reuben have a long history—they've worked on several bilateral projects in the past. It is rumored in both Bogota and Washington that Castenadas and Reuben are the real power brokers in the relationship between the two countries.

So when Reuben became ill, Castenadas felt devastated and distraught—he had to do something tangible to show his respect and admiration for this career diplomat and lifelong friend. The General remembers very well that morning when he got the call from CIA Director General Dumas. Since then, he has made several changes in his life—working less hours, making time for family and ensuring that he gets at least eight hours of rigorous physical exercise.

When Dumas told him that Reuben worked almost a twelve hour day, drank lots of booze and ate fast foods; Castenadas knew that the time for change in his own life had come. His new energy and high level of commitment has been a source of inspiration to fellow officers. Many of them are now using him as their role model. The man is now a fitness fanatic, thanks to Reuben's close brush with death.

The Colombian General always preferred a window seat when he boarded an airplane. On this flight he not only got his wish, but an ideal seat with an excellent view just around the middle of the fuselage. As he peered through the window, the faint outline of the Washington Monument and the DC skyline could be seen in the distance. Castenadas felt the drop in altitude as the 737 began its descent into Ronald Reagan National.

The aircraft shook slightly as a heavy patch of dark cloud streamed across its path; General Castenadas sat back feeling quite calm and relaxed. He is a veteran with decades of flight experience so a little turbulence has no impact on him. In any event, this flight consisted mainly of current and former military personnel, so the General did not expect too much excitement from the passengers.

As the aircraft descended, the General heard the muffled thud of the landing gear; this coincided with the inflight announcement by the flight attendant: "ladies and gentlemen, we are about to land at Ronald Reagan National Airport, in Arlington County, Virginia. In preparation for landing, please ensure that your seat belts are securely fastened; all electronic devices must be turned off at this time. It was truly a pleasure having you on board USAF Flight 189; enjoy your trip to our great city—and we hope to see you again."

From his seat over the wing, the General felt the impact of the aircraft tires scraping the runway; the sturdy Titanium landing gear holding strong under the impact. The wing flaps retracted fully, the jet thundered across the runway then taxied onto the tarmac.

USAF flight 189 landed safely at 2.07 pm on a cool October afternoon. General Castenadas now knew that he would be seeing his good old friend before the day is over and he felt elated.

The TSA officer escorted the General to an area for quick processing and within ten minutes the visiting Colombian Military man was on the road. The drive to the Hyatt Regency Cristal City, on 2799 Jefferson Davis Highway had a very soothing and therapeutic effect on Castenadas. The serene countryside and the magnificent trees certainly contributed to the tranquility of the surroundings. He was really enjoying the scenic and pristine beauty of this place. The General now felt he had to find a way to extend the length of the stay as his armored limousine pulled up into the driveway of the Hyatt Regency.

The driver remained in the limousine and the other security detail got out. He carried an Israeli made Uzi Submachine gun concealed beneath the thick long black coat. The mean CIA looks made even meaner by the pair of really dark shades fitting snugly on his nose. The man quickly scanned the entryway with two rapid movements of eyes before giving the General the all clear to alight from the limo.

A butler, dressed rather smartly in a brilliant red blazer with contrasting black trousers greeted the General, took his wheeled carry-on bag and escorted him to the receptionist desk. Soon, he was enjoying the ambiance of this magnificent hotel—and he couldn't find a better place to be before going to spend some real quality time with Mark Reuben. The General's visit had another dimension as well; he had some other news which would have more than a medicinal effect on the recuperating Chairman of the Joint Chiefs of Staff.

Chapter 23

Bradley made it back from the ridge well before darkness fell. His rendezvous with Captain Alvarez added a new dimension to the pending operation to free Christina Preston. The old seaman once again provided new and vitally important details on the mountainous terrain of the Sierra Nevada. He advised Bradley to bring forward the scheduled date of the mission by three days and gave very scientific reasoning for his assessment.

Alvarez told the American that the tide is usually very high around that time of the month. And since the back up plan includes an amphibious landing by a small commando unit from a US Navy ship positioned off the coast, Bradley felt that the Captain's admonition had merit. High tides usually mean more water turbulence and an increased risk of accident—especially in an operation at night.

Bradley gave the Captain one of the radios he retrieved from the duffel bag he left on the ridge above Santa Marta almost a month ago. He gave Alvarez extra batteries and a camouflage military flashlight as he slung the bag with the remaining gear over his shoulder. They continued the trek down the ridge and the retired Special Forces man continued to explain to Colombian seaman his role in the rescue operation.

"I would definitely go along with your suggestion and move the date; had no idea that the tide would be high on that night. Just didn't think about that—you're such a damn good man to have around."

"Thanks my American friend; I earned those gray hairs," replied Captain Alvarez, gently stroking the curly bearded chin.

"You must remember to purchase the fuel for the torches to mark the landing area for the unit coming from the ship. The lights are to be placed on bamboo poles along the landing zone." Bradley lifted his voice as he spoke.

"Don't worry, just leave that to me my friend, I will take care of everything," Alvarez said assertively as he steadied himself on the rocky gorge. "I would have all my supplies in place at least two days in advance; the machete, rope extra blankets and the thermos filled with hot coffee—you can count on me American."

Alverez and Bradley continued to rehearse the details of the pending mission as they made their way down the path. The American is maintaining a steady pace but not too far ahead of the seasoned Colombian seaman. Bradley reckoned that they should be back down at the port on the outskirts of Santa Marta within another half hour. That's important, since around this time of the year darkness falls over the land rather quickly and Captain Alvarez wants to back at his home base in Taganga Bay at least by 7.30 pm.

As they moved further down the ridge, Bradley stepped on some of the loose rocks strewn over the path. The ex Special Forces man threw out both hands to maintain his balance; he just couldn't afford an injury at this critical stage. With less than a week to go before the operation, Bradley knew he had to maintain maximum fitness.

As Bradley steadied himself he grabbed a nearby sapling and his fingers became snarled by the sharp tentacles on a coarse tree bark. The inch long barb tore deep into his left middle finger causing the American to wince in pain. A squirt of blood formed a tiny beaded droplet on the wound and Bradley quickly held his hand in an upright position to minimize the bleeding. Captain Alvarez offered a helping hand but his travelling companion refused. They travelled for about another two kilometers before the Santa Marta skyline became visible; Bradley saw from the corner of his eye the sprawling Port buildings around the harbor and lengthened his strides; forcing the older man to quicken his pace also

They got down to the harbor area around 5.00 pm; the conditions were rather overcast and murky but Bradley wanted to spend another 10 minutes discussing the details of the back up plan with his trusted Colombian buddy. The old seaman knelt beside the open canvas bag to make one final check; he felt the plastic wrapping on the batteries and the extra blanket. The seven inch hunting knife, flare gun and reflectors were all in place.

Once again Bradley is counting on this man he met in a chance encounter just over two months ago. The many years he spent in covert operations had taught him several lessons—and an important one was knowing when the right man has your back. From the start, Bradley felt very comfortable with Captain Alvarez so he had no second thoughts about the old man's expertise once again.

They shook hands and Bradley pressed twenty crisp US fifty dollar bills into the man's shirt pocket and watched as he made his way back to the water's edge to begin the journey back to Taganga Bay.

Bradley quickly hailed a taxi to take him back to his hotel. Tonight, there's quite a bit to do; he must make contact with the other players and, follow up on arrangements for logistical support.

The armored limousine pulled up in front of the Hyatt Regency on 2799 Jefferson Davis Highway just around 7:30 pm. General Castenadas took a bath earlier and had enjoyed the exquisite cuisine of the hotel. As he hurried out of the room, his knitted gray polyester scarf became trapped in the doorway. The Colombian military man yanked it free in one swift motion, slamming the door in the process. He strode briskly down the carpeted corridor then made his way to the elevator door, securing the scarf carefully this time. General Castenadas hit the G button and the cubicle descended quietly to the ground floor.

He quickly realized that it's the same limo and security detail waiting to pick him up. The man wearing the long trench coat and tinted shades looked even meaner and he made no effort to conceal the sub machine gun carried. The ominous looking weapon hung diagonally from a synthetic strap slung over his powerful shoulders. The Uzi Submachine gun has evolved to be the weapon of choice for several Secret Services units the world over. The improved UZI Micro carried by the CIA security detail, assigned to protect the visiting Colombian has awesome killing capacity—its muzzle capable of spitting out well over five hundred high velocity rounds per minute.

The CIA agent quickly opened the door of the black limousine and ushered the General in. Once seated, the vehicle sped out of the parking lot making its way onto highway 233, then headed further south towards George Washington Memorial Parkway. His security detail deviated from established protocol and engaged the General in some casual conversation as they drove along.

"Enjoying your visit so far? Hope you've got time for some good fun?"

"Sure, but it's a pity my stay is so short—you know what, maybe I'll come again; this time for a real holiday," replied the Colombian General as he rubbed his fingers over the leather upholstery.

"You guys take life too fucking serious man; I know you're here to see the big boss, but hey man—you got to relax amigo. Make some time—go clubbing; get a lap dance or better still, pay a broad a few bucks to suck your dick. I'm pretty darn sure you'll love that."

"General Castenadas took a long deep breath and looked at the agent as he replied." One day my boy you'll realize that when you're in certain positions, high risk behaviors—like having sex with prostitutes or extramarital affairs can really screw up things. Perhaps in my earlier years—but right now, I can't allow nothing to wreck my retirement plans; another three years and I am ready to call it a day."

The agent nodded in partial agreement as he thought about what the General just said. It certainly made a lot of sense. His mind flashed back on a recent scandal in Washington involving a high ranking military man—a five Star General. Just a few weeks before a Senate confirmation hearing to land him a top Government appointment, the news broke of an affair with a younger woman within the Service. Washington is still recovering from the shock and the furor over the incident, and the General withdrew from the race; and his resignation soon followed.

"Can you imagine a newspaper headline: "Visiting Colombian General hospitalized after prostitute chews off a piece of his dick!"

The CIA man almost broke his neck as he heaved out of his seat, barely able to contain his laughter. In the meantime the driver too became distracted, the sudden and sharp maneuver he made attested to this. They continued to travel along the George Washington Parkway for another 20 minutes before the man assigned by the CIA made a left turn into a gated secluded area lined with towering pine and fir trees. It's the middle of a really beautiful Autumn and General Castanedas couldn't help but admire the truly magnificent suburban scenery. Castenadas rolled the window down slightly to feel the cool crisp air as the limo driver reduced his speed.

The Party traveled for about another ten minutes; the road became slightly narrower at this point, and the CIA man informed the General that they are just a short distance away from the residence of the Chairman of the Joint Chiefs of Staff.

The agent sitting next to the General removed a radio from his coat pocket and spoke briefly. "Alpha 109 this is Murdoch 113, do you copy?" The voice at the other end was terse and alert: "Murdoch 113, copy that, what's your current position?"

"Arriving with Eagle in five minutes, please prepare for entry, over and out." The man stationed at the guard house picked up the remote control from the wall holster and pointed it at the large white metal gate demarcating the entrance to Reuben's sprawling mansion.

The driver approached the slight incline leading up to the residence as the two segments of the gate slowly swung open. General Castenadas looked at his watch; the time was 6:35 pm when the limo drove into Mark's Garage.

The mansion had all the markings of royalty and opulence; from expertly manicured shrubs in the surrounding gardens, colorful trees and the exquisite ambiance. One word sums it all up—awesome!

Mark sat in the recliner sipping a hot cup of organically grown herbal tea. Since his near brush with death, he has certainly made some major lifestyle changes. Gone are the cigarettes, the excessive alcohol use and the junk food. His Wife Mary insists that he eats lots of fruit and fresh vegetable. She no longer serves him fried foods—baking and grilling are the preferred methods of cooking these days, and so far the results have been phenomenal. Mark has made tremendous progress since the day he fell ill—he now walks unassisted and his speech is quite normal.

General Castenadas extended both hands to embrace his old buddy. Mark appeared to be a lot trimmer than before and this did not surprise Alvario.

"Hello my good old friend, it's so good to see you—how is your health these days?"

Mark took a good long look at his visiting Colombian counterpart and walked straight towards him as he replied. "Couldn't have been better, my friend—I am making great progress as you can see."

"I am so glad to see you" said the General as he hugged his American friend. Both men moved over to the large circular dining table; Castenadas paused for a short while and asked Mary to show him to the bathroom. The General emerged shortly afterwards still holding a quilted paper towel, Mrs Reuben quickly showed him the stainless steel garbage receptacle neatly tucked in the corner.

Mark had already taken up his position at the head of the table when General Castenadas took the chair closest to him. The chairman of the Joint Chiefs of staff asked Mary to seek God's blessings over the meal they were about to partake in.

"Oh God and eternal Father, we thank you for life and all your goodness. Lord, we pray your bountiful blessings for the meal we are about to share; we ask Lord that you continue to provide and nourish us through your divine provisions. Bless and keep our families Lord, and may we continue to dwell in your perfect peace and harmony. We thank you Lord."

Castenadas, a devout Catholic crossed himself and picked up the white folded serviette with the colorful embroidery trim. The table was quite impressive and Mark started off with a light non alcoholic grape wine. "Cheers to a great friend, a wonderful wife and to life and health," intoned Reuben as they all lifted their glasses in unison.

Mary helped the men with lavish servings of grilled baby carrots and fresh green beans; General Castenadas decided to help himself by picking up the stainless steel thong and slapped two large portions of the baked salmon over the servings of vegetables. The peach, onion and garlic sauces were already causing him to salivate incessantly. The food tasted so good, and the visitor showed no restraint. General Castenadas covered well over eight hours travelling from Bogata to Ronald Reagan National in Virginia. He had every reason to be tired—and hungry.

Reuben chipped in occasionally but generally the tone of the conversation centered mainly on family matters and Mark's remarkable recovery.

"At one point we thought we were going to lose him—but I always knew that the old stubborn ram would pull through," said Mary as she smiled at her husband.

"It's in times like these you realize how frail and vulnerable we are; you certainly learn to appreciate the little things in life—and most importantly you learn to see the value of good friends and a strong family," replied Mark as he filled another glass of the dark red brew.

"My friend, you could not have said it better; when I heard what happened to you, I started to make some real changes in my life as well," remarked General Castenadas.

After the meal, the two men went over to the living room; Mark changed the channel on the forty two inch flat screen TV to watch the Military show and shortly after, the Colombian General started to update the Chairman on events back home.

"Our Military and Special Forces are working with your man on the ground in Santa Marta—John Bradley."

"I understand the Police and Army have been making steady progress lately. Before I left, a usually reliable source indicated that a strike on a guerrilla base deep in the rugged interior was imminent."

Castanedas leaned back in the leather upholstered chair and took a sip of the cinnamon flavored herbal tea Mary had on the coffee table. He took a good look at Mark, and experienced a great feeling of satisfaction and inner peace. Here is a man—powerful and famous, who just only a few short weeks ago was fighting for his life, and now looking very healthy and robust again. General Castenadas placed the cup on the table as he spoke.

"Our guys are working around the clock, and yes I understand that your man Bradley is in charge of the operation. The Colombian military has placed at his disposal whatever assets he may need to mount a successful rescue."

Mark crossed his legs and filled the tall glass with water from the pitcher, placed besides the China teapot as he spoke.

"I know her father, Mike Preston very well—we were actually college buddies, so I really hope that the operation is successful."

"Don't worry mate, we are going to beat those bastards into submission, and your friend would soon have his beloved daughter back home."

General Castenadas sounded rather confident but as a military man with a career spanning well over thirty years, he knew that there is always a possibility that something could go dreadfully wrong. While Mark did not express similar sentiments, he too had some feelings of apprehension.

"Let's not try to be everywhere; the guys are capable of doing a good job—I don't think we need to worry," replied Reuben confidently.

"I agree with you Mark," said the General as he glanced at the clock positioned above the living room entrance.

It's been almost two hours since he arrived at the residence of the Chairman of the Joint Chiefs of Staff, and Castenadas wanted to talk more about Mark's amazing recovery and the complete revamping of his lifestyle.

"Mark, every time I think about your new approach to life and health I am quite thrilled. Tell me how you did it my friend?"

Reuben stood up almost immediately as if to reinforce the General's encouraging sentiments. "If I knew the answer, perhaps I would not be here," Mark replied assertively.

"My friend, you've got to take life one day at a time—as you grow older, you learn not to wrestle and fight with life. Rather, you sway with the punches and adopt a positive outlook on life. By accepting the things you cannot change, and letting go of anger and resentment, you simply help to ignite all the positive life force energies all around you. During my stay at the hospital, not for a moment did I harbor any feelings of self pity—I just kept on repeating positive and uplifting words; everyone was so amazed at my remarkable progress."

General Castenadas looked at his friend, took a few steps towards him before he replied.

"I always knew you were special Mark, and I am so privileged to have you as a friend and colleague—that's the reason why I travelled all the way from Bogota to Washington. I just had to let you know how much your friendship means to me."

General Castenadas walked over to where Mark stood and the two men hugged each other. Mary looked on keenly while retrieving the mug and saucer from the exquisitely carved mahogany coffee table. Both men had totally ignored the World War 2 action movie on the large screen perched high above the living room table. There were so many things to talk about, but the General knew that the time is limited.

There is a war being waged this very moment, and even as he enjoyed the opulence of the Virginia neighborhood, many lives are lost on the battlefields of his beloved homeland, Colombia.

It was a beautiful and memorable evening, and Defense Minister knew that the time had come for him to head back to his hotel. In another seven hours he'll be on the way back to Colombia. The growing insurgency, rumors, and festering allegations of collusion between corrupt officials and rebel leaders are high on his agenda.

The General dialed the number of his CIA security detail and sipped a cold glass of orange juice as he waited on the limousine to arrive.

Chapter 24

Christina found it difficult to sleep. The last time she felt like this, something dreadful happened. That's when the transfer from one camp to another took place. It's been close to four months since her captivity in this dense jungle. She had employed every tactic possible to stay alive and in shape; this meant personal sacrifice and sometimes unbearable pain, but she had endured. From the cold chilly nights and other nocturnal vermin, to the uncertainty of knowing that her life is in the hands of a bunch of ruthless desperados!

She just had this uncanny feeling that something's about to happen. Christina looked at the her watch, the time was 12:19 am. Immediately, she jumped out of bed and crawled on the creaky wooden floor until she got to a position close to the door. Christina could not believe her eyes—the night sentry was fast asleep on the tree trunk which served as the main barrier to the entrance to her log cabin. He was in a deep sleep and snoring like a wild boar.

Christina wasted no time. Sprinting back to her old log and timber framed bed, she quickly grabbed all her belongings and stuffed them into the soiled canvas bag. Her stained sneakers seemed a bit tight as she finished the worn and battered laces. Oh! Just a few more items—the hunting knife she had stolen and kept beneath the cloth mattress; two bottles of spring water and a few cans of poached salmon.

Peering through the small opening in the cabin, Christina could still see the sleeping guard. She slipped the hunting knife from the case; gripped the handle firmly and gently pried the piece of coarse wire loose. A slight push and Christina Preston got a whiff of the cool air and the possibility of freedom. Carefully, she wrapped the wire around the wooden door to ensure that it appeared to be closed. With the canvas bag slung diagonally over her shoulder; and the hunting knife strapped around waist, Christina sprinted away from the cabin and melted into the thick dense black forest.

Fear never crossed her mind. This tough American girl made a decision rather quickly. Remain a captive in the hands of an unpredictable guerrilla army, or make a desperate run through the jungles of the Sierra Nevada and hope to be rescued. Christina felt deep down inside, that her dad would spend his last dollar on some kind of rescue operation. She obviously could not be sure of the exact date and timing, but she just knew that her dad will not abandon her.

Christina continued moving swiftly through the dark, sometimes slamming into decaying tree trunks and other obstacles. For now, she just wanted to be as far away from the guerrilla base camp as possible. The terrain got a bit more rugged as Christina made it up a pretty steep gorge; she slipped as her right foot made contact with the top of a moss covered stone. Christina quickly regained her balance and kept a steady pace as she made her way up the rugged incline.

The American had no problems with fitness. While in captivity she found simple and effective ways of keeping fit. From vigorous knuckle pushups and fast repetition squats to skipping with a crude rope fashioned from old jute bags. Alfredo, her

Colombian guerrilla buddy had conveniently left one of his camouflage jackets and a small flashlight in her cabin a few days earlier. As she made her way further up the ridge, Christina remembered the insurgent fighter who had gone out of his way to make her comfortable.

The predawn rain came down suddenly and Christina reached into the backpack for the thick jacket. She hastily threw off the bag and fitted the oversized hooded military apparel. The sleeves were a bit out of size, but at this point it did matter. As the heavy tropical down pour pierced through the jungle foliage, a strong gusty wind blasted the high canopy, sending severed branches and shards of tree bark all over the area like missiles.

Christina had to find shelter from the torrential rain. She summoned all her energies to finish the climb up the ridge. Her jeans were soaking wet but the army jacket had an inner lining so her torso and arms remained dry. Christina knew that she had to find some shelter soon; another minute in this early morning downpour and with the rapidly dropping temperature, hyperthermia is a distinct possibility.

At the top of the ridge, Christina found a narrow path; it certainly had all the makings of frequent use. Evidence of recent traffic— plastic water bottles and other pieces of camping paraphernalia. The rain started to subside as she advanced further up the pathway. Keeping a shivering right hand on the flashlight, Christina stumbled on what appeared to be the entrance of a cave.

Before travelling to Colombia, she spent some time learning about the flora and fauna of the country. The presence of large venomous snakes and other deadly predators she remembered all too well—but right now this is the least of her worries. By now, Christina had made up her mind; she just wanted to get inside. Whatever lurked in the darkness on the inside, she'll deal with afterwards; the urge to find a warm spot and get some rest overrode any phobia at this point.

Using the sharp serrated blade of the hunting knife, Christina slashed the thick bush carpeting what appeared to be an entrance to the huge rocky canyon. One final push, and the American made it inside disturbing a nest of wild bats in the process.

Chapter 25

Miguel rolled and twisted as he stretched and rubbed his eyes. He had a good long sleep and the cool morning rain increased his inner urge to take another snooze. The man guarding Christina's cabin stood up, rubbed his eyes again, turned around and walked towards the cabin door. The old rusty chain appeared just as he had left it eight hours ago; Miguel prodded the top of the door with the bayonet of his M16 assault rifle and entered the room. He glanced at his watch; in the semi darkness he read from the black plastic rimmed digital screen: 2:58 am.

He took the flashlight from the loop attached to the left pocket of his jacket, pressed the on button and as the rays of light illuminated the cabin, Miguel froze—his jaw dropped as he stared in utter shock and disbelief at the empty bed. "No! No!" Shouted the guard. He inched closer to the bed; keeping both hands on the rifle as a precautionary measure. Miguel felt his chest tighten, he was sweating profusely—and seemed unable to support the weapon suspended from the shoulder strap. "Dios mío, la chica Americana se ha ido," said Miguel as he got closer to the bed.

Miguel knew he was in big trouble. How on earth is he going to explain her escape to Del Monte? This is only his third stint on the late shift assigned to guard the American. No amount of excuses could save him from justice—Del Monte Style. Of course he would be accused of collusion with the prisoner and ultimately assisting her to escape. The Colombian insurgent knew he had to act quickly; daylight was only a few hours away, so time is not on his side. Miguel turned around, switched off the flashlight and headed for the door.

In the pale morning light, he sprinted across the open field trying desperately not to attract the attention of the man in the guard tower. He knew that his comrade on duty is up and alert—the piercing beams of light coming from the powerful revolving search lights clearly reminded him of this. Miguel made it into the heavily wooded perimeter and quickly disappeared into the blackness of the undergrowth. Getting as far away as possible from the camp is crucial. The morning shift for the changing of the guards would begin in about an hour. The man continued to plow his way deeper and deeper into the jungle. He knew the terrain quite well and despite the poor visibility, still managed to keep a steady pace.

The fleeing insurgent observed that the vegetation became a bit sparse when he got to the brow of the hill and he used the opportunity to break into a sprint. It became much easier for him to maneuver through the light brush since the obstructions were much less. Miguel kept on going at a steady pace, all the while thinking about what would be his fate if caught. Over the years, Miguel had witnessed summary executions for mere suspicion of committing a crime—in his case, since he would have a great difficulty explaining why the female captive escaped while he kept guard. For sure, Del Monte would want to lead the firing squad to send him off to eternity. The renegade insurgent kicked on a fallen log as he advanced further. Despite the fatigue, he pushed on as hard as he could. The light appeared to be slightly better now and Miguel knew that's another reason why he had to press on. The animals of the wild were announcing the dawn of a new day. Indeed for Miguel it's the beginning of a new life; his plan is to find his way to the nearest Colombian Army outpost and turn himself in. The Government had an amnesty program, and he is quite sure that some consideration would be given to his case.

The gray pale pre dawn light got brighter as Miguel stumbled, exhaustion is really sapping his energy now. He fought the inner urges to stop for a break. The thought of Del Monte taunting him before they execute him in the parade square, gave Miguel an extra boost. There will be a lot of time to rest; the fleeing guerrilla fighter knew that El Capitan would have dispatched multiple search parties already; their orders—shoot the traitor on sight!

Miguel later found a rocky outcropping near a deep gully; the spot seemed perfect for a break, and once again the fleeing man resisted the temptation.

The man rushed into the hall were Del Monte and the group of guerrillas were meeting to discuss the plan to move Christina to another Jungle hideout. Normally, a meeting of this nature would never be interpreted unless a really grave and urgent situation had developed.

"Commandante! Commandante! The girl is gone and there is no sign of Miguel."

Del Monte grabbed his weapon and quickly led the men out of the room; they raced across the yard to the cabin where the American prisoner was kept for the last six weeks. Del Monte got inside first; he took a deep breath then trained the muzzle of the Uzi submachine gun on the empty bed and fired until the magazine had no more rounds.

"Fucking bitch! I will carve your pussy with my knife, then feed it to the alligators." The leader of the Colombian Black Devils became so enraged, even the other men in the cabin were fearful.

"That fucking traitor Miguel helped her to escape! I will cut off his balls, force it down his throat and watch him bleed to death. This will be a good lesson for anyone else with plans to double cross me. Alright men, lets get moving; I need four search parties; Ramon, Diaz and Alberto get moving. I'll take charge of the other party."

The stern command of Del Monte resonated right through the cabin, and as the men left the room an eerie silence descended on the area. As the early morning light slowly crept over the compound; men were heading in different directions, moving between buildings. Weapons were hastily checked and the respective teams soon fanned out into the nearby forest.

Del Monte's squad took a more southeasterly route—the area of the Sierra Nevada known for its towering peaks and extremely dense and rugged terrain. The leader of guerrilla group had a gut feeling that the renegade Miguel may have taken a more difficult and challenging route.

"Go! Go!" Shouted Carlos as he pushed the men up the slope. They had covered a significant amount of territory already and at that pace, Del Monte felt that his squad should be hot on the trail of either Miguel or Christina within the next two or three hours.

The last couple of weeks have not gone very well for the man leading the Colombian Black Devils. First, the debacle at the Santa Marta Police Compound and the subsequent capture of his right hand man, Alberto Gutieriez. And to complicate matters, his main source of intelligence within the military establishment, a high ranking officer code named Esmirlda simply vanished without a trace. The only piece of information he gathered, spoke of the presence of an American agent on the ground in Santa Marta and speculations of some type of operation to free the girl.

As a preemptive measure, Del Monte had taken a decision to transfer Christina to a new location. This action, scheduled for Thursday of this week has no relevance now—there is no longer a prisoner locked up in a jungle cabin. Christina had escaped under extremely mysterious circumstances; and now his world and everything around him seem to be falling apart. He had to find Miguel quickly, put him through a rigorous interrogation to find out what exactly happened while he kept guard duty last night.

Del Monte's squad pushed deeper and deeper up the mountain path; a plateau was spotted some distance away and the group wanted to get to that point quickly. The tall man leading the trail took a long machete from the leather sheath he carried and cleared the path of the encroaching thorny jungle vines. He handled the sharp tool rather efficiently, and in short order the pathway became clear and fully accessible.

They made it to the top and Del Monte ordered the men to take a ten minute break. They were travelling for well over three and a half hours and Carlos knew that they deserved rest. By now the sunlight had spread its warm rays all over the mountain side. A slight drizzle sprinkled the forest foliage as the gentle morning breeze wafted across the plateau.

The short recess was over, and they were on their way again. A few minutes into the trek across the marshland the man who had been wielding the machete stepped on a cluster of tin cans and plastic bottles. "El Capitan, look over here!" He shouted while pointing to the pile of debris.

"These fucking hikers have to respect for the environment," remarked Del Monte in an angry tone.

"Yes, that's so true; they come from all over just to pollute our beautiful country," replied Antonio as he pierced one of the cans with the sharp tip of the machete. He took a closer look at the tin and noticed that the label is very much intact, and although the print bore some signs of water damage, this did not render it illegible; he read the words printed on the label: "Poached Salmon in chili tomato sauce." The unfinished content of the tin appeared quite fresh. This can of Salmon was opened recently; the million dollar question—by whom?

Antonio paused for a while to allow his commander to take a good look at the item he had stumbled upon. Del Monte picked up the discarded salmon can and placed it close to his nose. "I think we are onto something here guys, keep following the trail. Come on guys, let's go! Let's go!"

Bradley stayed up for most of the night; his thoughts were on Mike Preston's daughter and the plan to free her from captivity, deep in the heart of the Sierra Nevada. John had good reason to be up this late anyway, and Mike was thrilled to hear about the details given by the Special Forces man. Preston couldn't believe the extreme measures Bradley had taken to ensure the success of the mission. After speaking with Bradley, Preston really understood why only the very best troops go on to be Navy Seals or United States Special Forces. The Texas Billionaire could barely contain his emotion as he counted down the hours for the start of Operation Jungle Rescue.

The American had a feeling of nostalgia as he packed his bags to move out of the Estelar Santamar Hotel. This was his home for the last four weeks or so and now that the time had come for him to leave, his feelings were punctuated with mixed emotions. Bradley had become so accustomed to the wonderful ambience and all the other comforts of Santamar. He knew that the opulence was temporary though as his main purpose on the Colombian mainland was not yet accomplished. John looked at the bedside clock; the time indicated—4:03 am. He sat on the edge of the bed before touching the switch on the coffee maker.

Steam spewed out of the top as the water came to a boil. Bradley dropped a sachet of Colombian coffee into the jar and allowed it to brew. He did a few stretches before going to the bathroom. He was just about to enter the shower door when his mobile phone rang. Bradley turned quickly and picked up the mobile handset.

The voice at the other end of the line had authoritative flare. "The men are on their way; they left from a secret location about forty-five minutes ago and should be picking you up around 5:00 a.m."

"Are we going to the prearranged rendezvous point to pick up all the weapons and other supplies?"

"Nothing has changed; the team is prepared and ready to go at midnight, and we are coming to pick you up as planned just for one final rehearsal before the assault"

"OK, let me take a shower; my stuff is already packed. I should be completing my check out in about a half hour, I'll be in the lobby downstairs."

Bradley rushed into the bathroom; he slammed his right shoulder against the stainless steel door frame as he entered. He is never late for any kind of engagement so this would be a rather quick one. John grabbed the towel from the shiny metal ring attached to the ceramic tiled wall and dried his skin vigorously. The American Special Forces man came out of the shower in a hurry. He picked up his favorite dark olive green denim suit; the trousers fitted quite snugly and for a moment he paused to admire himself by looking in the full length mirror on the bedroom wall.

Fully clothed, John made one final look around the room—now is not the time to make errors; he just could not forget anything at this point. His backpack looked quite stuffed; he made a sweeping glance at the countertop. All his personal effects seem to be accounted for and John Bradley picked up his bag and headed towards the door.

On the ground floor, hotel guests were already queuing up in front of the checkout counter. The elderly couple just ahead of Bradley appeared to be having some difficulty with their paperwork. John moved closer to the attendant's desk and hoped that whatever prevented the two seniors from being processed quickly would be resolved soon.

He gave a sigh of relief when for some strange reason the receptionist waved them through. Bradley stepped up to the desk and presented his credit card to the beautiful brunette.

"You're checking out rather early, Mr. Bradley," she said in fluent English while swiping his Master Card.

Bradley did not give any indication of surprise; he had encountered many of the Hotel Santamar staff who spoke excellent English.

"No, not really; got some other pressing matters to deal with. I'll be back soon my dear; the service here is fantastic."

"Thank you sir; you're welcome anytime," replied Bella with a radiant smile.

Bradley flung the backpack over his shoulder and headed straight for the door. The clock on the wall showed the time as 5: 05 am and the jeep provided by the Colombian Military was already in the parking lot. The American tossed in the back pack and quickly got in the back seat before the driver sped out of the hotel compound.

There were three other occupants including the driver; Bradley immediately recognized two of them from a previous encounter. At such an early hour, Bradley did not expect this high volume of traffic; he had gotten used to this anyway and experience had taught him that his Colombian hosts always had an alternative route. The man at the wheel maneuvered the vehicle with effortless ease as he stepped on the gas on approaching the slight incline. They soon entered a densely forested area; John couldn't recognize any distinguishing or outstanding features, and quietly concluded that the location is totally unfamiliar. The man at the wheel steered the jeep slightly to the left of the nondescript building located in the middle of the compound. As the party alighted, a heavyset man with a black curly mustache walked through the door. Bradley recognized him instantly while advancing towards the entrance—He had not seen Commander Nunez since that fateful day.

"How is my good American Buddy doing?" asked the Colombian Police Chief.

"Man, it's good to see you again; what have you been up to? Seems like you've been working out or doing some really rigorous training—damn, you look so good man!"

"Since the firefight at the Santa Marta Compound, I started to take my fitness a bit more seriously. The guys literally have to chase me out of the gym. Gone are the cigars, heavy drinking and the unhealthy diet."

The American paused momentarily to embrace the Police Chief; he just couldn't believe the transformation! The three other commandos walked pass and placed their gear in the far right hand corner of the building. Nunez and Bradley walked in moments later; three other Colombian Special Forces Commandos joined the party.

Nunez did a brief introduction and stressed the importance of the imminent assault on El Capitan's redoubt deep in Sierra Nevada, before handing over the team to the American Navy Seal.

"Gentlemen, in less than nine hours we begin what is perhaps for me the most important mission I have undertaken within the last ten years. This one is unique for several reasons; firstly an American citizen is at the center of the operation, and I gave her dad a commitment to take her back safely to the United States. Secondly, as a former Navy Seal, this is my first mission since retirement. I've got quite a lot to prove guys."

Bradley continued to brief the team on the rescue plans. He pointed to the heavily guarded guerrilla compound in the reconnaissance photo, keeping the stick on the log cabin located just to the left of center. He told the group of elite commandos that the primary objective of the mission is to snatch the American from the insurgents and take her back to the base camp.

The Special Forces man told the men that a lightening fast incursion is the optimum goal—in and out in a flash. But reminded them that if it does not work out as planned they've got to be prepared for a scorching firefight with the insurgents. Bradley pointed to the heavy machine gun emplacements and the other fortifications and explained the assault strategy in more detail.

Two commandos were responsible for placing the C-4 plastic explosives charges at the base of the perimeter guard towers. Another two man team had the responsibility for clearing booby traps, and the Claymour mines the insurgents had scattered around the southern corridor of the compound. This piece of intelligence extracted from Del Monte's right hand man— Gutierez who was snarled during the Santa Marta assault, proved to be invaluable.

Before wrapping up the briefing, Bradley reminded the men that a backup party would be supported by an Apache helicopter gunship and a Black Hawk UH-60 Sikorsky. These assets are to be deployed from the USS Antartica—a Virginia based naval vessel positioned in international waters off Santa Marta's Caribbean coast. The presence of the US ship in Colombian waters was no secret. According to a joint Communiqué released by the US and Colombian Navy, the exercises are planned to test the counter narcotics and drug interdiction capabilities of both countries. John noted the confident smiles on the faces of the men when he listed the supporting military assets.

Of particular significance to the team is the Apache helicopter gunship; one of the special forces Commandos described it as an aerial firestorm—an awesome and ruthlessly efficient killing machine. With that kind of firepower, John felt quite confident that the mission to rescue Christina had a good chance of success.

Nunez and Bradley walked briskly to the area where the other men sat. They had already opened up the folding table for breakfast. The piping hot oatmeal porridge laced with cinnamon powder and fragrant herbs immediately caught the attention of the retired Navy Seal.

"Nunez, I can't speak for you, but I am hungry." The American grabbed one of the large ceramic bowls and poured the hot porridge right up to the brim. Nunez looked at his friend and smiled sarcastically as he pointed to the small wooden tray holding the spoons and other cutlery.

"Thanks mate" said Bradley as he sat down. Not eating my friend?" Asked the former Special Forces man.

"I'll go with just bananas and the watermelons," replied the Police Chief as he eased his way onto the bench. Don't want to hear you and the guys making fun of me again."

"Yeah, but you don't have to be a fucking extremist, come on man—eat some shit!"

"Alright! Alright! Nunez reached over to the pot containing the spicy oatmeal and filled a bowl; then followed up with a large serving of baked beans and a huge chunk of the course flat bread.

John smiled approvingly. "That's my man; the next few hours we'll have very little time to eat, so let's fill up."

The remote abandoned Colombian Army base now serving as the staging point for the operation to free Christina Preston is now buzzing with activity. Heavily armed troops patrolled the perimeter; four 50 caliber machine guns and an anti aircraft battery positioned strategically on the concrete roof complimented the security of the compound. After the fiasco in Santa Marta, Bradley was leaving nothing to chance.

He suggested that the team check all their weapons and equipment before the scheduled three hour rest. In just a few short hours they'll be heading to the designated area located near the foothills of the Sierra Nevada to begin the ascent and the launch of operation Jungle Rescue.

Chapter 26

Christina paused and took a deep breath; she was travelling for the last four hours and really needed a break. Stopping now would perhaps narrow the gap between the fleeing American and the guerrillas, who by now were in hot pursuit. The months of captivity had really toughened up Preston's daughter, the decision to press on with minimal effort, and was symbolic of her tough indomitable fighting spirit.

She slashed at the loose decaying vegetation and entered through the small opening in the rocky cavity. The interior had a dark creepy look. Christina inched her way gingerly using the flashlight to avoid protruding objects. Less than a hundred meters inside, she struck her right foot on a hard partially immersed metal case. Wow! She screamed as the pain shot through her entire leg; Christina buckled and winced in pain and anguish.

Regaining her composure, the escaped prisoner reached for the knife, dropped down to her knees and started to scrape off the mangled undergrowth, revealing the top of a rectangular metal case. She continued to chip away at the debris until the entire lid became clear. This fearless girl had no intentions of stopping—she had to find a way to open up that container! Certainly it contained something, and Christina is going to find out one way or the other.

Christina removed enough of the slit and murk from the top of the rectangular box, to reveal a portion of a u-shaped piece of metal which securely fastened the lid to the sturdy box. A closer look confirmed her worst fears—the content of this mysterious box is fastened and secured by two heavy duty padlocks. Christina had to think quickly once again; she is absolutely certain that Del Monte and his men are already on her trail. Any unnecessary delay would certainly be to her disadvantage. Defiant, persistent and strong, the American girl soldiered on.

Fortune favors the brave, thought Christina as she sat on the edge of the metal box and pondered her next move. She did not have to wait for a long period; a short distance from where Christina sat, stood a cluster of stones. She placed the knife on the top of the box and headed towards the pile; she selected two of them and rushed back to find her mystery case. Christina summoned all her strength as she jammed the piece of wood into the base of the box. She managed to create a space large enough for one of the stones to fit. Christina then took a short plank from the surrounding shrubbery and pushed it deep beneath the box.

Taking a firm grip of the plank; Christina lifted with all her might until the box was flipped over—the bottom now became the front. She got a perfect view of the lock and fastening mechanism. The American exchange student straddled her legs over the container, picked up one of the stones and fitted it under the first padlock. With the other stone, Christina began to hammer down on the corroding metal. Bang! Bang! Whack! Whack! Christina delivered another powerful blow and the first lock snapped open.

She had to hurry now. Moving with great haste, Christina placed the other stone under the fettered padlock and started hammering again. This one appeared to be a bit tougher; but she persevered and continued to bang on the lock with her crude stone hammer. Christina paused, then lifted the stone with both hands; boom! Bang! Boom! "Yes! Yes! I did it!" Christina exclaimed as she let the hard rock slip from her tired fingers and roll to the side of the box. She could not contain her emotion— another challenge conquered; now it's time to flip open the cover. Christina tipped the heavy case over again before planning her next move.

The American exchange student, although tired from the heavy hammering picked up the hunting knife and pushed it under the edge of the lid. A tearing squeaky sound came from the old metal hinges; and Christina continued to push until the cover popped open. She ran her fingers along the molten green fabric lining the top and felt the hard metal objects beneath.

Christina couldn't believe her good fortune; oh my God! She screamed in excitement. She probed deeper with the tip of her hunting knife, exposing more of the fabric in the process. The new found assets certainly empowered Christina; she just couldn't find words to describe the emotions. This is not the time to drop her guard though. Aware that the insurgents were on her trail, she decided to select some of the items from the metal case and made a hasty retreat down the hill.

The newly found weapons and other military supplies weighed her down, but they are vitally important for her survival. Christina now looked like a seasoned guerilla fighter—ammo belt complete with extra pouches and magazines for the AKS 74 assault rifle. The arms and other military supplies she stumbled upon only moments ago, may be one of many caches hastily abandoned by retreating rebels during anti insurgency operations by Government troops. Christina flipped the folding stock of the weapon, strung it over her shoulder and continued her trek deep into the dense forest. Misty rays of sunlight seeped through the foliage as the American pushed forward;

aware that every stride she took brings her one step closer to total freedom.

At first, Christina thought her ears were playing tricks on her. She paused and listened again. Months of captivity had given her a rather keen sense of hearing—she knew virtually all the sounds of nature. That's why human voices in the bush are so easily picked up by her. Based on the wind direction and the area the sound came from, Christina estimated that a search party could be less than two kilometers away. She thought about taking a quick break but decided against it and continued up the trail. Christina had come to far to give up now. She was now an armed fighter in the bush so those who are pursuing her had better be aware—this exchange student had a taste of freedom and would fight tooth and nail to maintain it. She is prepared to die In the defense of her freedom if necessary.

Carlos radioed the other group to find out their position as he urged his party on; they had nothing significant to share. The guerrilla leader eagerly reported the findings of his group to the other search teams before directing the party further up the mountain. Along the way, fresh evidence of recent traffic at several points—newly cut vegetation, and in one instance some broken branches.

"Alright guys, let's keep on pushing I am sure you could do with some good American pussy, just keep that at the back of your mind. That's the special prize for the team which captures the fucking broad!" The words of the chief seem to energize the crew; the men literally started to sprint up the hill. The man with the machete picked up a discarded tissue ensnarled in a jungle thicket. He plucked it up and got a distinctive feminine scent. In great jubilation and excitement he shouted while making some wild gestures.

"We are definitely onto something here, I think we've got her cornered, let's go!"

Del Monte ran past two of the men to get closer to the man leading the group, he too felt that they were closing in on the American. "I think she's somewhere to the left of the ridge. Let's go! Let's go!" Riaz shouted at the top of his voice.

They got to the top of the mountain and headed straight through the shoulder high grass; someone had disturbed the tall grass not too long ago and the insurgents grew in confidence as they advanced—closing in on the target. At least so they thought.

Christina positioned herself behind two large rocks; from the vantage point just to the right of the advancing party she had a good view of them. They had no idea of what she had in store for them; this jungle hardened girl had laid a very simple but effective trap for the approaching insurgents. She kept the binoculars retrieved from the abandoned cache trained on the tall figure in front. Before securing her position behind the boulders, Christina deliberately disturbed a patch of grass in the direction to the far left of her location. Again, she is showing her natural survival instincts with great tenacity, cunning and guile. One day perhaps Christina may consider documenting her entire experience.

Concealed among the bush and tall grass were three hand grenades. The American became an expert at improvising. Earlier, she firmly secured the devices to the roots of surrounding trees by using the clear plastic string collected from the metal case. The grenades securely tied, Christina attached a piece of the string to the pin of each one and weaved the remainder through a protruding branch of a nearby tree. At the end of the string was a plastic water bottle, partially filled.

The bottle would be the trigger, and to ensure that the line gets the maximum thug to dislodge the pins from the grenades, Christina made a tight knot just under the rim of the bottle cap. As a back up she knotted some of the clear plastic string around a small piece of hardwood. Christina then inserted a full magazine, flipped the folding stock of the AKS-74, took up a comfortable firing position and waited.

This nasty assault rifle packs quite a punch; an improved version of the ubiquitous AK 47 assault rifle; the AKS 74 became extremely popular during the Soviet campaign in Afghanistan and was the preferred weapon for paratroopers and other airborne units, battling the much vaunted Mujahedin Resistance fighters.

The American read extensively on these matters and knew exactly how to handle the rifle. As the insurgents got closer to her booby trap, Christina leveled the weapon and waited. The guerrilla to the front saw the plastic bottle dangling from the tree and raced towards it. He beckoned to the other men—urging them to move in quickly.

As they closed in, the tall insurgent reached up for the plastic bottle strewn carelessly into the tree by another hiker and cursed loudly. He jerked the string vigorously and within seconds a deafening blast shattered the midday silence. The three exploding grenades had a murderous and deadly impact—especially on the two men right up at the front. Shrapnel flew in multiple directions as the stunned guerrillas tried to take cover. Christina had no intentions of showing mercy.

"This is my war and I write the fucking rules!" Christina shouted as she leveled the weapon and unleashed an unrelenting barrage of rifle fire on Del Monte's men.

The first burst ripped into the buttocks of a retreating insurgent knocking him down instantly. She quickly changed the firing sequence of the AKS 74 from semi automatic to single shot and pumped several more rounds in the field. Christina reverted to full automatic again, slammed in a new magazine and rained down more gunfire on her former captors. The guerrillas were in disarray and started a hasty retreat. Christina felt so empowered now. Only a few days ago her life was in the hands of the rebel fighters. Now she is a fearless fighter, prepared to kill anyone who threatens her freedom. This American hero has already decided to dedicate her victory to all the battered and abused women around the world.

Christina now stood up from behind the rocks which shielded her from the gunfire; she stretched her legs for a while, took a quick drink from the bottle in her backpack. The firefight lasted for just about thirty-five minutes, but it seemed like an eternity. This American had tasted freedom and had no intentions of giving it up. She checked the remaining magazines for the weapons, and although the ammunition pouches and military hardware slowed her down, never for a moment did Christina think about ditching any part of her arsenal.

Her weapons are now an integral part of this new life in the bush; she had just beaten back a band of seasoned guerrilla fighters and taken responsibility for her life. What made this possible—her tough Texan upbringing, loads of courage—and yes, the guns and ammunition she stumbled upon! Christina dusted herself off, sipped from the water bottle and took some time to savor the sweet victory.

In the mayhem, Del Monte tried to rally on his men; this proved quite difficult. The American was just laying down a carpet of sustained fire on them. Two of his men were dead, and the shell shocked and injured remnants didn't seem to have the stomach for this fight. Carlos dropped to one knee and trained a burst of fire from his .223 Bush Master in the direction from which the bullets were raining down on his troops. He was absolutely certain that they were being pinned down by the American Special Forces man who led the counter assault, and successfully repelled his earlier attack on the Santa Marta Police Head Quarters. The leader of the Colombian Black Devils did not realize that this firefight is all the work of a brave young American girl—his former hostage.

Fearing more losses among the search party, Del Monte ordered the remaining fighters to begin a full retreat. The loss of three of his men already had a devastating effect his troops; some had also suffered severe burns and other shrapnel wounds—a tactical withdrawal made perfect sense in the circumstances. Carlos spoke into the radio as he attempted to make contact with the other search parties.

"Abort mission and return to base, Alfa Eagle this is the Black Scorpion; do you copy?

"Black Scorpion, this is Cobra 87-Roger, copy that. What's your position?"

"On high ground some 58 degrees west longitude and 14 degrees north latitude," replied Carlos as he glanced at the GPS monitor strapped on his left upper arm.

"Roger that, we are on the way down travelling at a brisk and steady pace; should be making the rendezvous point at about fourteen hundred hours."

Del Monte rounded up the remaining men and they started the journey back to the base. As they pushed through the almost shoulder high reeds and grassy foliage, the guerrilla leader struggled to suppress the feelings of fear and depression which suddenly descended upon him. His world just seems to be falling apart—nothing is going his way these days.

His prize hostage escaped with the help of one of the guards assigned to her cabin—at least that's what he thought. The loss of the American meant that he no longer had a bargaining chip and is now extremely vulnerable to attack from Government troops. Carlos knew that as long as he had a hostage there would never be a massive bombardment of his camp. Any attempt at rescuing her while in captivity would then require a precise surgical strike. Now, he no longer has this human insurance policy—Christina is somewhere out there in this massive wilderness.

Carlos Del Monte bit his lips in an attempt to conceal his true feelings; the men must not have a clue of what's happening to him on the inside. After all, he still commanded a high level of respect and admiration among his loyal supporters. The image and persona of him being a strong and invincible leader must be preserved at all cost. These thoughts were uppermost in the mind of the guerrilla leader as they trekked back to the base. At their present pace he estimated that they should be back on the compound in about an hour and a half.

Del Monte had already decided that once the men were back on the base and the required period of rest received, then it was time to meet with the other group leaders. Collectively, a solution must be found to address the string of defeats the group has suffered over the past month.

Come on men, keep pushing; we are getting closer to home. Come on! Come on! The insurgents broke into a sprint following as always the instructions of their indomitable leader—Carlos Del Monte! They were quite anxious to get back to base after the ferocious firefight on the mountain plateau. A good rest, some solid food and a few bottles of booze and everything should be fine. At least that's what they thought.

The insurgents were approaching a patch of extremely rugged terrain so Del Monte and his men knew that they were just about three kilometers from Camp Diaz. As the guerrillas adjusted their pace to maneuver through the tangled undergrowth, they hadn't the faintest clue of what they were about to encounter.

Chapter 27

Bradley and his men were travelling for the last three and a half hours, on their current course they should be somewhere in the vicinity of Del Monte's hideout in about another two hours or so. That's the ideal time to be at the site where Christina was believed to be held hostage. The seven man initial rescue team had pushed really hard to be positioned deep in the Sierra Nevada mountains. The climb up the mountain paths really tested Bradley and his party.

Half way through a deep gorge on their way up, a massive tree came crashing down from an almost perpendicular rock face. How it grew so large from the side of the mountain was just another miracle of nature. The large roots had formed an intricate web and fanned out its long giant tentacles to form a secure tether to the surface. Bradley and his team blamed the progressive rock slippages for the accident which almost caused a major calamity for the group of commandos. Eduardo, the specialist trekker in the group, missed being hit by a falling branch by mere centimeters, and a dislodged boulder grazed the shoulder of another man. All things considered, they had covered a lot of ground and as darkness engulfed the area Bradley urged them on.

The commandos reached the designated staging area; Bradley decided to do one final briefing before the assault. All the weapons, material and other supplies were checked thoroughly; the arsenal looked quite impressive and included rocket propelled grenades, M16 Rifles fitted with M79 Grenade launchers, the rugged and battle tested AK 47's, Uzi submachine guns, M 60 E3 Machine guns, and several small arms. These commandos had an awesome amount of firepower; and for additional support they could call up other military assets like the Apache Helicopter gunships as well as the Black Hawk UH-60. Bradley and his unit came prepared for whatever the insurgents had in store.

Eduardo, the commando assigned with the responsibility of scout for the assault team paused briefly to remove a broken limb from the track. At first it appeared to have been broken, but after careful examination it looked like a freshly cut piece. The straight clean cut was certainly made with an extremely sharp and heavy blade; he focused the beam of his flashlight to get a better look, and nestled in the decaying foliage, Eduardo spotted something which did not fit into the jungle environment—a Cuban cigar almost in perfect condition.

"Bradley! Bradley! Look over here, see what I've found," he shouted. "Seems like we're onto something, hurry, come quickly!"

John rushed past the other guys to get to where the excited Colombian commando stood; he held the cigar to his nose as he smelt the strong pungent tobacco. The American Special Forces man assumed that the specimen had been lying in the bush for less than twelve hours, and that it came from one of the guerrilla fighters. Bradley's mind immediately went back to the captured insurgents interrogated after the raid on Santa Marta. The name came back to Bradley - Alberto Guiteirez! He was the source of quite a bit of intelligence on Carlos Del Monte. The captured insurgent spoke of the guerrilla leader's insatiable lust for Cuban cigars. Bradley knew immediately that they were onto something.

In the dull jungle abyss, the darkness appeared to be more intense. All of the commandos were outfitted with night vision goggles so the conditions really favored them. They got to the top of a ridge and again Eduardo picked up something—a sound, a bit faint at first; but then he heard it again. The voice appeared to be coming from somewhere to the west of their position. The scout tapped the stock of his rifle twice against the trunk of a tree and the men immediately hit the ground.

They were now on the outer fringes of Camp Diaz—Head Quarters of the legendary Carlos Del Monte and hopefully within reach of the captured American. Bradley felt a rush of adrenaline as he finished his camouflage paint; the other commandos soon joined in.

Using the light from his army flashlight, Bradley looked at the reconnaissance photos, and even in the darkness he marveled at the accuracy of the footage. They were just about a kilometer from the southern guard tower; Bradley joined Eduardo up front and scanned the area with his night vision goggles. He observed the silhouette of the guerrilla fighter perched atop the tower and felt a rush of excitement. The American got closer to his commando scout and whispered softly: "This one is for me amigo," while he unsheathed the long sharp hunting knife.

Bradley moved stealthily through the trees, almost hugging them to conceal his movements. Eduardo and the other eight commandos took up other offensive positions and waited. The American got to the base of the tower and slowly started to climb up the sturdy hardwood framing. Bradley estimated that this tower is about 50 meters high; a strong physique enabled him to pull his way up the dangling rope ladder at a rapid pace. He could hear the footsteps of the man at the top as he edged closer towards the platform. The sentry appeared oblivious of the danger lurking in the darkness as he leaned against the nylon rope rail.

The American Special Forces man took out the crossbow he carried, slipped a cyanide tipped arrow into the quiver and aimed carefully at the figure. In the hazy darkness, there was a deathly hiss as the arrow slammed into the guard's rib cage. A muffled gasping sound followed and the guerrilla fighter swayed, buckled at the knees and fell face down on the wooden platform; Bradley's deadly arrow protruding from his olive green military uniform. The sentry's stint with the Colombian black devils had come to rather swift end. Bradley had no doubts about this as he descended from the guard tower.

Once on the ground, Bradley signaled the other commandos and they gathered near a grassy mound. Just ahead, a dim light streaked through a tiny crevice in what appeared to be a long rectangular building; this looked like an extremely soft target thought Miguel, the rather muscular commando as he caressed the stock of his M60 machine gun. He really felt like opening up with a hellish salvo of 7.62 mm rounds on the building. Miguel loves to fire that beast of a weapon—the thrill and exhilarating feeling he gets from squeezing the trigger cannot be explained. He knew that it's just a matter of time before he gets his chance to blast away with his favorite weapon.

Eduardo and Bradley had other plans anyway. An all out frontal assault on the barracks would attract too much enemy fire. The plan then called for a three man team to place high explosive charges at the base of the building and blow it up using a delayed detonating technique Bradley had perfected several years ago. The group split into three as they approached in the darkness; night vision capabilities really made a difference for the assault team. Imagine being able to see your adversary and even decide where in his anatomy you want to place a bullet.

Two perimeter guards strolled leisurely along the side of the building unaware of the impending danger, a catastrophic wave of military might and fury is about to be unleashed on Del Monte and his rebel army. The taller of the two stopped for a while, leaned against a tree and unzipped his trousers then sprayed a burst of warm fluid onto the course tree bark. The urine careened of the bark and formed a small puddle at the base of the tree. Having relieved his bladder, the man then shook his penis vigorously to ensure that the last drop cleared his urethra. He quickly caught up with his comrade and they soon resumed their joint patrol around the compound.

In the meantime, Bradley and his team had already worked out the plan to rip the building apart with massive explosive charges. To get closer though, the two patrolmen had to be neutralized quickly. Bradley picked up the rifle with the sniper scope; the Mark 4/XM151 gave the weapon quite a lethal punch. The American up took up a firing position and waited while looking at the guard who had relieved himself against the tree earlier; he appeared to be slightly ahead of the other man. Bradley reached into the case and removed a six centimeter cylindrical object and screwed it onto the barrel of the Fielding M110 Sniper rifle.

The other commandos looked on anxiously, Bradley dug his boots firmly into the forest floor and took careful aim again. There was a muffled pop! Pop! Pop! The insurgent barely felt the 7.62mm round as it sliced through his carotid artery—death had struck him with ruthless efficiency. His partner, startled by the sudden collapse of the man who only six minutes ago paused to take a leak, panicked and broke into a run. He only managed to complete three strides. Bradley dropped him with a round smack in the back of his head—the impact of the slug literally ripping his skull open. Bone fragments and bits of soft cranial tissue were splattered against a nearby tree.

Quickly, the two-man team approached the building; at a glance well over one hundred insurgents could be housed in the structure. The two commandos inched their way closer and closer; the occasional obstacle popping up here and there—minor matters, nothing to shout about. They crawled under the structure and began to fix the explosives at strategic points along the structural beams and columns. Finally, they affixed and set the timing devices and headed back to the rendezvous point. The explosive charges were set and ready.

Eduardo, Enrique and Bradley looked quickly at the reconnaissance photos again. The log cabin where Christina was believed to be held by the guerrillas had to be somewhere in the North Eastern block. The team broke into two groups again and headed out in that direction. Moving along, the commander observed two other large barn-like structures on a ridge to the left of their position. The outline of another guard tower loomed over the treetops. The darkness and creepy night conditions were ideal for this operation; the commandos were moving with consummate ease as they got nearer to the log cabin.

The revolving lights from the tower positioned to the left threw a broad band of light through the forest. Three commandos, weapons drawn advanced close to the log cabin; Bradley led the way right up to the entrance. He wondered why there were no guards around the cabin; the former US Navy Seal continued his stealthy approach nevertheless, while keeping the Uzi submachine gun trained on the entrance at the same time.

As he got closer to the door the other commandos took up positions on both sides of the cabin, fanning out into the surrounding woods. The men were extremely surprised that no guards confronted them; perhaps the night shift hasn't begun as yet. Eduardo looked at his watch; they were well into the fifth hour of the operation, and so far they had encountered no resistance or any insurgent activity.

Bradley got up close to the door, still keeping the weapon leveled he kicked on the heavy wooden door. He pointed the flashlight straight at the small bunk bed in the corner of the room and froze for a moment. There was no sign of Christina. "What the hell, shit where is she!" Where did those bastards take her!"

The American Commando took a deep breath, knelt down on one knee and aimed the light under the wooden bed. Christina was gone! The guerrillas must have gotten wind of the assault and moved her to another part of the dense jungle. Bradley checked the room one more time just to be sure; he radioed the men waiting in the surrounding forest as he rushed out of the cabin.

As the team of commandos assembled again, Bradley told the guys that a new plan must be devised soon. Something had happened within the last week. How did the insurgents know that an assault was planned for Del Monte's jungle redoubt? Since the Santa Marta debacle, Bradley had a very uncomfortable feeling about some high ranking officers of the Colombian military. Is this latest development another sign of collusion between the military and the insurgents? Time alone will tell.

The revolving light of the Northern guard tower sprayed its brilliant rays all over the night sky and through the foliage. Eduardo and another commando moved quickly in that direction; they would plant explosive charges at the base of the tower and blast it to smithereens during their retreat from Camp Diaz.

As the lights of the Northern tower continued to shine through the dark jungle night, the commandos picked up some faint sounds in the distance. There seem to be some movements on the ridge overlooking the tower. The voices were a bit more audible now and a bright beam from a flashlight swept through the night sky.

They advanced rapidly towards the tower; again the commandos fixed a heavy payload of high explosives at strategic points on the structure without alerting the lone sentry at the top. The commandos had planted enough TNT on this compound to start a massive inferno. Bradley and his crew wanted to be absolutely sure that Del Monte's nest does not survive. All the devices were calibrated to explode at ten minute intervals; a tried and tested method, guaranteed to have the maximum explosive impact. Generally, the mortality rate for this type of detonation is around seventy-five percent.

Another beam of light appeared in the distance; Bradley and his men continued to move stealthily past the guard tower towards the area where the voices were coming from. As they approached the foot of the hill, the sounds became even louder. Bradley ordered his men to halt for a while to access the situation. As they crouched in the darkness, the American's mind just kept racing; what happened to Christina? He had searched the cabin and there was no sign of the kidnapped girl. Did the insurgents really move her to another location—or worse, is she still alive? There is only one way to know and Bradley had a plan. He signaled Eduardo to come over; the big Colombian commando walked briskly over to where Bradley sat and placed his backpack next to the American's.

•

Chapter 28

By now, Del Monte had made contact with the other search parties. They all met at the pre arranged rendezvous point at the top of the high ridge overlooking Camp Diaz. The leader of the Colombian Black Devils had a rather worried look on his face; nothing went right for the insurgents within the last three weeks. But the escape or release of the American girl has been most devastating; this is indeed a crushing blow!

Dwelling on their recent misfortune will only bring further misery, so Carlos shut out the depressing thoughts as they journeyed down the ridge, occasionally engaging them in conversation.

"Armando, when we get back to base, I think we should immediately increase the perimeter patrols; let us activate the emergency and defense plans, what do you think, comrade."

"Yes, Chief, I get the feeling the fucking American and his mercenaries are prowling around; maybe they played a part in her escape, we just can't take any more chances."

"You are so right, Armando; radio back to base and ask all the troops to be up and ready before we get back to camp. Tell them to turn on all the spot lamps and take up defensive positions in the designated areas."

"Right away Commander Del Monte," replied the newly promoted Armando as he rushed ahead of the group.

The men seemed to be moving down the hill with added gusto and fire now, some of them were even chanting.

"This is our land and no mercenary imperialist would make us run from it—fatherland or death!"

The chanting got louder as the guerrillas got closer to their base; in the distance the faint illumination from the camp became visible. In just about another forty-five minutes they'll be in the safety of Camp Diaz, ready and waiting for the enemy. An enemy who has been so elusive—almost ghostly and taunting.

Carlos felt that this is the time to make a stand; if he had to go down—certainly it should be with guns blazing! It's time to show his enemies what this tough Colombian guerrilla leader is really made of.

Eduardo and Bradley advanced ahead of the group of commandos; they heard the chanting and singing while concealed in the tall shrubs besides the tree-lined path. Bradley looked into the night vision goggles; and there they were—the guerrillas were travelling in two groups, moving parallel to each other at a rather brisk pace. The two commandos crept closer to the advancing guerrilla fighters who were no more than about a kilometer away.

While the American slithered on hands and knees ahead of Eduardo, the night sky south of their position became much brighter—some kind of explosives or fireworks—something really loud. Eduardo provided cover for the American Special Forces man as he continued to inch closer towards the advancing insurgents. The plan hatched by Bradley is quite a simple one. Simplicity and patience, he had perfected both skills over the many years he served with the Navy and Marines. Bradley shifted his body weight slightly to make the position a bit more comfortable.

Still crouching, he reached into his right jacket pocket; the American removed a glass test tube with a dark purple plastic lid, got to his feet and moved even closer to the approaching insurgents.

The chanting became more sporadic as the men moved past Bradley's position. Pressing firmly against the tree, he kept the rolled cotton swab removed earlier from the test tube firmly in his gloved left hand. Most of the guerrillas had moved past the concealed American commando; only a few stragglers were bringing up the rear. Bradley began to count silently. The man at the back of the line appeared to struggle with the bag slung over his shoulder. A fifteen second stop to do a minor strap adjustment created more than enough space between himself and the men just ahead of him.

One, two, three—now! Go, go! Bradley lunged hard at the man, slamming him down on the soft forest canopy. He quickly placed the cotton swab laced with a nasal anesthetic against the stricken man's nostrils, covering his mouth fully in the process. Bradley kept his hand firmly pressed in position until he felt the victim's body go limp. Another of Del Monte's men became ensnared in Bradley's dragnet!

Christina picked up her knapsack, ammo pouches and the AKS 74 assault rifle with the full magazine, and started out again. She had a good rest after the firefight, actually the adrenaline was still flowing but the last thing she wanted to do is become cocky or complacent. Her struggle for freedom has just begun, and the road ahead may be long and filled with danger and uncertainty. So despite this victory she knew that there were many challenges still ahead.

Moving quickly in the cool dark night, Christina thought she heard a sound, or maybe it's just her mind playing tricks on her. Anyway she could not spend too much time thinking about uncertainty. Whatever is the source, Christina felt that is not worth worrying about. Her primary focus is to get out of this wild jungle alive. In the darkness, it's not quite easy to determine location; she knew that initially the path had taken her in a Northeasterly direction from where the rebels had kept her. At 1:30 am—almost twenty-two hours since she broke out of Del Monte's jungle prison, Christina had some difficulty maintaining her bearing. Moving through the dense forest in the dead of night without some form of tracking device or GPS, presents quite a challenge.

The former hostage thought about her dad and the sprawling family estate in Texas. Oh how she missed her beautiful home and all the luxuries. Christina tripped over on a fallen branch as she tried to clear her mind. Remaining fully focused and alert is extremely important at this stage, despite her waning strength. Falling into the hands of the enemy again is just not an option!

She got to a small clearing in the forest; the area appeared to have been used within the last few days, maybe by hikers or mountain climbers. Christina took no chances though; she leveled the weapon and advanced gingerly. She flashed the light onto the clear patch of ground while advancing, pausing only briefly to observe anything unusual—an empty can or carelessly strewn food packaging.

Nothing appeared out of the ordinary, so Christina continued to work her way through the forest, moving at a much quicker pace to make up for any time lost. And then she heard that sound again; but this time more distinct than previously. Christina heard that sound before—oh yes, definitely. She broke into a trot, trying to move towards the general direction in which she thought the noise came from. The heavy backpack, extra magazines and other military gear wore her down, but Christina had only one thing on her mind – freedom! Preston's battle-hardened daughter won't be dropping her guard though.

She got to a deep rocky gorge in the forest and decided to tackle it head on. The last gorge-like canyon she entered unearthed a cache of weapons—a discovery which may well turn out to be of tremendous importance as her situation unfolds. Christina folded the stock of the AKS74 Assault Rifle just as she completed the special knot at the end of rope tied to the trunk of a nearby tree.

The American used the rope to control her descent into the rather deep gorge; once at the bottom a quick yank on the other end, and her makeshift device came crashing down. Christina quickly rolled up the rope for storage in her knapsack. In the valley, she decided to take at least a fifteen minute break. She knew that daylight is about another two or three hours away, and although the last eight hours were quite frenetic—amidst all the gunfire and adrenaline rush she felt like a super woman; but reality started to hit home. Christina needed to rest and fifteen minutes was just not enough. The villiant "Gung-ho" American girl threw her knapsack to the ground, then elevated her sore and tired feet onto the fallen tree trunk. Christina fell asleep within minutes.

As the captured man jerked his arm involuntarily; the effects of the nasal anesthetic started to diminish, and before long he began to mumble. Bradley slapped him on the cheeks as he quizzed the frightened man.

"What is your name, my friend? Now answer me quickly mother-fucker, I don't have much time. Hurry! Hurry!"

The man wriggled again, and took a slow shallow breath before responding.

"Marco, Gustavo Cristobal; guerrilla fighter, Colombian Black Devils."

Bradley leapt into the air, barely able to control his emotion. For a moment he wondered whether or not he was in a dream. The rest of his dialogue with the captured insurgent went on without a hitch; Marco offered no resistance and volunteered to give much more information to Bradley and Eduardo. For his full compliance, Bradley decided to spare Marco's life. The grateful man picked up the few things he was allowed to keep and headed back up the ridge, away from Camp Diaz. He soon melted away into the vast expanse of jungle.

The news of Christina's escape gave Bradley and his team added momentum and vigor. Bradley first broke the news to the Santa Marta Police Commander, Nunez stationed at the staging base camp about ten Kilometers from their present location. Nunez had strict instructions not to share this information until Christina's whereabouts were known.

This new development meant that some tactical changes are now necessary. Bradley and his commando team wanted to find Christina some time after daybreak—they were quite confident.

Bradley had some unfinished business to discuss with Carlos Del Monte before they set out to find Mike Preston's daughter.

Once again the men fanned out, this time in the direction from which they had travelled earlier. The plan is to split into three, three—man groups as they approached the base. Bradley had already radioed for back up support to be on standby if additional firepower becomes a necessity.

John Bradley was about to rain down fire and brimstone on Carlos Del Monte and his guerrilla army.

Camp Diaz had not seen so much activity so early on any day. Del Monte and the men had returned to base without realizing that another of their comrades did not make it back to base. Del Monte knew something wasn't right though. The Southern guard tower had no revolving lights and nobody could explain the absence of any guard detail around the compound of the main building.

In the predawn darkness, guerrilla fighters were rushing to take up defensive positions. The earlier message from the Chief's new right hand man, Ronaldo Diaz conveyed a great sense of urgency. The men were up and ready in record time. Heavy machine gun emplacements, 105 mm Howitzers and the modified, ubiquitous ZSU Shilka antiaircraft guns were all ready. Del Monte had a pretty impressive array of weaponry—and he intended to throw it all at any attacking force.

The morning light began to streak through the forest as Del Monte and his men huddled down and waited. They could not tell what time the attack would come—but the signs were all there. The bodies of two guards were discovered in the woods nearby; one mangled beyond recognition. Meanwhile, slung over the sturdy nylon rope railing atop the Southern guard tower, the lifeless body of the man had already attracted a few aerial predators. Their wings flapping furiously as they completed several strafing passes; It was a rather gruesome sight.

A commander positioned a short distance away saw the commotion. He radioed Del Monte before firing several rounds from his M16 Rifle to scare the birds away. The guerrilla leader quickly dispatched a two-man team to retrieve the body of the slain fighter.

As the warm morning sunlight shot its rays over Camp Diaz, the hustle and bustle around the compound continued at a frenetic pace. The team had already lowered the corpse with the protruding arrow through the neck from the platform of the guard tower. Some men were busy digging a large trench—Del Monte and his rebel guerrillas were staring mortality straight in the face.

The special forces commandos heard the rifle blast as they advanced through the dense forest. In the morning light the barracks of Camp Diaz were quite visible. Bradley and the team rehearsed the plan just to fine tune every minute detail. Team Delta, led by Bradley would attack the Eastern flank while Eduardo's men launch their attack from the Western fringes. Del Pino and the Storming Eagles took up the rear, providing cover and tactical support for the two advancing units.

Weapons at ready, the commandos advanced towards the camp. Bradley and his men waited for the other commando unit to take up positions.

"Delta 7 to Raging Lion, do you copy? Come in please, if you are hearing me."

"Copy you Delta 7, we are poised to take off in fifteen minutes."

"Great, Raging Lion, we fly ten minutes after you depart"

"Storming eagles to Delta 7, we are moving into position. Do you copy?"

"Got you, roger that" replied the American special forces man.

Eduardo and his team got to within half a kilometer of the main barracks. The Colombian fitted the sniper scope and silencer onto the Fielding M110 rifle and took up a firing position. Rafael and the other men kept their heavy machine guns trained on the main entrance of the large hall, waiting for the order.

A short distance away, three insurgents walked up to a sandbagged bunker. They delivered what looked like a crate containing heavy ammunition. Using his field glasses, Eduardo spotted the four barrels of the ZSU anti aircraft gun nestled ominously in the bunker. This had to be taken out fast!

Eduardo took aim and squeezed the trigger; a man swayed and toppled over. His partner dropped to one knee and started firing wildly. Another round from Eduardo tore right through his chest. The other insurgent turned and tried to take cover in the bunker;

he managed only to make it to the entrance before another round from the Colombian sniper opened up a big hole in the back of his neck. The slug catapulted the insurgent, landing him face down on the bunker floor.

In the meantime, the man inside the bunker had climbed onto the Shilka four barreled anti aircraft cannon and was spewing out a hail of deadly fire in the direction of the attacking commandos. The accuracy of the artillery fire pinned down the team for a while; they were not in any immediate danger though. At least not directly; for the moment the main threat came from the flying branches and chunks of wood busted up by the big gun.

Eduardo squeezed off a few more rounds, but his position and trajectory meant that the shots did not have the maximum impact. He tried to maneuver to a more elevated position to get a clearer shot but the heavy slugs kept on coming.

Bradley looked on from behind the thick cluster of trees; he got much closer to the compound than the other two commandos. John could hear the insurgents talking—he was so very close, less than seventy meters from the enemy. The heavy artillery fire from the western end of the perimeter had subsided by now. Guerrilla fighters were rushing to man some other bunkers— Camp Diaz looked like a macabre scene from a war zone.

Crouching low, Bradley settled the M60 Machine gun on its mounting then opened up with a deadly salvo; he mowed down at least seven insurgents in the first barrage before the remainder took cover behind a large concrete culvert in the courtyard. Slightly to the right, Bradley saw a tall slender man gesticulating frantically and shouting commands. He appeared to be directing the operations and had a flair of authority. The American Navy Seal was tempted to take a shot at Carlos Del Del Monte but opted not to—capturing him alive would be more of a major victory.

By now, the compound was raked by gunfire from three directions; Del Pino and his team had opened up with a wicked barrage from their rocket propelled grenades and heavy machine guns. Del Monte's gunners responded with an ear splitting salvo, pouring down a hail of hot lead on the Storming Eagles Team. One of the Commandos took a round in his left calf, and as blood gushed out of the gaping wound, Del Pino rushed to his aid. He pulled out his army knife and cut through the green camouflage to get a clear view of the wound. Thankfully, the slug just tore through the muscle but did not enter the Tibia. Del Pino wrapped a tourniquet around Enrique's injured calf to stop the bleeding. This good, time-tested and simple treatment had come to the aid of yet another combatant.

The gunfire continued as more of Del Monte's big guns began to open up; a lot of the fire appeared to be coming from a bunker nestled on the northern fringes of the sprawling compound. Bradley looked at his watch. Time is of great importance now; and as much as he wants to destroy the guerrilla base, Bradley had not forgotten the real purpose for his trip to Colombia—the rescue and safe repatriation of Christina Preston. John decided that this is the perfect time to up the ante.

Bradley changed his position quickly as a round from one of Del Monte's 105 mm howitzer careened and exploded harmlessly some fifty meters away.

"Fucking bastards, hope you could handle what's coming your way," shouted the American angrily as he returned fire in the direction from which the projectile came. Another thunderous blast ripped right through the top of a large tree, scattering chunks of timber in all directions. Bradley grabbed the radio and screamed his command.

"Raging Lion, this is Delta 7, do you copy?" Come in Raging Lion, it's time to smoke them out. Let's give these fucking bastards a taste of the real stuff! It's time to smoke the nest!"

Eduardo heard the crackling on his radio and responded to team Delta. "Raging Lion to Delta 7, Roger that, let's count down to fifteen." The Colombian commando remembered clearly what was meant by "time to smoke the nest"—detonation of the first set of explosive charges strategically placed beneath the buildings of Camp Diaz.

Eduardo removed a small electronic device from his backpack, keyed in nine digits and started to count. Moments later, there was a deafening explosion and a massive orange flame shot up through the air. The explosives ripped right through the main support structure of the building; mangled metal sheets and broken timber sailed through the air. The frantic screams of dazed and shocked guerilla fighters punctuated with the occasional machine gun blast, created a mad and chaotic scene. Carlos Del Monte's compound is being pulverized and blown to dust.

On the Eastern flank, Rafael held the electronic device firmly as he entered the numbers into the keypad. The first blast toppled a guard tower, sending the man at the top hurtling to his death in the forest beneath. As the splintered framing crashed landed onto an oil storage facility, a large tank exploded, shooting hot bursts of fire and fuel through the air. Sounds of death, destruction and chaos filled the area.

The second blast, proved to be the most deadly. When Bradley and the team planted the explosives earlier, they were unaware of the presence of an ammunition storage bay on that site. They had planted more than enough TNT to level the buildings and any peripheral structures. All this additional munitions further increased the destructive payload resulting in further mayhem. Screams of despair and panic filled the air—men were running desperately, some rolled on the hard surface to extinguish their flaming uniforms.

By now, the Colombian Black Devils were in total disarray and Bradley had no intentions of letting up. He decided to call in air support. A new and deadly dimension is about to enter the arena—the monstrous flying beast—the AC 130 Spectre gunship. Reports from other theatres of operations where this military asset was deployed previously spoke of enemy combatants defecating and freezing in their positions when this gunship opened up on their positions.

Chapter 29

When Christina first felt the heaviness in her right leg, she thought it might just be due to cramps caused by dehydration. She struggled to open her eyelids and tried to turn slightly to the left, but this seemed to be extremely difficult. Christina slowly opened her eyes and attempted to get up from her makeshift bed. "Oh my God! Oh my God!" Christina screamed in horror as she looked down at her right foot, and the bulging mass which entangled it.

A large Boa Constrictor had crept up on her while she slept and formed a tight coil around her entire foot, extending it's squeeze all the way up to her calf muscle. Christina had heard stories of hikers crushed to death by these ominous jungle creatures. She learnt very early in her wildlife training that the one thing you do not do in these situations is panic. Every jerky movement encourages the predator to increase the pressure further restricting blood flow to the affected area.

Her survival instincts kicked in almost like second nature, and despite the mounting pressure on her leg, Christina remained calm. Only part of the huge snake was wrapped around her foot, about a two meter portion remained on the old tree trunk.

Christina weighed her options, the hunting knife or the semi automatic; in the end, she chose the hunting knife.

She reached into the side holster and cleared the weapon; the blade still razor sharp, perfect for the job. Christina lifted the blade and drove down in a hard ninety degree thrust, the blade shearing into the muscle of the coiled reptile. She lifted it again, this time plunging the blade in two swift horizontal stabs. Blood gushed from the wounded beast as Christina felt the grip on her foot loosen slightly.

While the wounded reptile bled profusely, Christina spotted the head. By now her adrenaline was pumping and nothing could stop her from going for the kill. Christina waited for the wounded snake to push its head further away from her leg, then lifted the knife for one final lethal thrust!

The Texan heroine had prevailed once again. As the Boa wriggled in a feeble penultimate breath, the American kicked her foot free and the limp and lifeless creature fell off the old tree trunk. Christina dusted herself off, checked all her gear and continued on her journey through the valley. Judging by the height of the sun, she knew that the midday hour had already past. Somehow, the watch fell off her wrist at one point during the trek, so reverting to mother nature to determine the time of day made perfect sense.

Christina got to a point in the valley covered heavily with thick luxuriant tropical ferns, exotic wild plants and flowers. Wow! What a beautiful spectacle; the former hostage paused for a moment to capture a truly magnificent scene from nature. Despite her capture at the hands of the rebels, Christina still loves Colombia and would like to return when this terrible ordeal is over. She met some truly marvelous people, and to pass judgement on the entire population because of her situation won't be fair.

The journey through the forest got even better; Christina stumbled upon a patch of bananas. They had a sweet fragrant aroma which caused her taste buds to go haywire. But she had company; two monkeys were happily feasting on the yellow tropical delight. Christina decided that the primates would not be alone in the feast and joined in the healthy potassium rich lunch. Two quick whacks from the hunting knife and the soft stock of the banana plant folded over, scattering several fingers on the forest floor. Christina stuffed some of the goodies in her backpack before downing at least six of the delectable tropical snacks. Refueled and energized, she resumed her journey to freedom with added verve and energy.

Along the way, she kept hearing these sounds, she actually thought they were somewhat familiar—an aircraft, some type of helicopter perhaps. The heavy whirring noise seemed to be getting closer, Christina retracted the stock of AKS 74 and continued to advance with the weapon held in an offensive position. She had fought too hard for freedom to give it up now, no way!

Chapter 30

The AC130 Spectre gunship swooped down low over Camp Diaz; battered remnants of Del Monte's insurgents tried to engage the aerial monster with anti-aircraft and rocket fire. Making a sharp Easterly turn, the pilot opened up with multiple rounds from his rocket pods, blasting bunkers and other defenses into mangled rubble.

Moments earlier, Del Monte crept quietly through the forest. The American Special Forces man had dealt a crushing blow to his morale. His grandiose and elitist dreams of maintaining control over large swathes of territory deep in the Colombian jungle already came crashing down. For him the dream is over now, his best bet is to melt into the dense jungle. He had failed miserably, and there is no way he could face the insurgents again—at least what's left of them. Carlos shifted the canvas strap of the heavy bag to his other shoulder and continued to climb up the steep hill.

He had escaped with his life and soon the disappointment, pain and anguish of this defeat would fade away. Del Monte pushed, on trying desperately to get as far away from the debris of Camp Diaz. Getting out of the Sierra Nevada is his immediate concern. As the battered and shaken guerrilla leader pushed on, he pondered about what lies ahead for him. Certainly, being captured by the American or Colombian Government forces is not an option. Carlos Del Monte had already decided that no matter what happens, he'll never be taken alive!

Despite the exhaustion from lack of sleep and all the fighting, Del Monte continued on his rapid retreat through the mountains. He knew that his best chance of eluding the encroaching commandos or the army is to get down to the cost. Ideally, if he could make it down to the Guajira-Barranquilla on the Caribbean coast, then all his worries are over. Catching one of the many freighters plying the coast would be extremely easy for Del Monte. After all, he still had some connections—and, with close to half a million dollars stuffed in his rucksack, slipping out of the country would not be a challenge.

Del Monte got to an area with a large cluster of palm trees, for a moment he felt the urge to take a break; he decided against it and pressed on. His first priority is to get to the famous Cuchillo de San Lorenzo Trail. Once there, getting down to the Santa Marta Coast should be relatively easy. Carlos Del Monte knew that every stride which takes him closer to the trail brings him closer to his ultimate goal—escape and the beginning of new life.

John and his group of Commandos were about an hour into the trail. The scenes of death and destruction they left behind at Camp Diaz bore a macabre similarity to some of the experiences Bradley had in Chechnya and Somilia. Combat is ugly dirty and bloody business—that's just the way it is. Bradley had no remorse, why should he anyway? He never asked the rebels to kidnap Christina in the first place—their demise is simply payback or what Bradley aptly calls, collateral damage. Hopefully, their fate would send a strong message to America's enemies—the US takes care of its citizens, and kidnapping or holding them hostage has serious and dire consequences!

The men were tired; they did not have much time to rest. Although the fighting around Del Monte's compound stretched them to the limit, Bradley felt that rescuing Christina before nightfall is a critical priority. He really had a good group of men; even the injured man refused to remain behind. As Enrique pleaded with the American Commander, Bradley saw the passion and fire in his eyes and allowed him to remain with the search party.

Eduardo pushed on at a really fast pace. They got to a deep gorge in a lush green valley along a path bearing signs of very recent activity—fresh shoe prints and broken bits of vegetation. The lead scout and tracker had no doubt that they were onto something and before long he found it.

"Over here guys, come, come!" Eduardo screamed at the top of his voice as he picked up the object nestled between some dried twigs.

"Hey buddy, you found gold or something," asked Bradley as he sprinted to see what Eduardo had found.

"Well, right now I think this is worth much more than any gem." Eduardo picked up the watch, wiped the moisture on the surface and handed it to Bradley. The American could barely control his emotion as he took a good look at the timepiece. It certainly had the look of a camper's watch and the mini accessory attached to the band strongly suggested that the owner is female.

Enthused and energized by this vital clue, the search party pushed on; they reached the valley floor some three and a half hours after pulverizing Del Monte's camp. Bradley's experience in jungle conditions had taught him that daylight can disappear really fast and darkness can engulf the area with little or no warning.

They had to find Christina before another sunset. Since Bradley and the team had no idea of her health and physical condition, finding her soon is paramount. The American looked at his watch; he knew that he had to keep pushing the men if they are to accomplish this task before sunset. As the search party moved out of the valley, Bradley Spoke.

"Gentlemen, we've roughly another two and a half hours before darkness takes over this place and we must find the missing girl. We've got no other choice, those damn bastards have been badly bruised and battered but our real and true victory is yet to come."

The commandos broke into a run again after Bradley finished his motivational talk. They made it up to another ridge close to a grassy meadow teeming with wild birds and other creatures. Still ahead of the team, Eduardo gesticulated with a vigorous wave of his hand. He picked up the field glasses, placed it to his eyes and gazed into the distance. Something had caught his eye in the bushes about two kilometers away; the shioulette appeared to be that of a human figure carrying some kind of backpack. He turned around and shouted at the top of his voice: "We are definitely onto something guys, I think she's nearby!"

Bradley rushed ahead to where Eduardo stood and trained the field glasses on the area his Colombian counterpart had pointed to previously. "Yes! There is definitely a moving figure in the tall brush to the far west of our position," shouted the excited American.

By this time, all the men had gathered in a huddle; the light started to fade as Eduardo spoke.

"This has to be the last big push, I want to recommend that we split up into two teams just about now, since time is against us, we need to forge ahead at a more rapid pace."

"Let's hear more about the plan," quipped Bradley as he tossed his bag of gear on the ground.

"A five man unit should set up camp at this point; all the heavy equipment and other stuff stays here as well; this would lighten our load and increase speed and mobility."

"Great Eduardo, let's do it! Come on Guys let's go, time is slipping away," Bradley commanded.

The small group of men, now relieved of all the heavy gear and supplies were literally sprinting through the tall bush and trees. Each man carried a rifle and a Semi Automatic pistol; if they ran into any serious opposition the backup commandos were not too very far away. That's very unlikely though, Del Monte's Army has been virtually decimated, and the tattered remnants of his troops were tired—the battle is now over. It's time to melt quietly into the dense jungle forest.

They got to a slight incline at the end of the meadow, Bradley had maintained the lead all the way up to this point. Eduardo kept a steady pace just behind the American and was just about to go past him when a sudden burst of gunfire punctuated the silence.

"Get down, get down!" Shouted Bradley as the gunfire ricocheted into the nearby trees, spewing splinters and twigs in several directions. Bradley knew that weapon, it had a very familiar sound. He remembered it all too well—it is of Russian origin and he had used it just about four years ago while training Chechnyan rebels in the Caucasus. The AKS 74 made a distinctive chatter and Bradley had no difficulty recognizing this versatile and ubiquitous piece of military hardware. Whoever is firing it, certainly knew what they were doing. The firing continued, but the commandos did not fire a single round in retaliation.

Bradley pointed to the right, and Eduardo immediately started to crawl in that direction; the American followed within moments with a westerly movement. The hastily hatched plan called for both men to move in opposite directions and engage the shooter from the outside flank.

Chapter 31

Christina just couldn't take any chances at this stage; she slammed in another magazine this time using a mercury tip round. Her survival skills had really turned her into a serious combatant; the American girl learnt about the impact of such munitions especially in marshlands. It only takes a few rounds in the right places to trigger an inferno. Christina held her fire and wondered why the approaching men were not shooting at her. From her position at the base of a large mahogany tree, the former hostage could no longer see her pursuers.

In the fading light she tried to remain as still as possible to avoid drawing attention to her position. Less than ten hours ago she had a scary encounter with a large Boa Constrictor and now the approaching darkness gave her a rather creepy feeling. In the heart of the Colombian Jungle, predators like giant Anacondas, leopards, tigers and other huge cats abound. Christina had good reason to be fearful. She shifted her position slightly and waited, holding the rifle in a steady horizontal position.

Bradley just had a gut feeling that the shooter hid somewhere behind the huge tree a short distance from his position. The American commando had crawled on his hands on knees and got to within seventy meters of the massive tree. The darkness covered the marshland quickly and the special forces man knew that he now had the advantage. He took the night vision goggles from the pouch and focused in the direction of the sprawling tree.

Within minutes he observed some motion, someone or some creature moved, paused momentarily then disappeared behind the massive tree trunk. Bradley called up Eduardo on the radio and spoke in a muffled voice,

"Raging Lion, this is Delta 7, come in do you copy, about to engage adversary—do you read me?"

"Roger, delta 7, got you loud and clear, approach with caution."

"Sure, roger that," replied the American as he crept closer to the unknown quarry.

He had closed the gap quite quickly and by now Bradley was less than fifty meters away from the target. Despite all his years of Special Forces and US Navy Seal training, Bradley's heart raced and his palms sweated profusely causing the black leather mittens to become rather moist.

Is he about to experience the euphoria and the thrill of finding Christina Preston, or is he just chasing after another elusive ghost in the dark Colombian Jungle? He removed the Semi-Automatic from its holster and crept closer.

Mike Preston ended the day the same way every day; by now he had used up more than twenty spools of bright yellow ribbons to weave a massive and intricate web interspersed with several pieces of the Star-Spangled Banner. The Texas billionaire is just hoping and praying for the safe return of his daughter. In his last conversation with John Bradley, the retired American Navy Seal, Preston learnt that the search team had narrowed down the area where they think Christina might be held.

Since then, there hasn't been much news from the South American continent and Preston couldn't help his feeling of deep emotional pain and scarring.

Actually, today marks the one hundred and eighty-ninth day since Christina became a hostage at the hands of the anti government rebels. Preston's life had unraveled into chaos since that fateful Saturday October morning. Despite the recurring bouts of depression, he had managed to keep his sanity. Of course Sally, his efficient and dedicated assistant played a pivotal role in all of this. And the one time sizzling hot sexual tryst more than therapeutic value. Mike would be eternally grateful to her for taking care of his emotional and other needs.

Preston was struggling all week and he just didn't have the zeal for the upcoming appointments with visiting foreign executives. Sally had already put a red circle on the calendar to remind him, and as usual all the files for the upcoming meetings were on his desk.

Deep inside she relished the thought of another hot fling with Preston but decided that it could wait. There will be numerous other opportunities to satisfy her flirtatious cravings. The memories of the night she sneaked into his sprawling mansion at Oak Forrest Heights would be forever etched in her memory.

As her boss left office at the end of the day, Sally had to struggle to restrain herself; she knew that there is a lot on his mind but those inner cravings kept on resurging. Sally pushed the large glass sliding door as Preston was about to get up.

"Leaving early today?" inquired Sally as she walked across the room, her eyes fixed on the clock hanging above Preston's desk.

"Just need to get some rest, tomorrow's going to be quite hectic with all the meetings and stuff," replied Preston with a smile.

"I think you really deserve the rest, you've been so hard on yourself recently; with all that's happening—Christina's kidnapping, the business and other things. You definitely deserve some quality time for yourself."

Mike heard the sincerity in Sally's voice and wondered how he would have managed in her absence. She had his back in the midst of this monumental emotional crisis.

"You're so thoughtful caring and kind," remarked Preston as he strolled past a blushing Sally.

"Thanks, I'll stay on for a bit to sort out some of the files, see you in the morning Sir."

Preston got into his chauffeured limousine for the forty minute ride back to Oak Forest. On the way back home, he spoke with his buddy in the Washington—Chairman of the Joint Chiefs of staff, Mark Reuben.

"Mike, how you doing mate?" Reuben asked compassionately.

"In the present circumstances, not too bad—all things considered it could have been much worse."

"Agreed, I know that you're quite a tough nut—just hang in there man."

"Any new developments from the South?" asked the Texas business man as the limo driver took a detour to avoid incoming traffic.

"No, I've heard nothing since the last report; General Castenades promised to keep me posted."

"Well, I'am sure you'll update me whenever there is breaking news."

"You can definitely count on me all the way buddy," replied Reuben as he spun around in his chair.

The Limo driver swerved to the right keeping clear of the path of an incoming emergency service vehicle. Its flashing lights and wailing siren splitting the afternoon silence with a deafening crescendo.

Preston rolled the window a bit to catch a glimpse of the fleeting ambulance hurtling down the highway. A few minutes later the sleek black limousine pulled up the driveway leading to the sprawling magnificent mansion.

Chapter 32

Del Monte made it up to the Couchillo de San Lorenzo Trail a short while before sunset. By the time he started up the steep climb, darkness had already engulfed the area. He had done relatively well, covering large swaths of jungle territory in an attempt to reach the Caribbean gateway and sea port of Santa Marta. Once there, several options are available but the most plausible and realistic one is to get aboard one of the many freighters plying the waters around the historic coastal city.

His strength waning from the exhaustion of battle, Del Monte had to find the inner strength to push his tired legs up the rugged mountain path. He had no other choice; when the pain from extremely tired feet became almost unbearable, the Colombian guerrilla leader took a break to recuperate. This pattern continued for just over two and a half hours.

A short while after the last break, Del Monte saw the lights of the city and felt a sense of renewed energy and vigor. The pathway to another life, a new name and identity now appears to be well within his grasp. He pulled the zipper on his backpack to touch the thick stack of United States currency, tightly wrapped in sealed plastic bags as he pushed forward confidently. This is not the way Del Monte intended to go out, but circumstances and fate had dealt him a tough and uneven hand. As he pushed through the dark and narrow trail, Carlos reflected on how it all started.

The action by the Government to send in the bulldozers to wreck the family farm was certainly the catalyst for all his subsequent actions. Chances are, his parents would still be alive, and the university graduate might have been exporting his dream and vision to other parts of the country—and maybe even all of Latin America.

El Capitan quickly jolted himself back to reality, and cleared some protruding branches encroaching along the path. The former guerrilla leader lengthened his strides, despite the physical and emotional exhaustion; reaching the Santa Marta coast is so important now.

With the Semi Automatic pistol in his hand, Bradley moved in silence. He could see the figure crouching while holding the assault rifle pointed towards the southern side. Bradley then gave Eduardo the signal to fire several diversionary rounds. The figure crouching at the base of the tree immediately opened up with a return salvo.

Bradley made his move. Like a big jungle cat stalking an unsuspecting prey he lunged forward pinning the victim to the ground. Quickly the American Special Forces Man wrenched the rifle from the victim's grasp. Screaming frantically, the woman kicked and clawed in a feeble attempt to free herself from the Bradley's tight grip.

"Christina! Christina! I' am John Bradley, United States Special Forces and I'm here to take you back to the United States of America. Relax, you are in safe hands now.

Shaken, numb and dazed, the rescued American burst into tears, her words barely audible.

"My daddy, My sweet caring daddy; I knew you would not have left me to die in this place."

"Don't try to talk too much my dear; you're tired and totally exhausted from this terrible ordeal," remarked Bradley. Christina placed both hands on her head as the American soldier hung a campers light to illuminate the area. Bradley took a good look at her sweat streaked face, and despite the rough jungle conditions, her beautiful features still stood out.

The American soldier could hardly restrain his glee and excitement—five months of tough grueling work had finally paid off. Bradley spoke into the mouthpiece of the radio to alert the rest of the team.

"Raging Lion, this is Delta 7; come in please." Bradley waited for Eduardo to respond.

"Copy you Delta 7, anything to report?" The Colombian Special Forces trooper asked in anticipation.

"Mission accomplished, Christina is safe and sound, she's right here with me!" The elated American spoke crisply to his fellow commando.

"What! That's great news; let me radio the backup party and some air support immediately."

"Yes, get them here quickly, it's time to get Christina out of this place."

Bradley spoke to Nunez giving him the good news. The Santa Marta Police Chief screamed with excitement as he banged his fist on the hard wooden tabletop. "I just knew you were going to beat the shit out of these fucking bastards! Good work my American friend, very good work!"

Christina took the bottle of water from Bradley and poured it all over her face. She felt the refreshing trickle, as the water filtered through her hair and all the way down to her breast. Eduardo and the rest of the search party then arrived.

"Gentlemen, this is Christina Preston! Let's get ready to take her home; but before we do, I've got an important call to make."

Chapter 33

Captain Alvarez checked his gear before heading up the hill. His American friend had asked him a special favor once again. He had already placed the special markers and buoys on the designated beach as instructed. According to the plan drafted Bradley, Alvarez would travel just about half way up the Jungle trail and await further instructions from the former US Navy Seal.

Although outfitted with a military flashlight and other gear, Captain Alvarez prefers to travel in total darkness. The old seaman thinks that while a light can shine the path to be followed, it could also give away your position. Captain Alverez did not have a very long wait to validate his theory.

In the pitch-black darkness, he saw the flash of light, and at first he thought that some careless hiker had dropped a tin or other shiny object along the trail. The old man had done this several times before, and by now every square meter of the turf was familiar territory. He paused momentarily and saw a faint movement this time. The veteran seaman unsheathed the big hunting knife and took up a crouching position at the side of the trail. He waited as the tall dark figure approached.

Alvarez supported himself on the camouflage tote bag as he touched the tip of his knife while keeping his eyes on the approaching figure. The old seaman did not believe in ghost so fear never crossed his mind. The man stopped for a moment to relieve himself, placing the flashlight in a small shrub; he then picked up his tote bag and continued down the mountain trail. Captain Alvarez looked on in silence, occasionally shifting his body weight for comfort.

The wail of a commercial freighter leaving the Port of Santa Marta startled the man, the Captain saw him jerk and sway sideways. Who is this mysterious traveler on such a lonely and treacherous trail thought Alvarez? As the figure got closer, Captain Alvarez prepared to make his move. He got the urge to draw the pistol Bradley had given to him a few days earlier but decided not to. The knife is stealthier than the gun; the old seaman held his breath and waited as the figure kept coming towards him.

Gabriella sat at her desk at the Santa Marta Police compound just looking through her notes on the Christina Preston case. It has been a truly unusual experience for the female cop. Since the very first encounter with a Former US Special Forces man, so much has changed in her life. Gabriella waltzed in and out of a few rocky relationships before. However, after that chance meeting at the discotheque near El Radadero a few weeks ago, she just couldn't keep her mind off the American soldier.

It's been a while since they spoke; there has been no official announcement on the Preston matter, but Gabriella had an uncanny feeling that something was going on. This perhaps could explain the unusual silence from Bradley. She had dropped some hints earlier about him taking a vacation when his assignment is complete. Her only hope now is that the mission goes according to plan, and the man she wants to share her life with makes it back alive.

Gabriella found it very difficult to concentrate, her thoughts kept going back and forth. It's way past midday, but somehow she did not feel like eating anything. Sergeant Gabriella Carmelita Hernandez just wanted to see Bradley again. She really wanted to hold him close to her and make passionate love to him. Actually, she now regrets not being more open with him during their last encounter. Gabriella picked up her mobile phone and decided to try John's number one more time.

Chapter 34

Mike Preston sat by the pool and sipped a martini; he just got the urge to do something special this evening. Maybe he should invite Sally over to spend the evening with him. He knew that she wouldn't mind but he really didn't want to give her a false sense of hope. Inevitably the relationship or fling is going to crash and burn and the emotional fallout may have a devastating effect on Sally. She certainly deserves better, and Preston is too much of a caring boss to cause her any grief or pain.

Preston put aside is flirtatious thoughts and dived into the pool. At his age, the Texan can still cover the seventy-five meter pool in record time. He made several laps practicing his breast stroke, kicking and splashing like the Albatros. Quickly, he changed to the freestyle and finished with a good strong lap doing the butterfly.

He climbed out of the pool using the stainless steel ladder and hand rail and reached for the large white towel. He dried his wet hair Briskly and flung the damp towel over his shoulder.

Moments later his cell phone rang; Preston sprinted across the oak planks and grabbed the handset.

"Hello, Mike Preston." He took a deep breath as he waited for the caller to reply.

"Hey Mike, John Bradley—how are you today? You've got a minute?"

"Sure man, we can talk for as long as you like," replied Preston.

"Great! Then just hold for a minute," said Bradley as he passed the phone to Christina.

"Daddy Daddy it's me Christina! I am coming home, yes Daddy—I am free!"

Preston dropped to his knees, too stunned to say a word. He tried to open his mouth, tears streaming down his cheeks.

"Oh my God, Oh my God! Christina I can't believe it's you." Preston could barely keep the tears from flowing down his cheeks as he spoke."

Still sobbing, the wealthy Texan started to climb the flight of stairs to the balcony overlooking the swimming pool as he listened to the voice of his beloved daughter Christina.

"Are you hurt or in pain?" asked the overjoyed Preston as he walked through the doorway leading to the spacious kitchen.

"No dad, I am fine—just tired, and missing home so badly," replied Christina as Bradley handed her a napkin.

"My love, thank God you are safe and well, let me speak with John now, I've got to make urgent travel arrangements. Take care my sweet and loving angel—I'll see you soon.

"Can't wait to be home again daddy," said Christina as she handed the phone back to Bradley.

The silence was broken by whirring sounds of the rotor blades of the Sikorsky helicopter preparing to land a short distance away. The search party had already gathered all their equipment and gear for the flight out of then jungle. Christina was helped aboard first; Bradley followed behind her. Everyone now accounted for, the chopper lifted off from the jungle clearing and soon faded into the evening sky. The estimated flying time back to the command post is thirty five minutes. Christina fell asleep as soon as the Chinook became airborne.

Bradley's mind raced as the chopper made its way back, travelling low to avoid any hostile or enemy radar. Over five months of grueling work had finally paid off; he can now seriously consider retirement and travel the world. For now he'll just enjoy the thrill and excitement of this victory; the future is unpredictable and at this stage it's just too early to make any commitments.

Some other terrorist group may take another American hostage in a far away land and a call for help from a desperate but well connected business man may be on the way. For now, Bradley would just wait and see.

The chopper circled a few times as the pilot dropped altitude in preparation for landing on the huge gravel and dirt courtyard. Bradley could see Nunez and a few other men outside. As soon as the Chinook landed, a medical unit from the Colombian Armed Forces whisked Christina away. A special hot and cold shower unit recently installed by the Special Engineering and Technical Brigade provided a more than comfortable bath and toilet facility for Christina. For the American, this was like heaven—the warm shower felt so good; it certainly reminded her of what's in store when she gets home.

Showered and cleaned up, Christina had a thorough medical examination. Except for signs of dehydration, she appeared to be in excellent health. Later, the former hostage helped herself to the sumptuous dinner prepared to celebrate her release.

Bradley and the team were at the table long after Christina retired to her quarters; tonight she'll have a good long rest. Although the bed won't be as comfortable as her own in Texas, it's certainly better than the rough jungle conditions she had endured.

Bradley and the guys were about to retire; the plan is to leave the staging area early in the morning and head back to Santa Marta. From there, Christina would be taken aboard the USS Antartica, currently stationed off the coast for eventual repatriation to the United States.

Chapter 35

When Preston broke the news to Sally, she was ecstatic. "Oh My God. Are you sure?"

"Absolutely, I spoke with Christina for more than ten minutes; she's alive and well, and I am heading down there to pick her up in the morning."

"How about the meetings with the visiting executives?"

"I'm sure you know what to do—reschedule them; get on the phone—start calling tonight."

Sally hung up the phone, rushed to her bedside table and logged on to her iPad. Quickly, she signed into the Office email. She retrieved the required information and started to call the relevant executives.

"Good evening Mr. Lawson, this is Sally from Mike Preston's Office; sorry to call at this time."

"Actually, I am glad you called; something's turned up and I've got to return home early in the morning," replied Lawson.

"Ok, what a coincidence, Mr. Preston also has some urgent matters to deal with."

"I think the following week may be less hectic so we can look at that—if that's good for Mike, I won't mind," said Lawson.

"Great, I'll call you to confirm, thanks," Sally replied with a smile.

•

Things were happening so quickly, only yesterday Sally thought about comforting her boss and the possibility of another late night romantic romp in the plush Forrest Oaks Mansion. This no longer looks possible; anyway that's somewhat selfish she thought. Perhaps Preston may wish to make one final victory lap—after all he's got quite a lot to celebrate.

Sally pulled of the wrap, tossed it on the bed and headed to the shower. Her taunt nipples confirming her inner cravings; oh how she wanted to be caressed and cuddled. She turned the water on allowing the warm spray to cascade all over her shapely body. She lifted her right leg, resting her feet on the side of the bathtub. Sally stroked her vagina gently over and over again, moaning softly in erotic excitement and pleasure. Still moaning, Sally gripped the golden shower hand rail, her writhing voluptuous hips gyrating in wild fulfillment. Relieved by the rhythmic orgasmic convulsions she just experienced, Sally rinsed and stepped out of the shower, fully energized and rejuvenated.

Captain Alvarez waited in the darkness; crouching in the cover of the thick jungle undergrowth, he inched closer to the edge of the trail. He got the distinct smell of a strong cigar. He froze for a moment; this can't be true. He sniffed the cool night air again as the dark shadowy shape moved closer.

Then it all came back to him—a few years ago he was ambushed by bandits. He lost some of his men on that fateful night but survived only because the leader of the gang thought he was dead. Captain Alvarez touched the scar on his left cheek inflicted by the man wielding a sharp hunting knife. And as the tall shape got within touching distance, the old seaman struck hitting the man a thumping blow from behind.

The man fell over and screamed in agony; Alvarez followed up with a another smashing blow to the knee cap of the stricken late night traveler. For a moment, the Colombian fisherman thought about plunging the knife into the wounded man's chest, but then he remembered the old rosary beads he kept in his inner pocket; the blood of this man would not be on his hands.

Captain Alvarez tied up the wounded man securely then rummaged through the heavy tote bag; his fingers touched the tightly wrapped bundle strewn among the other personal belongings. Anxious to see what's in the package, Alvarez reached for the knife and ran the sharp blade right down the edge, severing the tightly bound bands in the process. He felt as though his heart stopped for a moment, he screamed with excitement. "Marabel! Marabel my dear! You won't believe my good luck."

Barely able to contain his excitement, Captain Alvarez decided that it's time to call his good American friend. The mysterious traveler, he ran into several months ago—a man who has left an indelible mark on his life and brought him such incredible fortune. Captain Alvarez reached for the radio in the pocket of his field jacket.

Chapter 36

Miami International Airport was abuzz with activity, flights were landing and taking off at frequent intervals. Preston's executive jet taxied out of the ramp and waited for air traffic control clearance before embarking on the two and a half hour flight to Aereopuerto Internacional Simon Bolivar, Magdalena, Colombia. The flight to Santa Marta was uneventful. Mark Reuben, retired Chairman of the Joint Chief of Staff sat next to Preston. The two men never stopped talking, covering topics from as far back as their boyhood days to events in the Middle East and the Korean Peninsular.

Sally read a fitness magazine and fell asleep at one point during the flight. The other close friends and associates of the Texas Billionaire found various ways to pass the time. When Mike Preston's Personal Assistant awoke, the pilot had already started the descent into Simon Bolivar International Airport.

For Mike, this is really a special occasion; the sleek Cessna SN525A, executive Jet touched down at exactly 1:55 pm local time. Preston and his entourage had high security clearance from the Colombian Government. A uniformed official quickly escorted the arriving party to a designated counter for immediate processing.

In the meantime Bradley, Christina and a group of high ranking Government and Military Officials including Minister of the Interior, Alvario Castenadas were waiting outside in the arrivals lounge. The former hostage wore a white cotton polo shirt with the American stars and stripes emblazoned on the front.

This is the moment she has been waiting for. During her six month long incarceration, Christina dreamt about the day she'll see her dad again. Now that this has become a reality, no amount of words can describe her feelings.

Bradley tapped Christina gently on her shoulder and pointed to the large glass doors through which Preston and his party were expected to emerge any moment now. Christina held on to Bradley's arm as they moved forward towards the metal barrier separating the lounge area from arriving passengers. Christina stared through the giant glass panels trying to get a glimpse of her father.

Finally, she saw him. The tall well built man wearing the blue blazer held a bright red bouquet of carnations accentuated with a brilliant yellow bow. He looked really good as he strode ahead of the party with Mark Reuben close behind. The automatic door slid open as Preston stepped out.

Christina ran towards her father, screaming at the top of her voice. "Dad, I knew you would be here—not for one moment did I think you were going to give up on me." Preston held his daughter as he handed her the bouquet of carnations. The relieved and happy dad embraced Christina and could not hold back the tears of joy streaming down his cheeks. His prayers were answered, and soon Christina would be back home at the sprawling Texas mansion.

While Preston and his daughter bonded; Bradley, General Castenadas and Police Chief Nunez were entertaining the former Chairman of the Joint Chiefs of Staff, Mark Reuben. The Colombian military band played a lively samba jive. Bradley couldn't keep his eyes of Gabriella; of course he made sure his dancing partner got invited to the ceremony marking Christina's freedom. As the group of dancers, decked in their traditional garb rolled their hips to the pulsating Latin sounds, Gabriella made eye contact with the American Navy man. She wondered if he'll take up her offer for a true vacation now that the mission has been accomplished. Certainly, she no longer had any inhibitions about her romantic feelings for the American Soldier.

San Andres islands on the Caribbean Coast sounds great for a romantic getaway. Or better still the exquisitely beautiful Spice Island of Grenada—so many of her friends had spoken about this magnificent vacation paradise. Gabriella waited for a lull in the music and walked over to Bradley. She deliberately spilled some of the Pina Colada while threading her way to where he stood, the American quickly offered her a napkin to wipe the white mixture off of her tightly fitted skirt. Gabriella, leant forward and whispered softly into Bradley's ear. The American smiled approvingly and walked back to his original position just as Mike Preston started to address the gathering.

"Minister of Defense and the Interior, General Alvario Castenadas, Santa Marta Police Chief Nunez, US Ambassador Martin, other Government and Military Officials, Former Chairman of Joint Chiefs of Staff, my good friend, Mark Reuben and of course the USMC/ US Special Forces man— John Bradley; friends and well wishers. Today is a reality only because of you—all of you. When my daughter was kidnapped almost seven months ago, my entire world came crashing down. I became helpless and hopeless—desperate to the point where I even lost the will to live. Thankfully, I had the right people around me—all of you. So today all I want to do is say thanks—Thank you all for giving me back my life, my all—my pride and joy, my daughter, Christina."

Preston stepped off the podium as the welcoming party erupted into a thunderous burst of applause. Just to the right, Mark Reuben and General Alvario Castenadas were already engaged in some serious discussion.

"Were you guys ever able to figure out who's been leaking information to the rebel guerrillas?" asked Reuben as he expertly balanced a bowl of tropical fruit salad.

"No, not really, we've had some success; you see these bastards are so well entrenched it is not always easy to root them out. I think that our counter insurgency operations have certainly pegged them back though."

Preston and Christina joined Bradley and Gabriella at the table in the beautifully decorated reception area. The American Soldier introduced the female Officer from the Santa Marta Police Department.

"Preston, this is the Officer who gave me the first lead on Christina," said Bradley as he placed his arm on Gabriella's shoulder displacing her scarf in the process.

"It's my pleasure to meet you, and for all your good work we'd like to offer you a trip to Texas anytime," quipped Preston.

"You're so generous; I just did what I had to do Sir—that's my job you know. I'd love to come to the United States again anyway. I'll take up your offer sometime in the future." Gabriella smiled as she replied to the Texas billionaire.

"Dad, that would be wonderful, she'll stay at the mansion and we'll have lots of fun—movies, hiking trails, rock climbing and all the good stuff."

"John, I'm sure you'd love to have Gabriella come up to the States." Mike interjected.

"Of course, that's the least we can do to show our appreciation for all the work she's done, I'd like to give her another reason to come to the United States," replied Bradley assertively.

Preston looked at Bradley, the Former Special Forces man had his eyes glued on the female cop.

"Are you dropping hints John, I've always wondered when you're going to tie the knot?"

John smiled and held Gabriella by the arm and walked over to a vacant table. "Don't worry mate, you'll be the first to know—this I promise you."

The proceedings continued for about another twenty minutes, as the band wound up its musical treat; the local and foreign press were still interviewing some members of the Colombian Military.

Bradley stepped aside briefly to respond to the crackle coming from his radio. "American! American! I have news for you, where are you?"

"My dear friend, Captain Alvarez—where have you been?"

"Just following your orders Sir but I caught a big fish along the Couchillo de San Lorenzo Trail. Got him all tied up and waiting for you,"

"Fishing on dry land now Captain?"

"American, I am actually down from the mountain, had to build a wooden ramp to drag the heavy catch down the rugged trail.

"Captain I don't understand, right now I am celebrating a great victory. Christina is now free—actually we are celebrating right now—her dad came down to take her back to the States."

"Wonderful news! I am so glad to hear that she's alright, so that's why I did not hear from you before."

"Let me know exactly where you are, Old Captain—I'll come and get you, want to check your catch."

"Do you remember that little cove just off the Santa Marta Harbor, we met there before."

"Of course, how could I forget," replied Bradley as Gabriella looked on rather anxiously.

She really didn't want anything to come between her and the American now. Although Bradley did not give a commitment, Gabriella felt that the idea of a juicy romantic escapade on San Andres Island or another Caribbean getaway would be most appealing. Gabriella looked on anxiously as Bradley pushed the radio back into his pocket and rushed over to where Christina and her dad were seated.

"Something's turned up guys, may have to stay on for a week or so," said Bradley.

"Thought you were coming back with us," Christina interjected as she pointed to the Departure Lounge.

"Planned to, but I've got some unfinished business to take care of; don't worry—would be heading home soon."

Preston stood up as he extended his hand to thank Bradley once again. The American Navy man had made up his mind about staying on a bit longer to enjoy the exhilarating beauty of Santa Marta, and of course spend some quality time with a very special woman. The possibility of a romantic trip to one of the many magnificent off shore Islands meant that no amount of cajoling can cause him to change his mind.

"John we'll be waiting for you—just call as soon as you get back and oh by the way, please get your friend to come along as well," said Preston as he pointed to Gabriella.

Christina got to her feet and walked over to Gabriella; the former hostage wanted to have a few words of her own with the Colombian. They spoke for about five minutes and Christina's body language suggested that Gabriella would be in Oak Forest, Texas sometime soon.

Bradley stepped in as both women were about to say goodbye, almost tripping over a chair in the process. "See you guys are having fun, but I guess it's time to go, don't want to keep an old mate waiting too long."

Christina hugged Bradley and smiled; a tear drop trickled down her left cheek, the emotion clearly audible as she spoke." Thank you John, thank you! You're my hero!"

The afternoon traffic at Simon Bolivar International Airport was quite extraordinary. Passengers catching connecting flights rushed in and out of souvenir shops with colorful bags filled with Colombian treats and goodies. Christina and Sally got in on the action as well; they picked up a few pieces of exquisite wooden carvings and other fine craft items. Christina already knew exactly where in the Texas mansion she'll be placing her Colombian trophies.

Moments later, they chipped across to the food court to order large servings of a mouth-watering tropical sorbet, topped with multiple layers of delectable fruit.

Christina had no intentions of deviating from her great eating habits, but she had to enjoy all the good things her freedom brought. Preston and Reuben walked over to check on Christina and Sally; Mark ordered ice tea while Mike asks the smiling attendant for a cup of coffee. The other members of Preston's entourage were also enjoying the ambiance. In that group, only

Peter had travelled to Colombia before, so for the others it's an excellent opportunity to experience a different culture.

Christina looked over her shoulder and sees Peter and the others; their weighted shopping bags brimming over with gifts and other souvenir items. She beckoned them to come over. Peter, whom she'd met before had done some work as an engineering consultant for her father sometime ago. Since then, the fit and health conscious New Yorker has always been close to the Preston family.

"Come on over guys, we need to start talking about the big party back at the mansion," Christina said. Peter acknowledged and waited for Linda to leave the jewelry store then strolled over. By then, Preston and Reuben decided to walk around the Departure lounge to chat for a while.

"Tell me something Mike, that beautiful woman—your assistant, where did you find her?"

"Hope, I'm not thinking what you're thinking?" asked the Wealthy Texan with a broad smile.

"She looks darn good man," Reuben replied as he gazed momentarily in Sally's direction.

"Thought you'd stop looking many years ago; don't tell me you're still shooting from the hip buddy?"

"Show me a man who does not look and I'll point to a dead man. You see old mate, our primal instincts were hardwired into our DNA eons ago, so don't be too hard on yourself. Back to my question though, tell me Mike. I saw the way she kept looking at you, are you fucking her?"

Preston mopped his brow with the soft napkin he held, and gave Reuben a strange rather perplexed look. His boyhood buddy was spot on—should he dance his way out of this or be straight and upfront. He fidgeted for a while, nudging the bright yellow necktie he wore.

"I guess you knew I had a lot of stress—dealing with Christina's kidnapping, and a whole bunch of other stuff. Sally's been like a solid rock; apart from her beauty, she's quite an intelligent girl— yes she comforted me from time to time. We only did it once though, and boy since then it's been difficult for me to keep my eyes off her."

"Mike, you did what you had to do to survive, I would have done the same thing—that's just life." Said Reuben, licking his lips as he thought about Preston's romantic tryst. "I am sure, now that Christina is back you'll not be returning to those old tricks."

Preston took a deep breath, tapped Reuben on the shoulder and they moved away from the window and walked towards the table where Christina, Sally and the others were chatting and having a great time. The Texas billionaire looked at his watch and interjected.

"Sorry guys, we've got to be on board in about fifteen minutes, let's get moving!"

Chapter 37

The cool morning breeze blew across the windswept coast as the couple waded in the shallow water. Since their arrival on the island yesterday the experience has been absolutely amazing. The three and a half hour long ferry ride offered a breathtaking view of the exotic tropical island. Surly their first night would always be remembered; they were really having a wonderful time. His female companion had an insatiable fire and passion for romance and fun. He held her gently as they continued to walk along the beautiful white sand beach, sometimes struggling to keep his eyes off her.

Bradley deserved every one of these blissful moments; the last six months had tested him to the maximum. He had no regrets though; the Colombian experience has rekindled a new kind of fire in him. When he got the call from Preston several months ago, the retired Navy Seal didn't have a clue that romance was a possibility. His chance encounter with an officer stationed at the Santa Marta Police Head Quarters, provided the spark for this fairy tale and truly exotic experience.

John decided that the rocky cove on the Northern side of the beach is an ideal spot to set up camp. Gabriella leapt from his arms and ran towards the shaded area. The large beach bag she carried brimmed over with snacks and other goodies. The couple had plans for a fun-filled day; Bradley wanted to do some snorkeling as well, while Gabriella just felt like splashing around in the warm soothing water.

"Hey honey, want to come fix my swimsuit?" Gabriella beckoned Bradley as she threw the bright tropical wrap onto a nearby coconut palm.

"Babes, you know what's going to happen when I start to touch you, can I pass on that?"

"No, come over now darling; you know what they say about keeping a woman waiting," replied Gabriella with a smile.

"Ok my love, I'll be right there with you."

Bradley walked over to the area where Gabriella was standing, as the light morning wind sprayed tiny shafts of sand into his face. He held her gently in his arms again, conveniently forgetting what he had to do. Instead he completely removed the garment, revealing the pair of firm nipples on her shapely breast.

Gabriella responded by placing her arms around Bradley, gently caressing his hairy chest. The waves rolled and churned as the couple enjoyed the passionate moments. Seagulls looked on approvingly, and as the warm morning sun poured out its shinny rays all around San Andres Island. Bradley never felt so good, this perhaps is the most fulfilling end he ever experienced on any mission.

The constant travel and military life had taken a toll on his family. Since his divorce well over ten years ago, the former Special Forces man opted to stay out of serious relationships. But by the way things are looking now, it seems like he's about to make a radical change.

As the couple continued to enjoy the island, other tourists were also basking in the tropical scenery. John took Gabriella by the hand again and led her to another stretch of white sandy beach, away from the many inquisitive onlookers.

"Darling, go take your swim now, I'll be snorkeling on the reef just off the other end."

"Be careful now my love, I've got plans for a great future with you."

"No need to worry darling—your man's very good beneath the waves—perhaps that's why I'll always be a navy man—a proud and brave United States Navy Seal."

Lightning Source UK Ltd.
Milton Keynes UK
UKOW04f1929111213

222850UK00002B/5/P